THE SIRENS OF SURRENTUM

THE ROMAN MYSTERIES

by Caroline Lawrence

I The Thieves of Ostia
II The Secrets of Vesuvius
III The Pirates of Pompeii
IV The Assassins of Rome
V The Dolphins of Laurentum
VI The Twelve Tasks of Flavia Gemina
VII The Enemies of Jupiter
VIII The Gladiators from Capua
IX The Colossus of Rhodes
X The Fugitive from Corinth
XI The Sirens of Surrentum

A Roman Mystery

THE SIRENS OF SURRENTUM

Caroline Lawrence

Orion
Children's Books

First published in Great Britain in 2006
by Orion Children's Books
a division of the Orion Publishing Group Ltd
Orion House
5 Upper St Martin's Lane
London WC2H 9EA

1 3 5 7 9 10 8 6 4 2

The Orion Publishing Group's policy is to use papers that
are natural, renewable and recyclable products and made
from wood grown in sustainable forests. The logging and
manufacturing processes are expected to conform to the
environmental regulations of the country of origin.

A catalogue record for this book is
available from the British Library.

ISBN–13 978 1 84255 255 1
ISBN–10 1 84255 255 4

Typeset at The Spartan Press Ltd,
Lymington, Hants

Printed in Great Britain by
Clays Ltd, St Ives plc

www.orionbooks.co.uk

To Kirsten, Penny and Trisha,
beautiful women and good friends

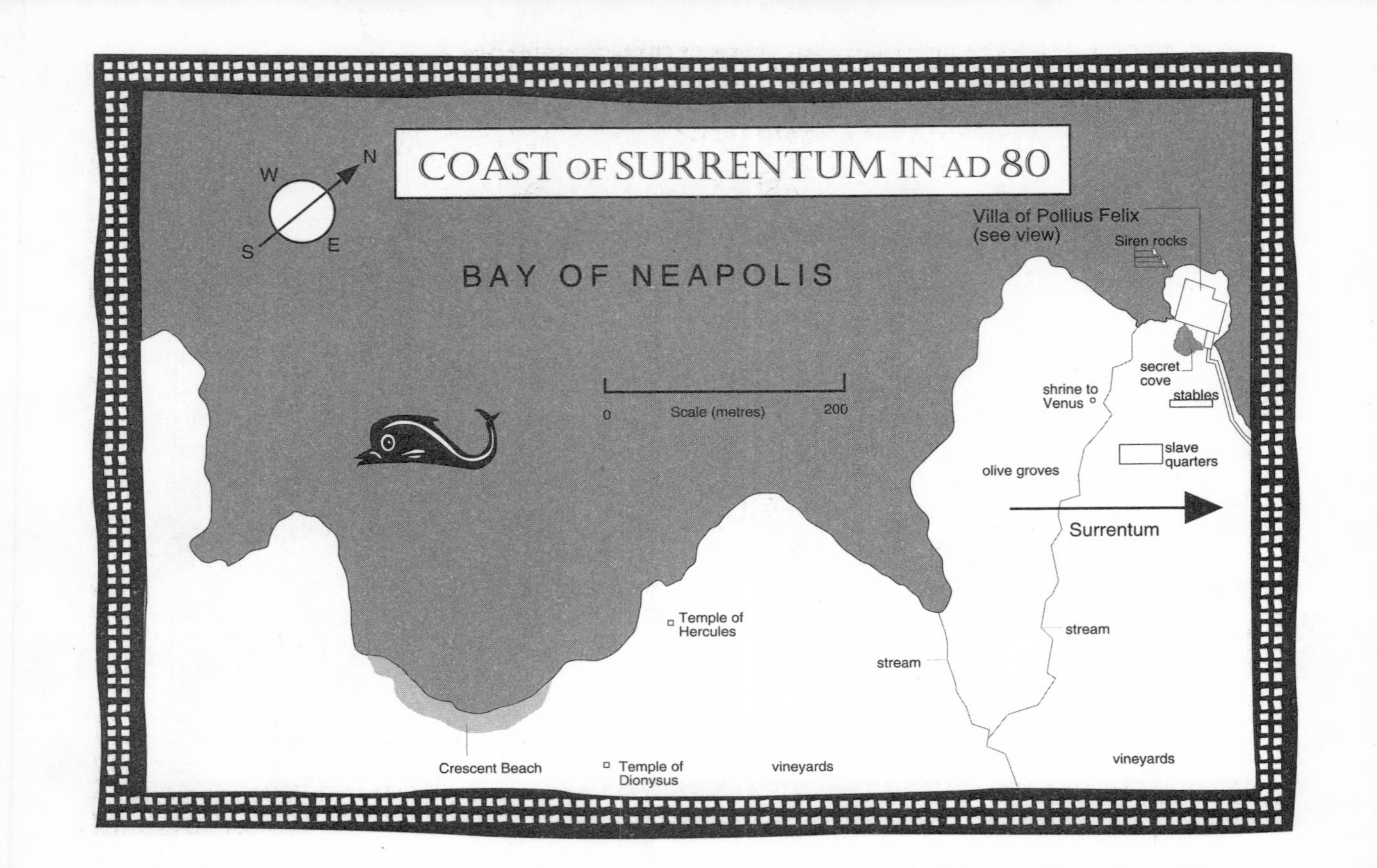
COAST OF SURRENTUM IN AD 80
N
W
E
S
BAY OF NEAPOLIS
0
Scale (metres)
200
Villa of Pollius Felix
(see view)
Siren rocks
secret cove
stables
shrine to Venus
slave quarters
olive groves
Surrentum
stream
stream
Temple of Hercules
Temple of Dionysus
Crescent Beach
vineyards
vineyards

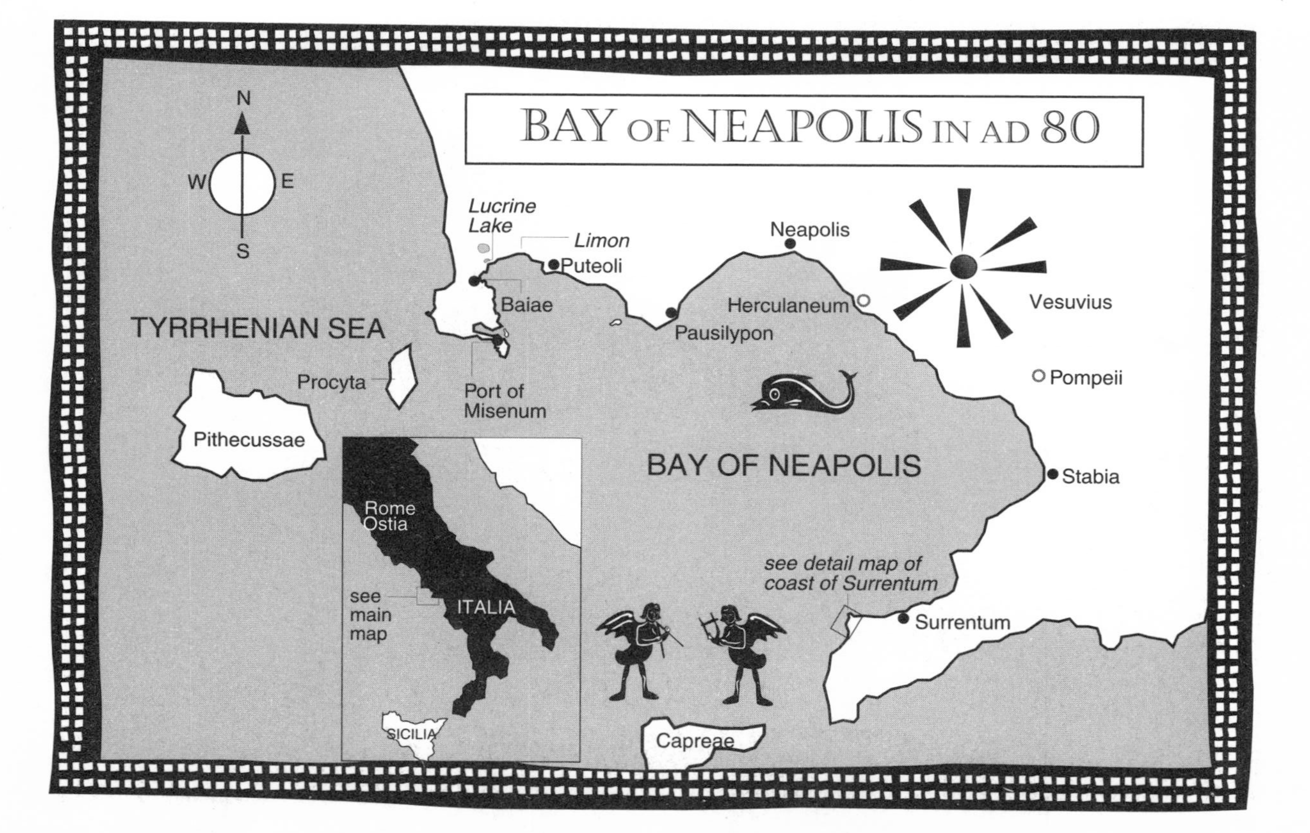
BAY OF NEAPOLIS IN AD 80
N
W
E
S
TYRRHENIAN SEA
Lucrine Lake
Limon
Puteoli
Baiae
Port of Misenum
Procyta
Pithecussae
Neapolis
Herculaneum
Pausilypon
Vesuvius
Pompeii
Stabia
BAY OF NEAPOLIS
see detail map of coast of Surrentum
Surrentum
Capreae
Rome
Ostia
see main map
ITALIA
SICILIA

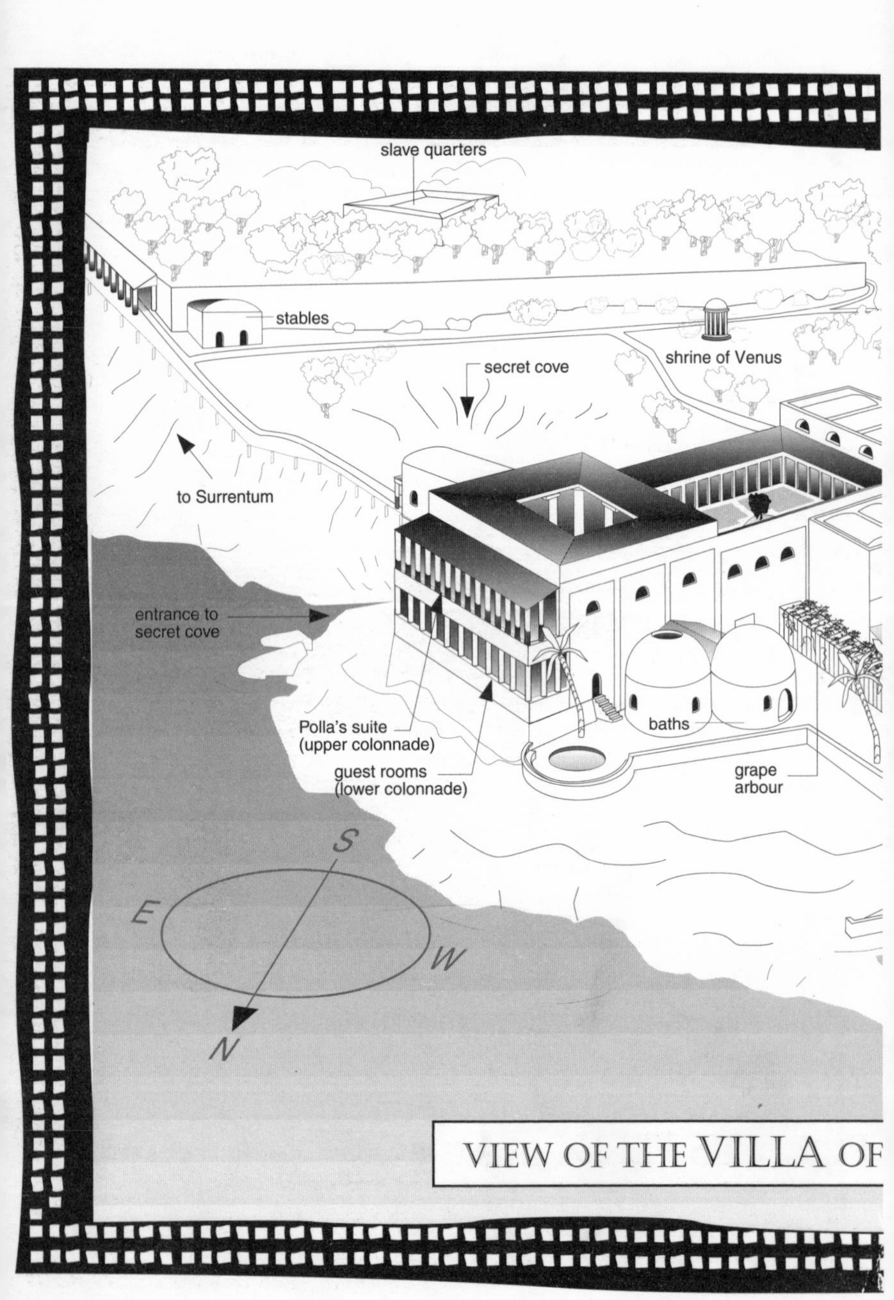

slave quarters
stables
shrine of Venus
secret cove
to Surrentum
entrance to
secret cove
Polla's suite
(upper colonnade)
guest rooms
(lower colonnade)
baths
grape
arbour
S
E
W
N
VIEW OF THE VILLA OF

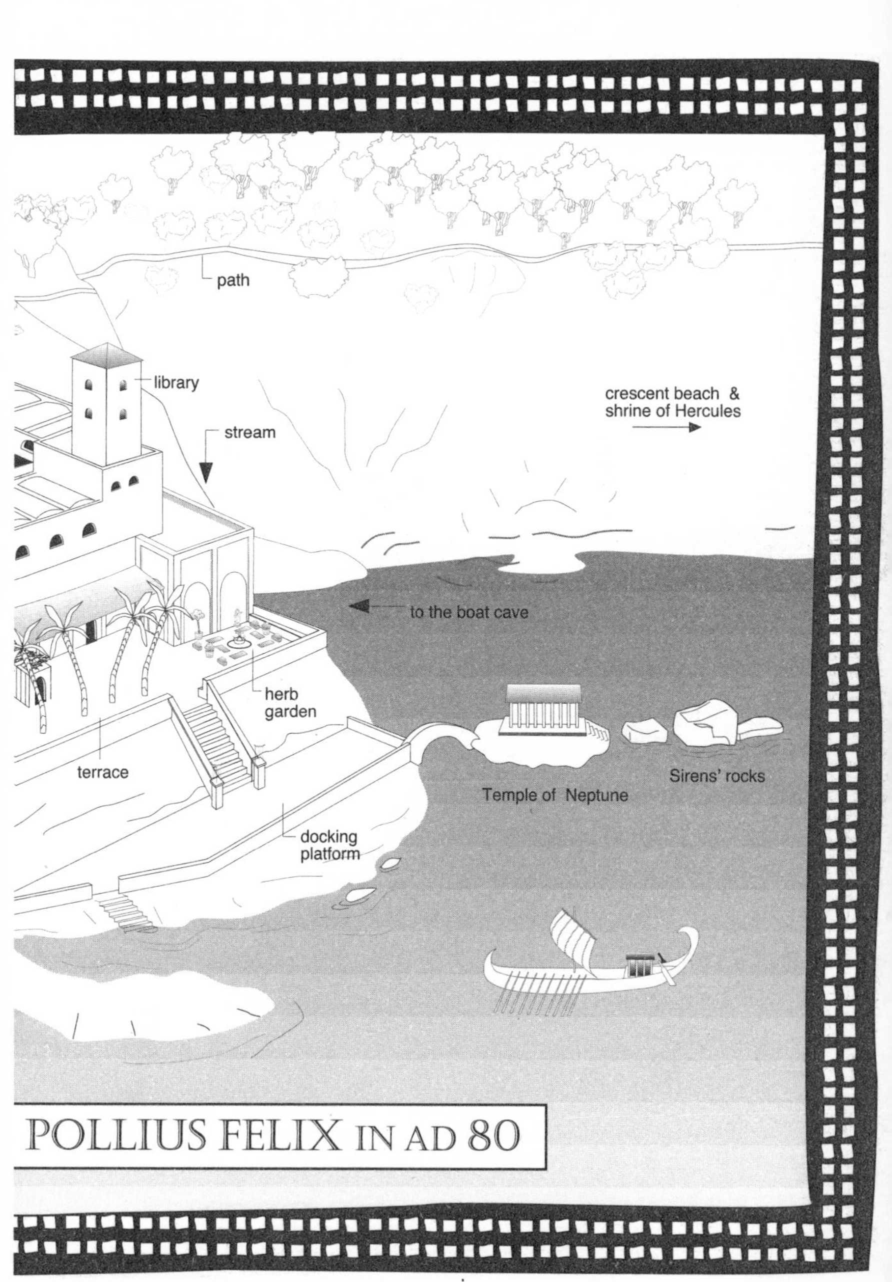
path
library
stream
crescent beach &
shrine of Hercules
to the boat cave
herb
garden
terrace
Temple of Neptune
Sirens' rocks
docking
platform
POLLIUS FELIX IN AD 80

This story takes place in ancient Roman times, so a few of the words may look strange.

If you don't know them, 'Aristo's Scroll' at the back of the book will tell you what they mean and how to pronounce them. It will also tell you about Roman names.

SCROLL I

Flavia Gemina and Jonathan ben Mordecai were kissing. They had been kissing for some time.

At least it felt like it to Flavia.

Finally she pulled back and gasped for air.

'That was my first time,' said Flavia. She was almost eleven years old, with grey eyes and light brown hair pinned up in a simple knot. She wore new leather sandals and a short, sleeveless tunic of sky-blue linen. The gold bulla hanging from a silver chain around her neck showed that she was both freeborn and rich.

'It was my first time, too.' Jonathan wiped his mouth with the back of his hand. He was eleven and a half, with curly dark hair and brown eyes. Like Flavia, Jonathan was freeborn, but he wore a small herb pouch rather than a bulla around his neck.

'So?' said Flavia. 'How was it?

Jonathan considered for a moment. 'Did you have salad for lunch?'

Flavia nodded. 'Why? Could you tell?'

'I could taste the vinegar.'

'And you had olives, didn't you?' said Flavia.

Jonathan nodded.

'But how was the kissing part?' asked Flavia, brushing away a strand of hair that had come unpinned.

'Well,' said Jonathan, 'apart from it being interesting because we could both tell what the other one had for lunch . . . I have to say it didn't clang my gong.'

'Me, too,' sighed Flavia. 'I mean, me neither. I mean, I like you, but not like that.'

'That's a relief,' said Jonathan, getting up from the marble bench and bending over the bubbling fountain at the centre of Flavia's inner garden. He took a long drink of water, then turned to look at her.

'So why *did* you want to kiss me?'

The jasmine bush beside the fountain trembled as a dark-haired boy in a sea-green tunic jumped out from behind it. He flourished a wax-tablet.

'Lupus!' Flavia jumped up from the marble bench. 'How long have you been spying on us?'

Lupus ignored her. He was dancing in front of Jonathan, laughing and waving his open wax tablet. Flavia saw the first words written on the tablet:

FLAVIA NEEDS TO PRACTISE

'No!' She lunged for the tablet, which Lupus was holding at arm's length.

'What?' said Jonathan. 'Why does Flavia need to practise? Give me that!'

He tackled Lupus and they rolled in the dust beneath the quince bush.

Flavia hovered over them, trying to snatch the tablet. 'Give me that, Lupus! Give it – OW!'

The wax tablet flew through the air and the three of

them scrambled towards the pebbled pathway where it lay.

Just as Flavia was about to grasp it – and she knew she would have been first – a sandalled foot and a walking stick appeared beside the tablet, and a man's hand closed over it. Flavia, Jonathan and Lupus looked up the folds of a toga into the amused eyes of the man who held the tablet.

'Pater!' stuttered Flavia, who should have been behaving like a proper Roman girl.

'Captain Geminus,' wheezed Jonathan, who suffered from asthma.

'Unnggh!' grunted Lupus, who had no tongue.

The three of them stood up.

Flavia's father handed the wax tablet to a dark-skinned girl standing next to him. 'Nubia,' he said, 'would you like to show me how much your Latin has improved in the past year?'

'No!' cried Flavia. 'Please don't let her read it, pater! It's private.'

'On the contrary,' said Captain Geminus pleasantly. 'I believe it concerns all of you. Nubia?'

The dark-skinned girl frowned down at the tablet. Flavia knew that although Nubia's reading was much improved, she could still only read if she pronounced the words out loud.

'*Flavia needs to practise*,' Nubia read haltingly, '*because we've been invited . . . to the Villa . . . Lim-o-na . . . and Pul-chra says there will be lots of highborn young men there.*'

'Excellent, Nubia,' said Captain Geminus. 'Isn't that nice? The four of you have been invited to spend the rest of June in Surrentum, at the villa of Publius Pollius

Felix. So, my little owl,' he said, turning to Flavia, 'what were you and Jonathan practising?'

'Hello, father,' said Jonathan. 'Hello, Tigris! How's my boy?' He bent to greet his large black puppy as Lupus bolted the front door behind them. 'Where's mother?' asked Jonathan, straightening up and looking around.

'Out. Again.' Jonathan's father sighed and turned to go back through the atrium. 'Shopping, I presume. I don't know why she doesn't let that slave-girl of hers do it.'

'I think she just likes to get out, because for ten years she was a slave and wasn't allowed to,' said Jonathan as they all moved into the tablinum.

'Yes.' His father picked up a green marble pestle and began to dig it fiercely into the small mortarium. 'I'm sure that's the reason your mother never spends time at home.'

Jonathan looked sharply at his father. Mordecai ben Ezra seemed to have aged in the past three months since Jonathan's mother had returned from Rome to live with them. His face was thinner and there were shadows under his dark eyes.

'Would you like me to make dinner tonight?' said Jonathan.

'Yes, please.' His father sighed. 'I need to finish preparing this medicine while the light is still good.'

'I think there's still some stew from last night. I can stretch it out with chickpeas and flatbread.'

Lupus cleared his throat and Jonathan saw he was looking at him with raised eyebrows.

'Father, there's something we wanted to ask you.'

'Yes?' Mordecai was still grinding and the scent of almonds filled the room.

'Flavia got a letter today from Surrentum. It was from Pulchra.'

Mordecai stopped grinding and looked up. 'Pollius Felix's daughter?'

'Yes. She's invited the four of us – Flavia, Nubia, Lupus and me – to stay with them for two weeks. Captain Geminus is sailing to Sicily the day after tomorrow and he could drop us off. But if you want Lupus and me to stay here and help . . .'

'No, my son.' Mordecai gave him a tired smile. 'You two go and have a holiday.'

'Are you sure?'

'Absolutely. A break will do you good. You've had a difficult year.'

So have you, Jonathan thought, but instead he said, 'Thank you, father.' He started to follow Lupus out of the tablinum, then stopped and turned back. 'Oh, father?' he said. 'Do you have any books about poison?'

'Poison?' Mordecai's dark eyebrows went up. 'Why do you want a book about poison?'

'There was a postscript at the bottom of Pulchra's letter,' said Jonathan. 'For some reason she asked us to bring any books on poison we might have.'

SCROLL II

'Nubia,' said Flavia later that night, 'Do you think the gods have destined a man for each of us?' Flavia lay on her back, staring up at her bedroom window. The lattice-work screen showed the night sky as diamonds of peacock blue, for it was almost midsummer.

'You mean one man for one woman? In all the whole world?' said Nubia from her bed.

'Yes. Like Aeneas was destined to marry the beautiful young princess Lavinia because the gods ordained it and so he had to abandon Queen Dido even though he loved her.'

'Are you reading the *Aeneid* again?' said Nubia. 'That is not our homework.'

'I know. But it's so romantic.' Flavia sighed and turned her head. In the flickering golden light of a tiny bronze oil-lamp she could just make out Nubia. 'Pulchra's invitation said there'll be some highborn young men at the Villa Limona,' said Flavia. 'Maybe one of them will be The One.'

'What The One?'

'The One the gods have destined for me.'

'I thought you renounced love.'

'I did. I renounced it until I was grown-up. In three more days I'll be eleven. That's grown-up.'

'I do not think eleven is grown-up.'

'But I *feel* completely grown-up,' said Flavia. 'And in only one year I can be married.'

'But why do you search for The One?' Nubia's bed creaked as she turned to look at Flavia. 'Your father has already chosen a person with whom you will be married. You told him you would obey.'

'I know.' Flavia sighed again and rolled onto her back. 'But I haven't even met him yet and pater won't tell me his name because he's afraid if he did then I'd investigate him, which of course I would. But if I meet my destined love before the betrothal ceremony then maybe I can become betrothed to him instead.'

'I do not think the gods ordain one man for one woman,' said Nubia. 'I think you can make happiness. I love someone who will never love me, but I will still marry and have babies.'

'You'd marry someone else?' said Flavia, and lowered her voice. 'Even though you love Aristo?' Aristo was the young Greek who tutored the four friends in Greek, philosophy, maths and music.

'Yes.'

'And you'd be happy?'

'I will try.'

'But don't you wish you could marry Aristo?'

In the pause which followed, Flavia could hear the cicadas creaking briskly in the pines outside the town walls; it was a warm night.

'Yes,' said Nubia at last. 'I wish it more than I can say. But I do not think that he will ever love me. And by the time I am ready for love, I think he will already be married.'

'But you'll be twelve in two months,' said Flavia. 'Under Roman law you're allowed to get married then.'

'In my country,' said Nubia, 'girls do not marry so early. We betroth very early but we marry late, at sixteen or seventeen. My cousin Qantala did not marry until twenty years of age.'

'That's ancient!' said Flavia.

'I know. But I think it is better.'

'What about Jonathan's sister Miriam? She's happy being married and she's only fourteen. Isn't it exciting that she's going to have a baby in December?'

'Yes,' said Nubia. 'Miriam will be a good mother. She is ready. But I am not. And you are not. Our bodies are not ready for babies.'

'That doesn't matter,' said Flavia. 'That's what betrothal is for. If you're betrothed then you're allowed to hold hands and kiss until you can have babies. My body might not be ready for love,' she sighed, 'but my heart is.'

Two days later, the merchant ship *Delphina* approached a maritime villa on the tip of a promontory south of Surrentum. The sea was smooth and blue, glittering with a million spangles of sunlight. A steady breeze had brought Flavia and her friends from Ostia to Surrentum in a day and a half. It was mid-morning, two days after the Ides of June.

'There it is!' said Flavia to her dog Scuto. 'The Villa Limona. Do you remember it from last summer?'

Scuto stood with his forepaws on the curved side of the ship, so that he could see over the polished oak rail. The wind ruffled his golden fur and his tongue flapped like a small pink flag. Despite the sea breeze it was already hot. Flavia could hear the cicadas throbbing in the olive groves behind the yellow and white villa.

'Of course it doesn't look exactly the same,' said Flavia to Scuto. 'The red roof tiles are brighter without all that ash on them, and the gardens look greener, too.'

'He will remember it when he smells it,' said Nubia, stroking the silky black fur of her own dog, Nipur. 'Dogs cannot see so well, but they can smell.'

'You smell, don't you, boy?' said Jonathan to his own dog Tigris. 'You smell terrible!' Lupus guffawed and Jonathan looked pleased. Tigris had short black fur like Nipur. They were brothers and almost identical, except that Tigris's eyes were brown, and Nipur's were golden, like the eyes of his mistress.

'Hey!' cried Flavia, pointing. 'What's that? It looks like a little temple.'

'Where?' said Jonathan.

'There! On one of those tiny islands close to the villa.'

'Oh, I see it. You know, I *thought* they were building something when we sailed by here in April.'

'It wasn't here last summer,' said Flavia, 'so it must be new. Oh, look! There's a little bridge leading from the villa to the temple.'

Lupus nodded his agreement and suddenly Scuto barked.

'Behold!' said Nubia. 'I see another dog by the villa.'

'Where?' cried Flavia. 'Oh, there! Coming down the steps from the terrace. Oh, isn't he sweet?'

'Looks more like a rat than a dog,' muttered Jonathan.

'And that must be Pulchra waving to us! With the pink tunic and matching parasol. Is that Pulchra, Jonathan?'

'Don't ask me.' Jonathan shrugged.

'Atticus! Punicus!' cried Captain Geminus behind them. 'Furl the mainsail!'

The four friends turned to watch two big sailors pull ropes which gathered up the linen sail, making the painted dolphin disappear.

'Alexandros! Drop the anchor!'

'But pater!' protested Flavia. 'We're not there yet.'

'We don't want to run aground!' he called from his place at the tiller. 'As close to the land as this, there could be rocks under the water.'

'We'll probably have to swim ashore,' grumbled Jonathan.

Lupus grunted 'no' and jerked his head in the direction of the little skiff that trailed behind the *Delphina*.

'We won't need the skiff,' said Captain Geminus. 'Look! They're sending a boat to meet us. It must have a shallow draft to navigate these waters.'

Emerging from behind the jewel-like villa was a sleek low ship with a yellow-and-white striped sail in the middle and a small temple-like deck-house at the rear. Twenty oars rose and fell – ten on each side – flashing like the wings of a bird.

Flavia suddenly felt sick. Was it the swinging deck of

the *Delphina* at anchor? Or was it something else? She filled her lungs with sea air and slowly exhaled.

The previous summer she had fallen in love with the powerful and charismatic owner of the Villa Limona, Publius Pollius Felix. A few months later, during the Saturnalia, she had purged her passion for him with a dance called the Little Tarantula. So why was her stomach twisting and her heart thudding? She took another breath and was relieved to feel her heartbeat slowing. She couldn't see Felix on the boat. He must be at the villa.

'Twenty oarsmen,' murmured her father, joining them at the rail. 'Imagine having twenty strong male slaves to spare.'

'He calls them his soldiers,' said Flavia, and added, 'They're not all slaves. I think some of them are freedmen.'

'Marcus Flavius Geminus?' called a man with a short beard, as the oared ship drew up alongside the *Delphina*.

'That's me!' cried her father, leaning over the rail.

'My name is Publius Pollius Justus,' said the bearded man in a Greek accent, 'freedman and secretary to Publius Pollius Felix. My patron sends his greetings and his apologies. He's been called away on business. But he offers his best regards and expresses pleasure in receiving the four children under your care' – here he referred to a papyrus scroll – 'as well as their three dogs, until the Kalends of July. He promises to attend to their needs and safety as if they were members of his own household.'

'Thank you, Justus!' replied Flavia's father in his captain's voice. 'Please extend my heartfelt gratitude to your patron and tell him I am in his debt.' And in a much lower voice he said. 'What a shame. I was hoping to meet this famous Felix who made such an impression on my daughter.'

Flavia waited for her face to cool and then turned to look up at him. 'Pater, you will look after yourself, won't you? You're still recovering from those stab wounds. Promise you'll be careful?'

'Don't worry, my little owl.' He kissed her on the forehead. 'The *Delphina* is only going to Sicily. I'll be staying with Cordius at his estate for most of the time so my feet will be on solid ground. I promise I'll be careful, if you promise me something in return.'

'What?'

'I don't want you going to Baiae.'

'What?'

'There's a town called Baiae to the west of Neapolis. It's a glirarium of licentiousness. I was hoping to mention it to your host.'

'It's a *what*?'

'Just promise me you won't go.' He lowered his voice. 'Even if you're invited.'

'All right, pater.' Flavia sighed. 'I promise I won't go to Baiae. Even if invited.'

'Make a vow,' he said.

'I vow to Castor and Pollux and all the gods that I will not go to Baiae.'

'Good girl,' he kissed her again. 'Promise to write to me, and remember what I said: if you want to go home early for any reason, just send a message to Aristo and he will come to fetch you all.'

'I'm sure that won't be necessary, pater. Besides,

poor Aristo deserves a rest after all that happened last month.'

Captain Geminus smiled fondly at his daughter. 'I agree,' he said, 'But even so, he's there if you need him. Now off you go, carefully down the rope ladder. I'll make an offering for your safety every morning. Oh, and Flavia!' he called. 'This time try not to get into trouble!'

As the yacht approached the rocky promontory, the Villa Limona seemed to rise above them. It was built on at least four levels with a red-roofed tower as its highest point. Flavia could not see the secret cove between the villa and the mainland, or its hidden entrance, but she could see the twin domes of the bath-house, along with palm trees, pergolas, colonnades and awnings, all designed to give cool shade on hot summer days.

At last the ship nudged steps going up to a docking platform and Flavia waved at Felix's eldest daughter. Although her real name was Polla Felicia, everyone called her Polla Pulchra – or simply Pulchra – because of her beautiful face and hair. She was a few months older than Flavia and far richer. Today she was wearing a sleeveless pink tunic and her blonde hair was tied up with a pink silk scarf. A small, bug-eyed lap-dog ran back and forth at her feet, yapping with excitement. Scuto, Tigris and Nipur responded with deep enthusiasm.

'Welcome!' laughed Pulchra, coming down the marble steps and taking Flavia's hand as Justus helped her off the side of the boat, 'I've been up in pater's library looking out for you. I saw your sail ages ago.' As

Pulchra kissed the air near Flavia's cheek she hissed, 'You're terribly tanned. You look like a field-slave!'

'We've been travelling round the Greek islands,' said Flavia, 'and mainland Greece, too. Do I really look like a field-slave?'

'Don't worry,' said Pulchra. 'I've got special cream that will bleach your skin. Meanwhile, take my parasol.'

Flavia accepted the pink parasol and moved up the steps so the others could disembark.

'Salve, Jonathan!' said Pulchra. 'You're so much taller and more muscular than the last time I saw you.' She stroked his shoulder. 'Have you been weight-lifting in the palaestra?'

'Jonathan was a gladiator,' said Flavia. 'We'll tell you all about it later.'

'A gladiator?' Pulchra's blue eyes grew wide. 'Oh, Jonathan! Yes, you must tell me everything.' She turned to greet Lupus and Nubia. 'Welcome back to the Villa Limona!' Pulchra looked down. 'Is this Nipur? He's so big! Look, Nipur! That's my new dog. Isn't he precious?'

Scuto, Tigris and Nipur gave the little dog sniffs of greeting and then began to follow other interesting smells up the steps towards the villa. Pulchra scooped up her lap-dog.

'I call him Ajax,' she said, bringing his bug-eyed face close to hers. 'Who's my little hero? Who's my little Ajax?' Pulchra giggled as the little dog licked her face with a wet pink tongue. As she went up the stairs she said to Nubia. 'After you left, I missed Nipur so much that I begged pater to buy me a dog.' She dimpled. 'And he did!'

'Where is your father?' asked Flavia, smoothing her hair and glancing around. 'And your mother?' she added quickly.

'Mater's in her chair and pater's at Limon.' Pulchra put Ajax down and he waddled off after the other three dogs. 'He should be back soon.'

'Limon?'

'His estate between Puteoli and Baiae.'

'Baiae?' gasped Flavia.

'That's right,' said Pulchra. 'Baiae. Now, come on. The slaves will see to the dogs and your luggage. Mater wants to see you. And then,' she whispered, 'I want to tell you about a mystery I'm desperate to solve.'

SCROLL III

They found Pulchra's mother resting in the shady colonnade outside her suite of rooms on an upper level of the Villa Limona. She was lying on a wicker lounge-chair and gazing out over the sea through red-based fluted white columns. With her pale blue stola and pink papyrus fan, Flavia thought Polla Argentaria looked lovely against the yellow linen cushions of the couch. Pulchra's mother had pale skin, high cheekbones and elegantly arched eyebrows. Her honey-coloured hair was pinned up in a simple but elegant twist.

'Flavia Gemina.' Polla made an attempt to rise, then sank back onto the yellow cushions. 'Greetings.'

Flavia took Polla's extended hand. It was cool and smelt faintly of balsam and cardamom. 'Salve, Polla Argentaria,' said Flavia politely. 'Thank you for inviting us to your home.'

'Not at all,' murmured Polla. 'Nubia, hello. Jonathan, welcome. And dear Lupus.' She greeted each of them in turn and then said over her shoulder, 'Parthenope? Are you there?'

A pretty curly-haired slave-girl of fifteen or sixteen stepped out of the shadows. 'Yes, domina?'

'Bring us another pitcher of Surrentinum, would

you? Chilled and very well-watered. Oh, and some honeyed lemon-cakes.'

The slave-girl nodded and swayed gracefully off down the colonnade.

'Please sit,' said Polla, taking a sip from a gold and sapphire wine cup. Flavia and her friends sat gratefully in wicker chairs and Pulchra perched at the foot of her mother's couch.

'Look at it.' Polla lifted her arm vaguely in the direction of the sea. 'Still smoking after nearly a year.'

They turned to look through the shaded columns at the brilliant vista. Across the blue bay loomed the truncated shape of an enormous grey mountain. It was Vesuvius, the volcano which had erupted the previous summer. A third of it had been blown away and even now an ominous cloud hung over it, a dirty brown smudge in the pure summer sky.

'It's been nearly a year since its eruption,' murmured Polla, 'but its effects are still being felt. Every night the sunsets are a lurid blood-red. And just last week the bones of some wretched man washed up on the beach near Puteoli. That mountain is a constant reminder that our days here on earth are numbered. *One moment we are fruitful and calm, the next disaster strikes. Events have tears,'* she quoted, *'and thoughts of death touch the soul.'*

Flavia leaned over and whispered in Nubia's ear. 'I'm not the only one who's been reading too much Virgil recently.'

'And they call me a pessimist,' said Jonathan a short time later.

'I'm sorry about mater,' sighed Pulchra. 'She's not well.'

Jonathan glanced at Flavia. She silently mouthed the words: *barking mad*, and he had to turn away to hide the smile on his face. He pretended to stare at a lemon tree which stood at the centre of the villa's largest inner garden. 'I thought the elixir my father prescribed was helping your mother's depression,' he said.

Lupus grunted his agreement.

'Your father's elixir helped for a while,' said Pulchra, 'but it's not doing any good now. And I think I know why.'

'Why?' said Jonathan.

'I don't think mater's just depressed,' said Pulchra. 'I think someone is trying to poison her.'

'So that's why you wanted books on poison!' cried Flavia.

'Shhh!' said Pulchra. She glanced around and said in a low voice, 'Did you bring any?'

'I brought one of my father's best books on medicine,' said Jonathan. 'It has lots about poison in it.'

'And I brought several scrolls of Pliny's *Natural History*,' said Flavia.

'Praise Juno!' breathed Pulchra and closed her eyes for a moment. Then she looked at each of them in turn. 'I was trying to work it out like Flavia does, and I realised mater only gets ill when we have house-guests, so I asked pater to invite back some of the guests we've had over the past year. The ones who accepted happen to be three bachelors and three young widows, so pater and I have told mater we're doing some matchmaking.

I don't want her to know the real reason we invited them. I don't want to worry her.'

'But you told your father what you suspect?' asked Flavia.

'Yes,' said Pulchra. 'He thinks I could be right. When I suggested inviting you to help us solve the mystery he agreed at once. He always talks about how clever and brave you were when you solved that mystery of the kidnapped children last summer.'

'He says I'm clever and brave?' said Flavia, and Jonathan noticed her cheeks were bright pink.

Pulchra nodded. 'He admires all of you.'

'Pulchra,' said Jonathan. 'Just because your mother gets depressed around house-guests, that doesn't necessarily mean someone is poisoning her.'

'No, Jonathan!' Pulchra put her hand on his arm. 'She doesn't just get depressed. Sometimes she has terrible stomach pains and once she couldn't move her legs, and she went all cold and blue around the mouth. She almost died!' Pulchra's blue eyes welled with tears. 'It was terrible!'

'That does sound like poison,' admitted Jonathan.

Lupus had been scribbling on his wax tablet. Now he held it up:

SO YOU'VE INVITED SIX POSSIBLE POISONERS TO STAY HERE?

Pulchra nodded and blinked away her tears. 'I know it's a risk but I don't know what else to do!'

'Don't worry, Pulchra,' said Flavia, putting an arm around her. 'We'll do everything we can to solve this mystery and save your mother! Now take us to the suspects!'

Pulchra led them up some pink marble stairs towards the highest floor of the villa. 'The bachelors arrived yesterday from Rome,' she said. 'I think they're in pater's library now. They were going up as I was coming down.' She linked her arm in Flavia's and whispered, 'Now that you're betrothed I've been thinking about a future husband, too. One of the bachelors is very handsome and highborn and rich. If he's not the culprit, I might ask pater to arrange a marriage.'

A moment later they moved through polished columns of purple-speckled porphyry into the highest room of the tower. It was a library, with small arched windows and walls covered with scroll-filled pigeon-holes. Flavia stared in wonder. Not even in the Emperor Titus's palace had she seen a room like this, made entirely of coloured marble.

Three young men stood around a table with a grass-green marble top and bronze legs. They were bent over a scroll.

'See if you can guess which one I like,' Pulchra breathed in Flavia's ear.

The men looked up as they heard the scuff of leather sandals on the marble floor.

'Flavia Gemina?' said one of them in a deep voice, squinting at the doorway.

Flavia gasped. 'Floppy! What are you doing here?'

The look of pleasure on the handsome young man's face faded and Flavia clapped her hand over her mouth.

'Oh, I'm sorry . . . I didn't mean to—'

'Floppy?' A red-haired young man with heavy-lidded eyes turned to look at him. 'Did she call you *Floppy*?' He began to laugh.

Pulchra rounded on Flavia. 'You two know each other?'

'Yes,' stammered Flavia. 'We sailed to Rhodes together a few months ago. I'm sorry, um . . . Gaius Valerius Flaccus.'

'It doesn't matter,' Flaccus replied stiffly, and gestured to the red-haired man on his right. 'Flavia Gemina, I'd like you to meet my friends Publius Manilius Vopiscus and Lucius Calpurnius Philodemus.' Here he indicated a man with alert brown eyes in a shiny face. 'Vopiscus and Philodemus,' he sighed, 'allow me to introduce Flavia Gemina and her friends Jonathan, Lupus and Nubia. It appears they'll be joining us this week.'

'Oh, Nubia! Why do I always say such stupid things?'

'You are not always saying stupid things,' said Nubia, opening a cedarwood chest at the foot of one of the two beds. 'But you are always saying what you think. This is your bed,' she added. 'The slaves have put your things here.'

'You don't think Floppy could be the poisoner, do you? Pollux! I did it again. I promised not to call him "Floppy" anymore.'

'I think you should keep that promise and not call him that even in privacy.' Nubia sat on her bed and the dogs padded over to her, tails wagging.

'You're right,' Flavia sighed. 'His hair's hardly floppy now that he's had it cut. But look at *my* hair. It's a tangled mess. Why didn't you tell me?' She leaned forward and peered into the silver mirror over their dressing table.

'Your hair is lovely,' said Nubia loyally.

'Nubia, do you think someone's really trying to poison Polla Argentaria? Or is Pulchra just trying to find an excuse for her mother being so strange and feeble?'

'I do not know,' said Nubia, scratching Scuto with one hand and Nipur with the other. 'But Pulchra says her mother's stomach is unhappy sometimes.'

'We all get unhappy stomachs from time to time,' said Flavia. 'Dear Juno! This mirror is awful! It shows every tiny spot.' Without taking her eyes from her reflection, Flavia turned her head to the left and then to the right. 'Nubia? Do you think my nose is too big?'

'No. It is perfect. It is Flavia-sized.'

'I think it's too big. Also, Pulchra's right: my skin is too tanned.'

'My skin is much darker than yours,' said Nubia.

'But on you it looks exotic and beautiful, especially with your hair plaited like that. And you have lovely golden-brown eyes. Mine are just grey. Dull old grey. Flaccus looked well, didn't he?'

'Flavia! Nubia!' wheezed Jonathan from the doorway. Lupus stood behind him, his chest rising and falling as if he had just been running. 'You've got to see this. The women guests have just arrived and one of them has a wild animal on a leash! Come quickly; you can see them from the library!'

*

As Flavia, Nubia and their two dogs followed Jonathan and Lupus along the colonnade, they passed several guest bedrooms. Some had folding lattice-work screens which could be rolled across the doorway for extra privacy. The boys' room had such a screen so they quickly stopped to shut Scuto and Nipur in with Tigris. 'We don't want the dogs running free,' Jonathan wheezed. 'Trust me.'

Lupus led them up marble stairs to the upper colonnade, through the villa's large bright atrium, then along a peristyle skirting the lemon-tree garden. Finally he ran up the pink stairs to the library of coloured marble, now deserted. The four friends crowded into an arched window and looked east towards the olive groves and the main approach to the villa.

Lupus pointed to the space between the stables and the drive. Flavia could see several elegant women and some slaves moving around a litter with leopard-skin curtains. Another litter with blue curtains was disappearing beneath the covered road, its four bearers jogging. It must be empty, she thought.

Suddenly Flavia gasped. As four Ethiopian slaves lifted the poles of the leopard-skin litter and carried it away, a woman in a red stola was revealed. She had pale skin, a mass of jet-black curls and an enormous black cat on a red leather leash.

'She's beautiful!' said Flavia.

'It is beautiful,' said Nubia.

'Let's get a closer look!' wheezed Jonathan.

Lupus nodded and beckoned enthusiastically, as if to say, *Come on, then!* He ran out of the library and down the stairs. Jonathan and Nubia followed and Flavia took up the rear. She went carefully down the polished marble steps because her sandals were brand new and the leather soles very slippery, but once at the foot of the stairs she broke into a sprint to catch up with her friends.

But she was going too fast, and as she rounded a corner she skidded straight into a grey-haired man emerging from another corridor. Flavia squealed and flailed as she fell backwards. But strong arms caught her and she found herself looking up into the amused dark eyes of Publius Pollius Felix, the Patron.

SCROLL IV

Pulchra's father was not as tall as she remembered but he was just as handsome. And being in his presence still took her breath away. He was smiling and holding her bare shoulders with strong, cool hands. Her knees were trembling and she felt her face grow hot.

'Hello, Flavia Gemina.' Felix's dark eyebrows went up and he leant towards her slightly. 'Investigating another mystery?' He was so close she could smell the citron-scented oil he used on his hair.

'I . . . um . . . we just . . . that is, I . . . hello, Patron.' Flavia knew her cheeks must be bright pink.

He laughed and released his grip on her shoulders.

'Come,' he said. 'I'll introduce you to the exotic Voluptua and her black panther. How was your journey down? I'm sorry I missed your father.' Felix led her through the atrium to the villa's elegant vaulted vestibule, with its arched windows overlooking the sea on the left and the secret cove on the right. As they reached the open double-doors, he stood aside. 'After you, my dear,' he said with a heart-stopping smile. 'After you.'

*

Flavia Gemina to her dearest pater M. Flavius Geminus.

Greetings from Surrentum, pater! I hope you are well. We are all well. I'm not sure when you'll receive this letter – or even if I'll be able to send it – but I promised to write and so I am scribbling a hasty note before dusk fades to night.

The Villa Limona is just as beautiful as I remember it, maybe even more so! The spring rains have washed away all the ash from the trees and plants in the gardens. Everything seems so much greener than it did last August after the eruption of Vesuvius. I have also discovered some new rooms in the villa, including a library!

As well as the four of us, Pulchra's father and mother have invited some other guests to stay. There are three young widows and three eligible bachelors. Pater, you know one of them! Remember Gaius Valerius Flaccus, the young patrician who sailed with us on the Delphina *a few months ago? He is here with his two friends Vopiscus and Philodemus. Vopiscus reminds me of a sleepy-eyed fox and Philodemus is like an eager hunting-dog. They are both about Flaccus's age (18) and they are also studying Rhetoric and Law.*

The three widows are very beautiful. Annia Serena is plump and fair, Claudia Casta is a tawny beauty with eyes like a doe, and Clodia Voluptua is dark and exotic. Voluptua caused quite a stir when she arrived in a leopard-skin litter with a black panther on a leash! Pulchra says her father calls them 'the Sirens' and predicts that the three bachelors will 'run hopelessly aground on the shores of love.' Isn't that clever and funny of him?

We spent most of today settling in. Pulchra showed us a little temple to Neptune which her father erected on an tiny island near the villa, and also a circular shrine to Venus, which her mother paid for. It is perched among the olive groves on the hillside above us. We made a small offering at each shrine and then had a picnic lunch beside the villa's secret cove. It was very hot so we women stayed there to swim while the boys and men used the baths.

Well, I must go. Pulchra's slave-girl Leda has just come to take us to dinner.

Don't forget to take the tonic Dr Mordecai prescribed and to put the balm on your wounds twice a day. And use your walking stick, even if it does make you 'feel like an old man'.

Farewell, dearest pater. I will try to write again tomorrow. Cura ut valeas.

'So, Flavia,' whispered Pulchra. 'Have you devised a plan to solve the mystery?'

'Mystery . . . ?' Flavia was reclining between Pulchra and Nubia on the central couch of the girls' private dining room. She had been thinking about Felix and it took her a moment to take in Pulchra's words. 'Oh! The *mystery*. The mystery of who's trying to poison—'

'Ajax!' cried Pulchra. She glanced pointedly at the couch where her little sisters Pollina and Pollinilla reclined. 'The mystery of who's trying to hurt *Ajax*.'

'Is someone trying to hurt Ajax?' cried Pollina, Pulchra's seven-year-old sister.

'Yes,' said Pulchra, 'Ajax is in danger.'

'Oh, poor puppy!' Six-year-old Pollinilla slid off her dining couch and wrapped her arms around Ajax, who had been snuffling at the dining room floor with the other dogs, looking for old scraps.

'Put down the dog, Pollinilla,' said the girls' pretty young Egyptian nursemaid. She gently lifted the little girl back onto the couch.

'Don't worry,' said Pulchra to her sisters, 'Flavia here is very clever and she's promised to think of a plan to stop the bad . . . animal . . . from hurting Ajax.' Pulchra looked at Flavia. 'You do have a plan, don't you?'

'I suppose the best plan,' said Flavia, 'would be for each of us to choose a suspect . . . I mean one of the er . . . *animals*, and watch them carefully for any suspicious behaviour. For example, I could take the tawny doe.'

Nubia looked puzzled.

Jonathan grinned. 'I'll take the dog. The one with brown eyes and hair – I mean fur. I have a feeling he's from my part of the world.'

I WILL TAKE THE FOX wrote Lupus.

Suddenly Nubia's eyes lit up. 'Oh! I understand! I will take the panther,' she announced.

'I suppose that leaves me with the sheep,' sighed Pulchra.

'Yes, those sheep can be vicious,' said Jonathan.

'What about the um . . . horse?' said Flavia. 'The horse with the *floppy* mane?'

'I don't think he's a suspect,' said Jonathan.

'Still,' said Pulchra, 'one of us should watch him, just to be sure.' She blushed prettily. 'I volunteer.'

'I'll watch pater's cockerel,' announced Pollina in a solemn voice. 'Sometimes he chases Ajax.'

'Good idea,' said Pulchra with a smile.

'I'll watch the chickens!' piped little Pollinilla. 'They are bad chickens!'

Everyone laughed.

'I'll watch the pigeons, too,' she cried, delighted at their reaction. 'And the goldfish in the fish-pond and all the flies and the bugs and every single animal in the whole world!'

'With help like that,' said Flavia with a smile, 'I'm sure we'll find the culprit in no time.'

Later that night Flavia lay on her bed staring up at the stucco ceiling. The pretty roundels painted on it flickered in the dim light of a small bronze oil-lamp. Nubia had been asleep for nearly an hour, and the dogs were snoring gently, but Hypnos refused to visit her.

Flavia sat up, fluffed her pillow, then flopped down on her other side.

It was no good: she was not the least bit sleepy. Rising from her bed, she moved out into the colonnade and rested her forearms on the cool marble parapet. The sea was as black as polished marble and the sky above it was peppered with a million stars. A lopsided moon hung overhead, throwing a path of silver across the inky water.

It was a deliciously warm night, and above the pulsing of the cicadas she thought she heard music. The sound drew her along the colonnade and up the marble stairs. Reaching the upper level, she could clearly hear the textured chords of a lyre and the laughter of adults at a dinner party.

She moved forward on silent bare feet, keeping to the shadows. Presently she found herself in the lemon-tree courtyard. At the far end of this inner garden she saw an illuminated triclinium with three couches and eight diners. So this was why she and her friends had been given an early dinner and hustled to bed: the adults were having a banquet!

Flavia crept closer. Crouching behind a potted rosebush, she gazed into the triclinium. Bronze oil-lamps made the red frescoed walls glow and cast a flattering rosy light on the diners. Felix and his wife reclined on the central couch; she wore a pale blue stola and he looked elegant in a synthesis of the same colour. On the couch to their right – the lectus imus – reclined the three young men in cream tunics. On the lectus summus opposite the men were the women; blonde Annia Serena in dark blue, doe-eyed Claudia in brown silk shot with gold, and raven-haired Voluptua in a filmy red stola. Voluptua's black panther lay chained to one of the legs of the dining couch on which his mistress reclined. Flavia's throat tightened with longing. Oh, to be grown-up and beautiful, reclining in that room on a couch near *him*.

She could tell it was near the end of the meal, for the diners were wearing their garlands and drinking wine. Red-haired Vopiscus was strumming a lyre and reciting verses in Greek which Flavia did not recognise. Everyone smiled and applauded as he finished his poem and handed the lyre on to Flaccus.

'After my recent trip to Rhodes,' said Flaccus in his deep voice, 'I've decided to compose a Latin version of the *Argonautica*. I'd like to recite the first few lines for you now.'

Flavia was about to move closer when a silent figure appeared a few paces away. It was only a barefoot slave-girl moving along the path, but Flavia didn't want to be seen crouching behind a bush in an unbelted tunic with her hair loose around her shoulders.

Reluctantly, she backed out of the garden and left by the nearest exit: stairs leading down to a long grape arbour.

This leafy moon-dappled tunnel led her down onto the villa's western terrace, which smelt of lavender and jasmine. The Bay of Surrentum lay before her, framed by tall, moonlit palm trees. From here she could see a smudge of light on the black water down below. Was someone down there? No. It was probably just the god's lamp burning inside the little Temple of Neptune.

The sound of splashing water led Flavia to the left. She found the fountain at the centre of a herb garden. This garden faced south-west, for maximum exposure to the sun during the day. It smelt wonderful here, for the sun-warmed plants were still releasing their fragrance into the night air.

Suddenly she saw a grey-haired man in a toga standing by the brick wall. Her heart thudded: it was Felix! But how could he be here? He was upstairs dining with the others.

Drawing closer, she saw that it was not the Patron, but a sculpture of him, done in metal and stone. The long toga was white marble but the hands and head were Corinthian bronze. In the light of the half moon she could see that the hair was made of silver, the lips of reddish bronze and the eyes of white onyx, inlaid with black. The sculptor had made Felix handsome as a god, gazing nobly towards the horizon. Tentatively, Flavia reached out to touch the statue's bronze cheek. The polished metal was deliciously smooth, and still warm from the heat of the day.

Flavia took a deep breath and glanced around. When she was sure that she was alone and unobserved, she stepped up onto the marble base, slipped her arms around the statue's neck and kissed his warm bronze lips.

The morning of Flavia's eleventh birthday dawned warm and misty.

She stretched and yawned and pressed her bare feet against Scuto's bulk. He lifted his big head and thumped his tail. From somewhere near the villa, a cock crowed exultantly.

'Good morning, Flavia!' Nubia came to sit on the end of Flavia's bed. 'Happy Birthday.' Nipur put his paws on the mattress and gave Flavia a wet birthday kiss.

Flavia sat up and stretched again. 'Thank you, Nubia.' She took the papyrus twist which Nubia was holding out to her. 'May I open it? Oh! It's a little ebony hairpin with a face that looks like yours on the end! It's beautiful.'

She leaned forward to kiss Nubia's dark cheek.

'You know,' she said softly, staring at the hairpin, 'I was thinking that today is special for you, too. Do you remember it was exactly a year ago that I bought you in order to save you from a fate worse than death?'

'How could I forget?' said Nubia. 'I remember how kind you were to me that day. You put your cloak around me to cover my nakedness and you put balm on the sore places on my neck and you fed me and gave me cool water to drink.'

Flavia nodded and tried to swallow a sudden tightness in her throat.

'And it was here in the Villa Limona,' continued Nubia, 'that you set me free. I will never forget that, too.'

'Happy Birthday, Flavia!' Jonathan and Lupus stood in the doorway. Tigris squeezed between them to greet Nipur and Scuto. 'We brought you our presents now', said Jonathan, 'because Pulchra will probably have bought you something that cost five million sesterces and we didn't want to be humiliated.'

Flavia laughed and patted the bed beside her. The boys sat and Jonathan handed her a scroll.

'No big surprise there,' he said. 'It's a book.'

'What is it?' cried Flavia, slipping the scroll out of its red linen case.

He shrugged. 'It's just a volume of Seneca's letters. You probably won't like it.'

'Oh, I'm sure I will. Thank you, Jonathan!' Flavia planted a kiss on his surprised cheek.

Lupus dropped his rectangular parcel on Flavia's lap and ran to the other side of the room, a look of alarm on his face.

'Don't worry, Lupus!' laughed Flavia as she pulled the papyrus wrapping off his gift. 'I promise I won't kiss you. Oh look! You painted portraits of the four of us on a limewood panel! Oh, Lupus, it's wonderful!' She jumped up. 'I *am* going to give you a kiss!'

Lupus gave a mock yelp of terror and ran out of the bedroom. Flavia ran after him, laughing. Jonathan, Nubia and the barking dogs followed close behind. They chased Lupus along the lower colonnade and up the stairs through the atrium and into the garden with the lemon tree.

'I'm Atalanta,' Flavia cried, 'and I can run faster than any man! I'm going to catch you, Lupus, and I'm going to kiss you!'

Flavia pursued Lupus around the garden and finally they ended up on either side of Felix's prized lemon tree. As Flavia ran left, Lupus dodged right, and tumbled backwards over Tigris, who was barking with excitement. Flavia seized her chance and leapt on top of the younger boy and lowered her head to kiss his cheek. Lupus yelled and thrashed his head from side to side. By this time Flavia was laughing so hard that he easily pushed her off.

She lay on her back, laughing and staring up at the leaves of the lemon tree and the pure blue sky beyond as the three dogs licked her face.

'Edepol!' said a voice. 'That's not very ladylike behaviour. I certainly hope you won't act like that when we're betrothed.'

Flavia pushed the dogs away and raised herself up on her elbows. Pulchra was standing beside a boy about their own age, a horrified look on her face.

'What did you say?' said Flavia, scrambling to her feet and brushing the dust off her tunic. 'Who are you?'

'My name is Tranquillus,' said the boy with a smirk. He had straight brown hair and pale arched eyebrows and although he was a good two inches shorter than Flavia he managed to look at her with a superior air. 'I believe you and I are to be married.'

SCROLL V

'What?!' gasped Flavia Gemina. 'You're the boy my father wants me to marry?' She glanced at Pulchra, who nodded and then closed her eyes and shook her head in despair.

'I am.' The boy folded his arms and looked her up and down with obvious disapproval. 'And I hope you'll behave with more decorum when you're my wife.'

'Why you . . . you . . .'

'Flavia!' cried Pulchra, a note of pleading in her voice.

Flavia ignored Pulchra. 'Why, you smug little runt! I'd rather jump off the top of that tower than marry you!'

Flavia heard laughter and she turned to see four men watching from the peristyle: Publius Pollius Felix and the three bachelors.

'Oh Nubia!' groaned Flavia Gemina. 'This is the worst day of my life!'

They were back in the girls' bedroom and Flavia sat before the mirror, her head in her hands.

'Was not the worst day of your life the day when you were almost devoured by hippos and crocs in the amphitheatre?' asked Nubia, patting Flavia's shoulder.

'No! This is far worse than that.' She lifted her head. 'Pater wants me to marry that arrogant boy! And Felix saw me in my sleeping tunic with my hair down all covered in dust. How could you let me go out looking like this?'

'Don't blame Nubia,' said Pulchra crisply from the bedroom door. 'It was entirely your own fault!'

'I know!' wailed Flavia, resting her head on her arms. 'I'm so stupid!'

'How is your mother today?' Nubia asked Pulchra. 'Is her stomach happy?'

'Mater's stomach is perfectly happy today, Nubia,' said Pulchra. 'Thank you for asking.' She looked pointedly at Flavia, then sighed. 'You really are your own worst enemy,' she said to Flavia. 'What on earth have you done to your hair? It's all sticky and clumped together.'

'Before we left Ostia I tried out a new rinse to make it shiny.'

'What new rinse?'

'Honey and hot water. It's what Jonathan's sister Miriam uses after she washes her hair. It makes her curls bouncy and glossy.'

'Well it doesn't work for you. Your hair looks terrible. And that colour! Neither blonde nor brown. You should probably bleach it with lye.'

'Do you think so?' said Flavia doubtfully.

'And you should eat lots of hare.'

'Hare?' said Nubia. 'Like rabbit?'

'Yes. Everybody knows that eating hare makes you more attractive. Don't worry; I've asked Coqua to get lots in.'

Flavia frowned. 'You think I need to eat more hare?'

Pulchra nodded and then sighed. 'Flavia, listen to me. I'm about to tell you something nobody else will. You are not beautiful and you never will be.'

Flavia stared at Pulchra.

'I'm sorry to be the one to tell you.' Pulchra pulled up a stool and sat down beside the girls. 'Nubia is beautiful but you are not. Your nose is too big and your mouth is too wide. You have knobbly knees and big feet. Your brow is too high, and if you're not careful' – she pushed the hair away from Flavia's forehead – 'you'll be getting spots, soon.'

Flavia opened her mouth and then closed it.

'Don't look at me like that. Beauty is not everything. And you don't really need it. Mater says girls who are dull need to be beautiful. You are not dull. You are clever and witty. But if you had a mother,' said Pulchra gently, 'she would tell you to make the best of your looks so that your inner beauty could shine through. She would teach you to be well-groomed.'

'Well-groomed?' said Flavia. 'That makes me sound like a horse.'

'Not at all. Being well-groomed means having attractive, well-coiffed hair, smooth limbs and flawless pale skin.' Pulchra glanced at her own reflection and touched her silky golden hair, done up in an elegant twist. Then she turned back to Flavia. 'Cheer up! I'm going to start transforming you right now. The boys and men and dogs have gone off hunting so we women have all morning to beautify ourselves in the baths.'

'All right,' said Flavia with a resigned sigh. 'I'm in your hands.'

*

'It's the wrong season for hunting,' grumbled Jonathan to Flaccus as he snapped a thrush's neck, 'It's far too hot for any sensible animal to be out. I'll be surprised if we'll find anything much apart from these.'

Jonathan and most of the hunting party were stood in a clearing, plucking birds from a rod held by one of Felix's hunt-slaves. The tip of this long, flexible rod had been smeared with sticky yellow bird-lime. Once the birds alighted they could not escape. The hunt-slave lifted the rod back up to the tree and gave a convincing bird call.

'I wouldn't be too sure this is all we'll find,' said Flaccus with a chuckle. He nodded over at Felix, who was showing Lupus how to throw a javelin at the edge of the clearing. 'This is only the gustatio. I'm sure our host will have sent his slaves ahead with orders to loose the main course just as we approach. A dozen hare or a small deer, I'd wager.'

'I'm just not used to having everything done for me,' muttered Jonathan.

'That's because you're a real hunter.'

Jonathan gave Flaccus a grudging smile, then turned to the man on his left. He was supposed to be finding out whether Philodemus might be a suspect or not.

'So, Philodemus?' asked Jonathan in a low voice. 'What do you think of our host and hostess?'

'Felix and my father were good friends,' replied Philodemus. 'The Patron has been very kind to me.'

'And Polla Argentaria?'

'A beautiful and gracious hostess,' said Philodemus carefully.

Jonathan tried a different approach. 'Do you like hunting?' he asked, watching Felix's hunt-slave move the long rod to the top of another tree.

'Yes,' said Philodemus. 'Though I prefer gardening.'

'Gardening? You mean plants and flowers and um . . . medicinal herbs?'

'Yes.' Philodemus's large brown eyes were suddenly moist. 'Our villa had a magnificent garden. But it was destroyed by the volcano.'

'Philodemus was up in Rome with me when Vesuvius erupted last summer,' said Flaccus softly. 'He and his family lost everything.'

'I'm sorry,' said Jonathan. 'Very sorry.'

Philodemus nodded sadly. 'The Lord gives and the Lord takes away,' he quoted softly.

Jonathan looked up sharply. He had suspected that Philodemus was a fellow Jew, now he was sure of it.

'You had that enormous library full of Epicureans, didn't you?' said a voice behind them. It was red-haired Vopiscus, emerging from the bushes where he had gone to relieve himself.

'Yes,' said Philodemus. 'That I do not regret so much. It was my grandfather's philosophy, and my father's. It is not mine.'

'Still, that library must have been worth a fortune.' Vopiscus shaded his eyes with his hand and gazed up into the tops of the trees. 'I'd give anything for just a dozen scrolls from that library.'

'But it sounds as if you miss the garden more than the library,' said Jonathan, hoping to steer the topic around to poison.

'Yes,' said Philodemus.

'Do you know a lot about plants?'

'I know a little.'

'Do you happen to know what that one is?' Jonathan casually pointed at a plant with dark blue berries which he knew to be poisonous.

'That's belladonna,' said Philodemus. 'A very deadly plant. And this one over here—' Philodemus moved across the clearing, 'is aconite. If you rub the juice of this on the tip of your arrows it will make them ten times more lethal. They call it wolfsbane, because if you shoot a wolf with an arrowhead tipped with this, then it will certainly die.'

Jonathan squatted to examine the plant. 'I didn't know that,' he said, plucking a leaf and smelling it.

'Why do you use a bow and arrow anyway?' asked Tranquillus, coming up to join them. 'It's a girly weapon.'

'What?' Jonathan turned to stare at the boy Flavia was supposed to marry.

Tranquillus shrugged. 'I was just wondering why you didn't take a javelin like Lupus and me. Or a hunting-spear, like the men.'

Jonathan shrugged. 'I prefer the bow,' he said as he unwrapped Tigris's lead from an olive tree. 'It's what I'm used to.'

'Archery is for girls,' said Tranquillus contemptuously. 'Or barbarians. Or girl barbarians, like the Amazons.' He looked round at the others in the hunting party. 'Did you know that the Amazons cut off their right breasts to pull the bowstring more easily? That's why they call them Amazons.' He giggled.

'Just ignore him,' said Philodemus to Jonathan under his breath. 'Turn the other cheek.'

Jonathan stared at Philodemus. He was about to ask what philosophy he followed when there was a loud burst of laughter; Vopiscus had just made an amusing remark.

'What did he say?' asked Jonathan.

Flaccus turned and grinned down at him. 'Amazons or sirens,' he said. 'Which would you rather do battle with?'

'Sirens, I suppose,' said Jonathan.

Flaccus slapped him on the back, 'Good man,' he said. 'That would be my choice, too.'

'Amazons,' said Tranquillus, his face flushed with pleasure at the success of his topic. 'I'd like to do battle with Amazons.'

Everyone laughed as Lupus mimed a girl firing an arrow and then made kissing noises. He had left Felix, who was giving instructions to one of his slaves.

'I'll tell you who I'd like to do battle with,' said Vopiscus. 'Voluptua. A little bed-wrestling, I think.'

'Watch out for that one, my friend,' said Flaccus. 'They say she's a legacy-hunter.'

'Then I'll take the fluffy blonde one.' Vopiscus grinned. 'Or haughty Claudia.'

'You have a very casual approach to marriage,' said Philodemus quietly.

'They're all pretty, and they all look fertile,' said Vopiscus, and added with a shrug, 'If your expectations are low, you won't be disappointed.'

For some reason Jonathan thought of his mother. When he had gone to Rome to find her and bring her home, his expectations had been so high. He had imagined that his reunited parents would live happily together in Ostia, his father curing people's illnesses and his mother weaving at home. Instead, his mother spent most of the day out of the house and his father looked ten years older. And the price of bringing her back had been so great. He thought of the flames and shuddered.

At that moment one of the hunt-slaves came crashing through the shrubbery onto the path up ahead.

'Master!' he ran up to Felix. 'The nets on the south ridge! We've caught something! The biggest boar I've ever seen!'

SCROLL VI

'So Flavia,' whispered Pulchra, as she stripped off her tunic and placed it in a shell-shaped marble niche, 'do you have any theories?'

'Theories?' Flavia's voice was muffled as she pulled her own tunic over her head. The three girls were in the domed apodyterium in the baths of the Villa Limona. 'Theories about what?'

'About who's trying to poison mater!'

'Oh, that,' Flavia paused, her head still covered by her tunic. She doubted that Polla Argentaria was in danger, but just in case Pulchra was right . . . 'Motive,' she said, pulling off her tunic and folding it carefully. 'I suggest we start with motive. Why would anyone want to poison your mother?'

'I've thought and thought,' said Pulchra, 'but I don't know.' She sat on the curved marble bench to undo her sandals. 'All she ever does is sleep and read and sit in her chair staring out at that mountain. Here.' She reached up into one of the niches and brought down a tin box shaped like the top of a scroll case. 'Use this instead of oil. It's the bleaching cream I was telling you about.'

Opening the tin, Flavia saw something like lard. 'Mmmm,' she said. 'It smells nice, like lemons.' She held it out for Nubia to sniff. 'What if it isn't one of the house-guests?' mused Flavia. 'What if it's your cook? She's the most obvious suspect because she's always around the food.'

'Coqua? Impossible,' said Pulchra, handing a bronze jar of scented oil to Nubia and taking one for herself. 'Coqua has been with mater's family since she was a little girl. She's a verna, a home-grown slave. She's completely trustworthy.'

'I like Coqua,' said Nubia, anointing herself with lemon-scented oil. 'She is kind.'

'Could it be one of the slaves?' asked Flavia in a low voice. She glanced at Pulchra's drab slave-girl Leda, who was folding bath-towels on the other side of the room.

'We make the serving-girls taste all the food,' said Pulchra. 'We do the same with the wine-stewards and the wine. If there was poison in either the food or wine, the tasters would take ill first.'

'Hmmn,' said Flavia thoughtfully, as she smoothed the lemon-scented cream on her arms. 'I suppose we should research different poisons and their symptoms. We'll have a look at the scrolls we brought. And maybe there will be something useful in your father's library.' The thought of Felix made her flush. 'Oh, Pulchra, why did you invite him?'

'Who?'

'That horrible boy. The one I'm supposed to marry. It was so humiliating!'

'Tranquillus? I thought you'd be pleased. Pater's friends in Rome went to a lot of trouble to find out who your betrothed was and track him down. How was

I to know his first glimpse of his future wife would be of her rolling about on the ground with a pack of dogs? Oh, don't put that cream on your legs; I'm going to give you a depilatory.'

Flavia scowled. 'He's an arrogant patrician snob.'

'You shouldn't scorn patricians, Flavia. You and I are of the equestrian class. We should set our sights on the next rung of the ladder. Come on.' Pulchra rose and led the two girls out of the apodyterium.

'I thought your father was a patrician,' said Flavia as she followed Nubia and Pulchra into a warm rectangular room. The three widows were stretched out on marble slabs; slave-girls were massaging them.

'Hello, ladies!' said Pulchra brightly. 'Are you happy?'

The three widows made noises of contentment and Pulchra turned back to Flavia. 'Our family may be powerful and rich,' she said, 'but we're only equestrians like you. However, I plan to marry into the highest class and raise patrician children.'

'Bravo,' purred Voluptua from her massage-slab. 'That's what I intend to do. Marry a rich patrician.'

'You should make that your goal, too,' said Pulchra to Flavia. They sat down on a polished wooden bench beneath a frescoed wall with blue and yellow panels. 'Tranquillus comes from an illustrious family with cartloads of money. He has excellent prospects of becoming a senator. And they say he's very clever.'

'I don't like him,' said Flavia. 'And he's shorter than I am.'

'Oh Flavia, Flavia, Flavia!' said Pulchra. 'Can't you look ahead more than a month or two?' She snapped her fingers. 'Leda! Bring the depilatory.' Pulchra turned back to Flavia. 'I know Tranquillus is just a boy now, but he'll grow. That's what boys do. And you know, I think he'll turn out quite nicely. His father's very presentable.'

'That's true,' said Annia Serena, the woolly blonde. She turned over on her marble bench and wrapped a towel around herself. 'I've seen that boy's father in Rome and he's quite handsome.'

'But what if Tranquillus isn't my destined love?'

'What in Juno's name are you babbling about?' said Pulchra. 'One doesn't marry for love. One marries for position, stability and children. Right ladies?'

Voluptua grunted her assent, Annia Serena giggled and Claudia Casta said nothing.

'Oh there you are, Leda,' said Pulchra. 'The depilatory's for Flavia.'

'What's a depilatory?'

'It's for your hairy legs. They are so unattractive.'

'But it's hardly noticeable on me,' protested Flavia, stretching out one leg. 'All my leg-hairs are very pale and little. You can barely see them.'

'Flavia, in a certain light they're completely visible. Roman men don't like hairy women. You and Nubia don't want furry monkey-legs, do you?'

'How can you not believe in love?' sighed Flavia, as Pulchra's slave-girl knelt and began to apply the sticky brown paste to her legs. 'What about Dido and Aeneas?'

'That is the perfect example. Which one succumbed to passion?'

'Dido.'

'And what happened to her?'

'She killed herself with a big sword.'

'And which one overcame his passion to do what was right?'

'Pious Aeneas.'

'And what happened to him?'

'He sailed to Italia and married the beautiful young Roman princess Lavinia and became the father of the Roman race.'

'There you are.'

'But what about Catullus and Propertius and Ovid and all the other poets who write so passionately about the women they love?'

'Pater says all love-poets are strange little men,' said Pulchra. 'He says real men don't give in to their passions. It makes them weak. Pater believes in *ataraxia*, freedom from passion.'

Abruptly, Claudia rose naked from her bench and disappeared through a small arched doorway into the caldarium next door. The pretty freckled slave-girl who had been massaging her looked at Pulchra in alarm.

'Don't worry about her, Leucosia,' said Pulchra to the slave-girl. 'Come and do Nubia's legs.'

'Ugh!' Flavia wrinkled her nose. 'That depilatory doesn't smell as nice as the bleaching cream. What's it made of, anyway?'

'That particular depilatory,' said Pulchra, 'is made of turpentine and boars' blood.'

Jonathan smelled the boar before he saw it: a pungent aroma of rank pig, mouldy leaves and fear that set his heart pounding. Then he saw a dark shape struggling in a net lashed between two oak trees. The creature had coarse black hair, curved yellow tusks and little red eyes. He stopped thrashing when the three baying dogs burst into the clearing, straining against their leads.

'Back, Tigris! Stay back!' grunted Jonathan, and to Flaccus, 'I don't think this is part of Felix's plan to give us a jolly hunting party.'

'Certainly not,' growled Flaccus, who held Scuto's lead. 'That net isn't even secured properly.'

Vopiscus snorted. 'As Ovid says: *A loose-netted boar that breaks free is not good.*'

'It doesn't look that big,' said Tranquillus.

It was much darker in this dense copse of holm-oaks than in the dappled olive groves, and at first Jonathan didn't notice two of Felix's slaves off to one side. One was crouching over the other, who lay moaning on the ground. The ugly gash in his thigh was still pouring blood onto the dark leafy earth.

'I'm sorry, Patron!' The wounded slave struggled to his feet. 'I was trying to secure the net and the beast got me.'

'Careful, everyone,' said Felix, without taking his eyes from the net. 'He's going to make a bolt for freedom.'

'He's mine!' cried a high excited voice, and Jonathan saw Tranquillus rush past Felix and aim his javelin at the boar.

'No!' cried Felix, 'Don't provoke it!'

But his warning came too late, and instead of striking the boar, the javelin hit one of the loose net ties, releasing it from the tree trunk. The boar twisted free, and as Tranquillus staggered back, he tripped and fell.

If the boar had chosen to, Jonathan knew it could

have ended Tranquillus's life by goring him in the neck or groin. But Lupus had loosed Nipur and the boar was running away from the clamouring dog, up the hill towards the deepest part of the copse. Unfortunately, the boar's escape route took it to a hunt-rope strung across that part of the path and the bright dangling feathers did their job.

'Roll over!' Felix shouted at Tranquillus, as the boar turned back. 'Protect your stomach!'

In the time it took Jonathan to release Tigris and notch an arrow, the creature was charging back down the slope towards Tranquillus.

Flavia's future husband lay face down on the ground, and the biggest boar Jonathan had ever seen was charging straight towards him.

In one fluid movement Jonathan's bow was up and he felt the tickle of feathers on his cheek and then the twanging release. The boar squealed and veered away from Tranquillus and towards Jonathan. The arrow was embedded in its bristling neck but still the creature advanced. Jonathan had never seen anything move so fast.

Before he could notch another arrow, the dogs were on the boar. But they only slowed the boar's charge for a moment. Then the ugly creature threw them away like a dog shaking off drops of water. The dogs yelped and a man cried out. Jonathan loosed his second arrow but it only struck the boar's flank as the creature veered to charge someone on Jonathan's right.

Flaccus.

He had called out to divert the beast's attention from Jonathan and now the boar was impaled on his spear. If it had not been for the cross-bar, the furious animal would have run up its full length. Flaccus's muscles bulged and his handsome face was set in a grim mask.

Jonathan marvelled that a creature no bigger than Tigris should have such power; Flaccus was one of the strongest men he knew.

Suddenly Felix was beside Flaccus. He brought his own hunting-spear down in a powerful arc, impaling the squealing pig at the base of its neck and pinning it to the earth.

For ten long heartbeats the boar continued to scrabble at the ground, squealing in impotent rage. Lupus, Vopiscus and Philodemus came up cautiously to watch. The dogs circled warily and Jonathan glanced at them, relieved that none had been gored. Finally the boar shuddered, slumped and lay still. A slow trickle of blood oozed from its mouth onto the dark earth.

Laughing with relief, Felix and Flaccus clasped hands over the boar's body. Then Felix turned to Jonathan. 'Well done, Jonathan,' he said, his chest still rising and falling and his dark eyes full of approval. 'Your quick action saved Tranquillus's life.'

'Yes, well done!' echoed Philodemus.

Flaccus patted Jonathan on the back and Lupus gave him a beaming thumbs-up.

'I owe you an apology,' said Tranquillus, coming up to Jonathan. There were leaves in his hair and a smear of earth across his smooth cheek. 'I have reconsidered my previous opinion. I now think your girly bow and arrows are a very good thing.' He held out his hand. 'Pax?'

'Pax,' said Jonathan with a grin, and they shook hands.

Flavia put down her new scroll of Seneca's letters and stared out through the bright square of her doorway. In the intense heat of mid-afternoon the cicadas' grating chant was as slow as a heartbeat. Everyone in the villa was napping, but Flavia felt restless.

She went out of her room into the shaded colonnade with its cool breeze to see if the boys and dogs were back from hunting. But their room was empty and quiet, the lattice-work screen pulled back, everything made neat and clean by the household slaves.

Flavia entered a dim corridor and took the stairs that led down to the marble fish-pond and the baths. Shading her eyes against the dazzling surface of the sea before her, she turned left and went past the baths complex and along the terrace to the sunny herb garden. A slave must have just finished watering the plants because she could smell hot wet brick and the green scent of leaves being cooked by sunshine. Tall sunflowers gazed up at Helios as he slowly arced across the sky.

Flavia's feet took her to the statue of Felix.

With the afternoon sun gleaming on his bronze features and silver hair, he looked like a god. *Oh Felix*, she said in her mind, *You're far too old for me and you're married and it's so wrong . . .* She wanted to kiss his bronze lips again but she knew the metal would be burning hot. Instead, she contented herself with gazing at his dazzling image through half-closed eyes. Presently she heard footsteps on the marble terrace behind her. *Oh please, Venus*, she prayed, *please let it be him.*

She turned and her heart sank. It was Claudia Casta, one of the young widows. Flavia felt a sudden pang of guilt. She was supposed to be watching the house-guests for unusual behaviour, not worshipping the statue of Felix. And Claudia was the one she herself had chosen to keep an eye on. She looked beautiful and cool in a mustard-coloured silk tunic with a matching parasol.

'Hello, Claudia!' said Flavia. 'Isn't it wonderful here?'

Claudia looked sharply from Flavia to the statue of Felix and back at Flavia. 'I suppose.' She turned away to examine a potted pomegranate.

'They're pretty, aren't they?' said Flavia, coming up to join Claudia. 'I love the little orange trumpet-shaped flowers.'

Claudia shrugged and moved away towards a low pot of lavender. Some of the herbs were arranged in beds around the fountain, others were in pots, clipped into different geometrical shapes: cubes, cones and spheres.

Flavia followed her. 'I like gardens,' she said. 'And this one smells so wonderful. Do you have a garden at your house?'

'Oh, yes,' said Claudia, taking a sprig of lavender. 'I wish I was there now.' Her beautiful mink-coloured hair was pinned up in a way that allowed glossy tendrils to fall loose and brush her shoulders.

'If you'd rather be there, then why are you here?'

'One doesn't refuse an invitation from the Patron.'

'Oh,' said Flavia, and after a pause, 'Where do you live?

'I have a villa near Neapolis,' said Claudia, pinching off some of the herb. 'In a place called Pausilypon.'

'Was it damaged by the volcano?'

'Not really.' Claudia bent to pluck a feathery spray of

fennel from one of the borders. 'But my husband died in the eruption.'

'Oh. I'm sorry.'

'Don't be. He was with one of his mistresses in Herculaneum when the volcano erupted. He left me everything. I am a very rich woman.' For the first time Claudia looked directly at Flavia. Her long-lashed brown eyes were full of something close to hatred.

'I . . . I'm sorry,' repeated Flavia in a faltering voice. She wondered what she had done to make this beautiful woman dislike her so much.

'And you?' said Claudia, with forced brightness. 'Where do you live?'

'In Ostia. But we were in Stabia when the volcano erupted and we only just survived. We came here afterwards. That's how we know Felix and Polla,' she added.

'Yes,' said Claudia flatly, plucking a sprig of rosemary. 'He was a friend of my husband. I think he hopes I'll find another and re-marry.'

'Will you?' said Flavia. 'Will you marry again?'

Claudia turned to face her. 'Tell me, Flavia Gemina,' she said. 'Have you ever been in love?'

Flavia stared at Claudia open-mouthed. She felt her cheeks burning.

'I thought so,' said Claudia.

'Just because I'm only eleven doesn't mean I can't love someone!' said Flavia angrily.

'Oh, I wasn't questioning that.' Claudia glanced at the statue of Felix. 'I fell in love for the first time when I was your age. I have never known such intensity of feeling before or since.'

'What happened?'

Claudia moved to the white marble parapet and looked out over the water. 'He seduced me and discarded me.' Claudia crushed the herbs in her hand and let them drift slowly down to the rocks below. 'Then he married me off to one of his friends. No, Flavia Gemina,' she said, without turning around. 'I will never marry again.'

Later that evening, at her birthday banquet in the girls' triclinium, Flavia began to cry.

'Flavia!' cried Pulchra. 'What's the matter? Don't you like the make-up kit I got you? I know it only looks like a piece of slate with a mortar and pestle and some chunks of red and blue rock, but when I show you how to use it, I promise you'll love it.'

'Don't you like our bangles?' cried Pollina from the little girls' couch.

'They jingle when you wear them,' said Pollinilla.

'Don't you like the signet ring with Minerva on it?' said Tranquillus. 'I know it's only glass, but it belonged to my grandmother.' He and Jonathan and Lupus had spent the afternoon in the baths, washing off the dust and sweat of the hunt.

'I love all your presents,' sniffed Flavia. 'But Pulchra said she had a birthday surprise planned and I thought she meant we were going to eat with the adults.'

Pulchra sighed patiently. 'Pater and mater don't usually eat with children. Except for the beach banquet, of course. Last year was an exception,' she added.

Tranquillus gave a sheepish grin: 'I think I was supposed to be the birthday surprise,' he said.

Flavia ignored him. 'But Pulchra, I'm almost grown-up. I'll be twelve next year.'

'Flavia, until you marry and dedicate your bulla to the gods, you're still a child.'

Flavia bit her lip.

'Oh, Flavia. Does it really mean that much to you?'

Flavia nodded and tried to hold back the tears that were welling up again. She had spent most of the afternoon memorising passages from the *Aeneid* so that she could impress Felix with her knowledge.

'Stop making that face,' said Pulchra. 'I have an idea, and another present for you.' She went out of the dining room just as a serving girl brought in the gustatio, a dozen stuffed thrushes lying on a bed of peppery-green rocket.

'Do you think we'll have some of your boar tonight as well?' said Tranquillus to Jonathan.

Lupus took a thrush and echoed the question with a grunt.

Jonathan shook his head. 'It will take at least a day to roast that thing.'

'Did I tell you how Jonathan saved my life today, Flavia?' asked Tranquillus cheerfully.

'Only three times.' She sighed, then looked up eagerly as Pulchra clomped back into the dining room. Pulchra was wearing gilded sandals with thick cork soles that made her tower above Flavia on the couch.

'Good news,' said Pulchra breathlessly. 'Pater and mater say the two of us can join them for the secunda mensa, as your special birthday treat. And I've decided to give you a pair of sandals like mine. They're the latest fashion in Rome. I bought an extra pair, so here! You have them. They'll make you look very grown-up.'

'Oh Pulchra, thank you!' cried Flavia. She accepted the gilded sandals and happily kissed Pulchra's extended cheek.

'I hope you boys don't mind!' said Pulchra over her shoulder as she slipped off her shoes and climbed up onto the couch beside Flavia.

Lupus shrugged.

'Well, I mind!' said Tranquillus.

'I don't,' said Jonathan. 'That means there'll be more of those honey lemon-cakes for the rest of us.'

'Happy Birthday, Flavia Gemina!' said Publius Pollius Felix from his couch. He raised his eyebrows at her platform shoes. 'How you've grown. And in one afternoon. Come! Recline here at the fulcrum of our couch.'

Flavia tried to control a grin that felt as wide as a comic mask's.

'You, too, my little nightingale,' said Felix to Pulchra.

'Happy Birthday!' cried the others, as Flavia tottered after Pulchra into the red-walled triclinium.

Flavia slipped off her cork-soled shoes and climbed up onto the wave-like wooden end of the cushioned dining couch. She stretched out at an angle, so that her head was pointed towards the centre of the room and her feet almost touched the back wall. Pulchra reclined beside and in front of her. Then came the Patron and his wife. Flavia was so close to Felix that she could see his back muscles moving beneath his sky-blue synthesis as he shifted on the couch.

A long-haired slave-boy of about Jonathan's age brought Flavia and Pulchra ceramic wine cups with images in red-figure on the wide flat bowls. The previous summer Felix had given Flavia just such a kylix, a fabulously expensive Greek antique which showed Dionysus and the pirates. This cup had a simpler design – a running hare – but Flavia could tell it was also old and valuable. The slave-boy poured in a splash of dark red wine and then added water until the cup was full of clear pink liquid.

As he stepped back, a pretty freckled slave-girl moved forward and extended a plate of honeyed lemon-cakes. It was the same slave-girl who had given Nubia her depilatory that morning. Flavia remembered her name was Leucosia.

'Thank you, Leucosia,' said Flavia, taking a cake and smiling politely at the girl. But Leucosia ignored Flavia; her eyes were fixed on her master.

Felix took a cake from the platter and started to bite into it. Then he paused and extended it so that it almost touched the pretty slave-girl's mouth. Her eyes still boldly fixed on his, Leucosia took a bite, then slowly licked her lips. Felix smiled at her. He took a bite from the same cake, then passed it on to Polla.

'Giton,' he snapped his fingers at the long-haired wine-steward. 'Bring me that *oenochoe*.'

The slave-boy picked up a wine jug and handed it to Felix, who passed it to Flavia. 'What do you make of that, Flavia Gemina?' said Felix, looking over his left shoulder at her.

Flavia took the jug carefully, for it was full of wine, and heavy. She knew this was a kind of test.

'It's a red-figure wine-jug, an *oenochoe*,' she said carefully, using the Greek term as he had done, 'so it must be about five hundred years old.'

'Excellent,' said Felix and she noticed him raise his eyebrows at Flaccus, as if they had been discussing this earlier. 'And the subject matter?'

'It's the Greek hero Odysseus, tied to the mast of his ship,' said Flavia, 'with his head thrown back as he listens to the sirens' song. The sirens were mythical creatures who were half women and half bird,' she explained. 'They lived on a rocky island, and they sang so beautifully that no man could resist their song. But whenever sailors tried to get to the sirens they crashed and drowned. On his way home from Troy, Odysseus had a clever idea of how he could hear the sirens' song and live.' Flavia looked up to see Flaccus give her an encouraging smile.

Flavia took a breath and continued. 'Odysseus got his sailors to tie him to the mast of his ship and he commanded them not to untie him, no matter how hard he struggled. Then he told his men to plug their ears with wax and row past the Sirens' Rock. When Odysseus heard the haunting song of the sirens he struggled and cried out to his men. He begged them to let him go to the sirens. But they couldn't hear him – or the sirens – and so they just kept on rowing. And that's how Odysseus became the only mortal to hear the sirens' song and live.'

Flavia looked up. All eyes were on her, including Felix's. She felt something more was required. Of course! A literary quote; something witty and relevant to the story. But none of the passages she had learnt from the *Aeneid* applied. Then she remembered that her tutor Aristo had made them memorise the first few lines of the *Odyssey* in the original Greek, so she quoted part of that:

'Sing, Muse, the story of the wily hero who, having taken Troy, was driven to wander near and far . . . he suffered anguish on the high seas in his struggles . . .'

Flavia trailed off, unsure how to finish. But Flaccus led the others in applause and she breathed a sigh of relief and a silent thank-you to Aristo.

Felix took the jug from her and examined it for a moment. 'The expression on his face looks more like ecstasy than anguish,' he said, raising an eyebrow and handed it back to the slave-boy.

'Are the two not very similar?' said Flaccus in his deep soft voice, and quoted something in Greek that Flavia did not understand.

Everyone laughed and applauded again.

'Now that our guest of honour has proved herself,' said Felix, 'I have a small request. I'm going to ask each of you to share a confidence. Something you've never told anyone before.'

Pulchra leant back to whisper in Flavia's ear. 'I love it when he does this!'

'Of course,' said Felix, 'anything you share will remain a secret between those of us here in this room. And we must send the slaves away.' Felix dismissed the slaves with a wave of his hand.

Pulchra was leaning back again. 'Pater says people rarely refuse. They love to confess.'

'No whispering!' Felix gave Pulchra a mock frown. Then he looked at Flavia. 'Would our birthday girl like to go first? I know you're very brave, my dear, but are you brave enough to share something about yourself that you've never told anyone before?'

Flavia stared at him.

Felix was asking her to share a secret about herself and there was only one possible reply: *Last night I kissed your statue.*

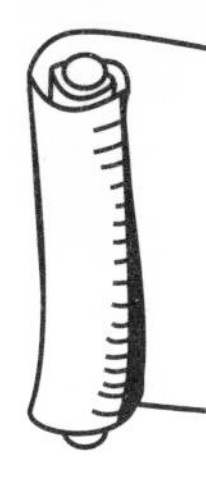

SCROLL VIII

Publius Pollius Felix had dared Flavia to confess a secret in front of all the adult guests. Her mind was frozen like a deer surrounded by hunting-dogs. She knew there were a dozen exploits she could share: breathtaking accounts of her recent adventures, private meetings with the Emperor, the solving of crimes. But only one secret. She saw herself standing on tiptoe, kissing his bronze lips and she felt her cheeks grow hotter and hotter.

'I'll share,' said a deep voice.

'Valerius Flaccus!' said Felix, turning away from Flavia with a smile. 'You'd tell us a secret about yourself?'

The young man nodded and smiled. As all eyes turned from Flavia to Flaccus, she almost sobbed with relief.

'Two months ago,' said Flaccus, 'I discovered that my personal slave, a boy I've had since I was ten, was not the son of a captured barbarian as my father and I had been told, but rather a freeborn Roman boy who'd been illegally kidnapped by slave-traders.'

The three women on the left-hand couch gasped and Polla closed her eyes, as if in pain.

Sleepy-eyed Vopiscus put down his wine cup and raised an eyebrow at Flaccus. 'You mean that pretty blond boy of yours is highborn?'

'Yes. Of the patrician class. It turns out his father was prefect of the fleet at Ravenna.'

'My dear Valerius!' murmured Polla. 'How terrible that must have been for you!'

'It was.' Flaccus hung his head. 'It makes the words of Seneca all the more relevant: *They are slaves, yes, but they are friends and comrades, and our fellow-servants.*'

'Only in this case it turns out he wasn't a slave,' snorted Vopiscus.

'But who would do such a terrible thing?' said Annia Serena, her blue eyes wide with concern. 'Who would kidnap and sell freeborn children? Have they caught and punished him?'

'Many people do such things,' said Flaccus, 'but the mastermind behind these illegal operations – the man who buys and sells freeborn children – is still at large somewhere in Asia. However, I mean to track him down and bring him to justice. With the help of some friends,' he added, flashing Flavia a quick smile.

'Oh, how brave!' Pulchra gazed adoringly at Flaccus.

'Is that why you didn't bring a slave with you?' asked brown-eyed Philodemus.

'Yes. I only have one slave in my service now. An old man who's been in our household since birth. I left him back in Rome.'

'How noble of you,' said Voluptua, looking up from her wine cup like a cat from a bowl of cream.

'Well, Valerius Flaccus,' said Felix, 'that was quite a confession. Thank you for sharing it. Who will go next?'

*

'I'll go next,' said Annia Serena. Her woolly yellow hair had been done up in seven large ringlets, three over her forehead and two dangling at each side.

'I have an unusually acute sense of smell,' she began in a breathy voice. 'For example, I can tell that Polla Argentaria is wearing metopium, a blend of cardamom, myrrh and balsam. Whereas you, Patron, are wearing citron-oil mixed with musk, a unique scent which suits you very well.'

'Extraordinary!' breathed Polla Argentaria, and Felix looked impressed.

'Ever since I was a little girl,' said Annia Serena, fanning herself, 'I have loved perfumes and scented oils. My earliest memory is of eating rose petals. I remember being terribly disappointed that something which smelt so sweet should taste so bitter.' She looked round at the diners. 'My mother had a collection of perfumes in exquisite little bottles. One day when I was seven years old, she received a new perfume in the shape of a bird: a delicate blue glass bird that fit in the palm of her hand. You had to snap off the tip of the beak to release the perfume. Susinum – as I'm sure you all know – is one of the most expensive perfumes you can buy. It's a blend of rose, myrrh and cinnamon, with saffron its main ingredient. Mater allowed me to smell it, but she wouldn't let me hold the little glass bird or try even one drop. Later, when she was at the baths, I crept into her room and applied a little, dabbing it here,' Annia Serena touched the base of her white throat. 'It was glorious and I almost swooned with pleasure.'

'I believe you're wearing it now,' said Vopiscus suavely.

Annia Serena's seven woolly curls bobbed as she nodded. 'But I dropped the little bird and it shattered,' she continued. 'My tunic was soaked with it and of course my mother smelled it on me. I was sent to my room with no dinner, which was a terrible punishment for me. You see, my father was giving a great banquet for friends and family. It was shortly after Piso's attempt on Nero's life and pater was trying to raise people's spirits.'

'Being sent to your room with no dinner is not a very terrible secret,' said Voluptua, showing sharp little teeth in a cat-like yawn.

'Oh, but it is,' said Annia Serena dramatically. 'You see, that night our cook prepared mushrooms. But what he didn't know is that they were poisonous, and every person at the banquet who ate them, including my entire family, died in agony that night.'

'Oh!' cried Claudia and her kylix shattered on the mosaic floor. There were no slaves to clean it up and Flavia saw the pool of red wine slowly bleed into the narrow spaces between the tesserae. Voluptua's panther padded over to the wine, sniffed it, then returned to lie beneath the couch again.

'What makes my tale even more tragic,' said Annia Serena, 'is that once before, when our cook prepared bad pork, my acute sense of smell warned me and saved my family. If I had not been disobedient that day, and if I had gone to the banquet, I might have saved them all.'

*

'My secret is even more shocking than Annia Serena's,' said Claudia, 'but first, I wonder if our host would share *his* secret?'

Everyone gasped, but Claudia stared defiantly at Felix with her tawny eyes.

Felix raised a dark eyebrow and smiled. 'Of course. It wouldn't be fair for me to ask for your intimate confessions without giving one of my own.'

Flavia glanced at Pulchra, who was gazing at her father with shining eyes. She had obviously heard his secret before and was not worried.

'You may have noticed,' said Felix, 'that although I'm still relatively young, my hair is completely grey.'

'Very striking with your tanned skin, Patron,' said Annia Serena, and then covered her flushing cheeks with her fan.

He smiled. 'Thank you. They say it goes back to a distant ancestor of mine from Greece. He was a brave hero who fought in the Trojan War.'

Flavia gazed at Felix's handsome profile. She could easily imagine him as a Greek hero.

'One evening,' continued Felix, 'during the tenth year of the siege of Troy, my ancestor went to drink at the banks of Scamander and there he came across the goddess Athena bathing. Captivated by her beauty, he tried to steal a kiss from the immortal one.'

'Oh, how very naughty of him,' purred Voluptua.

Red-haired Vopiscus snorted and quoted something in Greek.

'Well-put,' said Felix, when the laughter subsided. 'Athena is indeed the maiden goddess, who wants nothing to do with men. As a punishment for his insolence, she turned his hair grey, the colour of her eyes. Since then, every male descendent of his has woken on their eighteenth birthday to find their hair prematurely grey.'

'Is that what happened to you, Patron?' asked Annia Serena, gazing at Felix over the rim of her fan.

'Yes,' he said. 'On the eve of my eighteenth birthday I went to bed with dark hair and the next morning I woke to find it as you see it today. Just like my ancestor.'

'And do his descendants still assault maidens?' asked Claudia, lifting her chin a fraction.

Someone gasped and everyone looked at Felix. His smile did not fade but Flavia saw his eyes narrow at Claudia.

'You've told your secret, Patron,' she said. 'Now I will tell mine.'

'Oh!' cried Polla, from the end of Flavia's couch. 'Oh, it hurts!'

'What is it, my dear?' said Felix, putting a hand on his wife's shoulder.

Polla cried out again, her face very pale, and clutched her stomach as if she had been speared. Then she slumped onto the couch, unconscious.

'Not again!' whispered Pulchra fiercely, and gripped Flavia's hand. 'Oh please, Juno! Not again!'

'Was it poison?' said Flavia to Pulchra an hour later. 'Does the doctor think it was poison?'

After Polla collapsed, Felix had gathered his wife's unconscious body in his arms and carried her to her rooms. All the others had followed, but only Pulchra and Flavia had been allowed into Polla's suite. They waited in the outer dressing-room while Felix took Polla into her bedroom, where the slave-girl Parthenope was waiting. Presently the doctor and his assistant arrived grim-faced from Surrentum. Not long after that, Flavia and Pulchra saw the assistant leave the room with a bowlful of blood. Finally the doctor appeared in the doorway and beckoned for Pulchra.

Flavia edged forward far enough to see Pulchra's mother propped up on silk cushions, looking very pale but conscious. The curly-haired slave-girl Parthenope stood wringing her hands at one side of the low bed and Felix stood on the other side, still wearing his long blue synthesis. Pulchra threw herself sobbing on her mother's lap. As Polla weakly stroked her daughter's head, Flavia saw that the crook of her elbow had been bandaged, where the doctor had bled her.

Presently Felix helped Pulchra to her feet and said a few words to her in a low voice. Pulchra gazed solemnly up into her father's face and nodded.

'Come with me?' she said to Flavia a few moments later.

'Of course.'

Pulchra caught Flavia's hand and pulled her out of Polla's dressing room into the colonnade. All the guests were there, as well as Jonathan, Nubia, Lupus and Tranquillus. Voluptua and her cat stopped pacing and all eyes turned towards Pulchra.

'Pater says to tell you all that mater will be fine,' said Pulchra in a clear voice. 'She's just had a stomach upset and needs to rest. Please retire to your rooms. Pater says he will see you in the morning. Thank you for your prayers and your concern.'

She turned and embraced Flavia as if weeping. 'Tell me when they've gone,' she murmured into Flavia's ear, 'I can't bear to speak to anyone now.'

'They've gone,' said Flavia a moment later. 'Now tell me . . .' She pulled Pulchra back into Polla's dressing room and turned to her grimly, 'Was it poison?'

'Oh Flavia! The doctor doesn't know. He couldn't tell pater anything.'

'Stupid doctor,' muttered Flavia. She looked at Pulchra. 'I think you were right. It must be poison. If it was bad food, then we'd all be suffering. And you know what else you were right about? The house-guests. The poisoner must be one of them!'

SCROLL IX

'We were lucky,' said Flavia Gemina the next morning, 'that Polla didn't die.'

The four friends were sitting on the beds in the girls' room with the dogs milling about their feet. 'The gods have given us another chance to save her.'

'And the doctor didn't know which poison was used?' asked Jonathan.

'No,' said Flavia. 'He just bled Polla and gave her a tonic.'

'Pollux!' swore Jonathan. 'We need to find out what kind of poison it was, so that we can prepare an antidote.'

'What is anti boat?' asked Nubia.

'An antidote,' said Flavia, 'is something which makes poison harmless. If you've drunk poison, you have to drink the antidote as soon as possible. There are different antidotes for different poisons.'

'And that,' said Jonathan, 'is why we have to find out which poison she's been given. So that if it happens again we'll have the correct antidote ready.'

'Jonathan's right,' said Pulchra, coming into the room with her little dog Ajax on a gilded lead. 'Another attack might kill mater. We've got two days to find the antidote.'

'Or better yet, the poisoner,' said Tranquillus, who had come in behind Pulchra.

Flavia glared at Tranquillus. 'What's *he* doing here?'

'Why two days?' asked Jonathan.

'Tranquillus has kindly agreed to help us,' said Pulchra, sitting beside Jonathan on Nubia's bed. 'And we have two days because that's how long the doctor has told mater to go without food.'

Flavia narrowed her eyes at Tranquillus.

He grinned back. 'You can trust me,' he said cheerfully. 'I like mysteries.'

'How is your mother this morning?' Nubia asked Pulchra.

'Much better, Nubia, thank you. Ajax! Bad dog! Stop bothering Tigris!' Pulchra scooped up Ajax and turned back to Nubia. 'The doctor prescribed a clyster and a fast and told her not to leave her bed for two days.'

'I know a fast is not to eat,' said Nubia with a frown, 'but what is a clyster?'

'I'll tell you later,' said Jonathan in her ear, then turned to the others. 'I've been reading my father's scroll on poison. There are at least ten deadly plants within a mile's radius of the Villa Limona. There are even some here in your gardens,' he said to Pulchra. 'Lupus and I have made a list of them.'

They all bent over Lupus's wax tablet to see the list written there:

BELLADONNA
ACONITE
YEW
HEMLOCK

OLEANDER
HENBANE
HELLEBORE
MANDRAKE
OPIUM POPPIES
MUSHROOMS

'Impressive list,' said Tranquillus, raising his pale eyebrows.

'These bad things are all nearby?' said Nubia, her golden eyes wide.

'All of them,' said Jonathan. 'We need to list their symptoms and find the antidotes. Just in case we don't find the poisoner in time.'

'I brought three of Pliny's scrolls about trees and plants,' said Flavia, 'and there might be some books on plants in your father's library.'

'I don't think you'll find anything useful there,' said Pulchra, stroking Ajax's silky ears. 'Pater's collection is mainly poetry and philosophy. But you're welcome to look.'

'He won't mind?' said Flavia.

Pulchra shook her head. 'He always lets his guests use the library. We can go now if you like. Pater is receiving clients this morning in the tablinum, so we won't disturb him.'

'Good!' said Flavia. 'Who wants to go to the library with me?'

'I'll go with you,' said Tranquillus. 'I like doing research.'

'I'll come up with you,' said Jonathan, brushing breakfast crumbs from the front of his tunic and standing up. 'I haven't finished going through my father's scroll on medicine.'

'Shall I walk dogs?' asked Nubia. 'I am not so good at research and they are needing of exercise.'

'Wonderful idea, Nubia,' said Pulchra, depositing Ajax in her arms, 'Make sure you don't let the others leave my little hero behind. He's not as big as they are.'

Lupus wrote something on his wax tablet then held it up. IS THERE STILL A SPYHOLE FOR YOUR FATHER'S STUDY?

'How do you know about the spyhole?' Pulchra's blue eyes opened wide and she rounded accusingly on Jonathan. 'That was a secret!' she hissed. 'How could you tell them?'

'Sorry.' Jonathan shrugged. 'I didn't think it was that important.'

'I suppose it doesn't matter,' said Pulchra. 'It was last year. Besides, we're too big to squeeze between those walls now.'

I'M NOT wrote Lupus, his eyes gleaming.

'You don't think pater is the one trying to poison mater?' exclaimed Pulchra.

'Of course not,' said Flavia. 'But we've got to look out for any suspicious behaviour, and it wouldn't hurt for Lupus to watch your father receive his clients. The poisoner might be one of them.'

'All right,' said Pulchra, and turned to Lupus. 'To get to the spyhole you go through the storehouse by the kitchen. There's a narrow opening just past the three big amphoras leaning against the wall.'

Lupus gave her a thumbs-up.

'I'll come to the library with you three,' said Pulchra to Flavia, then looked round at the others. 'This afternoon pater has invited the men and boys to join him in the baths. He has something special planned. We women will bathe in the sea. We have something special, too, as it's going to be very hot today. Bye-bye my little hero!' This last was addressed to Ajax, panting happily in Nubia's arms.

'Let's meet back here at midday, then,' said Flavia. 'Good hunting everyone! Remember, watch out for any suspicious behaviour.'

BELLADONNA

Description: *woody shrub with glossy dark blue berries.*

Uses: *priests use highly diluted juice of the root to go into a trance.*

Poison: *every part of this plant is poisonous: roots, berries, leaves, stems.*

Symptoms: *large black pupils, frothing at the mouth, loss of voice, bending forward at waist, twitching of fingers, death.*

Antidote: *swallow a large beaker of warm vinegar or mustard diluted in water to induce vomiting, then keep warm and still in a dark, quiet room.*

ACONITE

Description: *medium-sized shrub with dark green leaves that look like palm fronds; blue flowers in the shape of a helmet.*

Uses: *can be smeared on arrowheads to ensure quick death of wolves, hence the nickname 'wolfsbane'.*

Poison: *the juice in the leaves is violently toxic and is said to be foam from the mouth of Cerberus.*

Symptoms: *sweating, tingling then numbness of lips and mouth, painful muscle spasms, cold limbs, irregular heartbeat, drowsiness, convulsions, stupor, death.*

Antidote: *victim should be given a clyster and be made to drink tincture of digitalis, then laid horizontally while body is rubbed.*

YEW

Description: *large evergreen tree with very dark green leaves, a thick trunk and rough reddish bark, bright red poisonous berries and no sap.*

Uses: *the wood is very useful for bows.*

Poison: *the male berries are poisonous.*

Symptoms: *dizziness, vomiting, rapid heartbeat, large black pupils, red face, shallow breathing, paralysis of lungs, death.*

Antidote: *according to Pliny, if a copper nail is hammered into the tree then it becomes harmless.*

HEMLOCK

Description: *plant with feathery leaves and tiny sprays of white flowers which smell like mice.*

Uses: *the reed-like stems are often used to make panpipes or dipped in tallow for candles.*

Poison: *the leaves, root and fruit are all poisonous if eaten.*

Symptoms: *drowsiness, paralysis of limbs progressing from feet up, staggering gait, thick speech, rapid heartbeat, failure of lungs, death.*

Antidote: *warm vinegar in water; the victim should walk about and keep moving as much as possible.*

HENBANE

Description: *sticky, hairy shrub with a yellow bell-shaped flower and a fetid smell. Grows in sandy wastelands. Hogs love the beans but its seeds kill hens.*

Uses: *a poultice of the leaves cools inflamed eyes and joints, and eases headaches; the oil of the seed can be dropped in ears against worms.*

Poison: *if eaten, the leaves, seeds and juice cause a deep deadly sleep.*

Symptoms: *rapid heartbeat, dry mouth, delirium, paralysis, coma, death.*

Antidote: *a mustard clyster, followed by large beakers of warm water with powdered charcoal; the victim should be rubbed and made to walk about.*

HELLEBORE

Description: *a low-growing plant with dark glossy leaves and white flowers which bloom in mid-winter.*

Uses: *to calm hysteria and to terminate pregnancies.*

Poison: *the leaves must be gathered while facing east with no eagles overhead.*

Symptoms: *tingling mouth, salivation, vomiting, stomach pain, diarrhoea, large black pupils, slowed heartbeat.*

Antidote: *after a clyster, drink charcoal powder mixed in castor oil.*

MANDRAKE

Description: *plant with large dark green leaves and*

root like a forked parsnip; in the autumn it bears a smooth round yellow fruit.

Uses: *the leaves are useful in ointments and cooling poultices, the root can be chewed before operations as an anaesthetic.*

Poison: *eating too much of the root puts you in a sleep from which you never wake; ie. death! The roots are said to scream when they are dug out of the ground.*

Symptoms: *dry mouth, erratic heart beat, drowsiness, depression, heavy sleep, coma, death.*

Antidote: *a clyster followed by large beakers of vinegar or mustard in warm water to induce vomiting.*

POPPY

Description: *pretty flower with big petals and a furry stem.*

Uses: *the milky juice is plentiful and can be fashioned into pastilles, then dried in the shade to be taken as pain killer, sedative and cough mixture.*

Poison: *if too much is swallowed, it brings about a fatal coma.*

Symptoms: *drowsiness, slow heartbeat and breathing, tiny pupils, coma, death.*

Antidote: *clyster followed by a tincture of gall-nuts; keep victim awake and moving around.*

MUSHROOMS

Description: *fungi that grow in moist damp places, they look like fat parasols.*

Uses: *mushrooms are prized as food.*

Poison: *according to Pliny, mushrooms become poisonous* *after a snake has breathed on them, so they are best eaten in winter when snakes hibernate. NB mushrooms which are naturally poisonous are called toadstools.*

Symptoms: *salivation, tears, breathing problems, stomach pain, diarrhoea, vertigo, delirium, excitement, coma, death.*

Antidote: *vomiting must be induced by drinking mustard in hot water. Agrippina used mushrooms to poison Claudius, so that her son Nero could become Emperor.*

OLEANDER

Description: *shrub with silvery green leaves and white, pink or magenta flowers.*

Uses: *as hedges and borders, because goats and sheep will not eat this plant.*

Poison: *all parts are poisonous and even its smoke can irritate; hunters have been known to die after eating meat roasted on skewers made of oleander wood.*

Symptoms: *severe diarrhoea, stomach pain, sweating, trembling, irregular heartbeat, paralysis, coma, death.*

Antidote: *No known antidote.*

'No known antidote,' murmured Flavia as she copied the words on her wax tablet. 'Those are three very terrible words.' She looked around the library table at Jonathan, Pulchra and Tranquillus.

Jonathan looked thoughtful. 'What if the poison isn't in the food?' he said.

'Where else would it be?' said Pulchra.

'Lining her cup!' cried Flavia. 'If someone smeared

the inside of your mother's cup with poison then poured normal wine into it . . .'

'No,' said Pulchra. 'She often gets the slave-girls to drink from her goblet first.'

'I've heard of someone having poison poured in their ears as they slept,' said Jonathan. 'Or it could be put in perfume.'

'But wouldn't you have to dab a lot of poisoned perfume on for it to have any effect?' asked Tranquillus.

Suddenly Flavia gasped. 'Some people drink perfume to make their breath smell sweet! Pulchra, does your mother ever drink perfume?'

'I don't think so,' said Pulchra.

'No,' said Flavia after a pause. 'It *must* be in the food because Polla was at dinner just before she took ill last night.'

Tranquillus looked around at them. 'I've just had a disturbing thought,' he said. 'What if the would-be killer decides not to stick to poison? What if he – or she – tries something else?'

'Like a knife or a blunt instrument?' said Flavia.

'Or,' said Tranquillus, 'something that would still make it look like an accident. Like pushing her off the upper colonnade, onto the rocks below.'

Pulchra shuddered.

'Or making it seem as if she slipped in the baths and hit her head and drowned!' said Jonathan.

'Or,' said Flavia, her grey eyes growing wide, 'being eaten by a panther!'

Nubia smiled as she followed the four dogs into the woven shade of the olive groves. She loved walking them on these fragrant hills, so full of plants and animals and insects. Tigris was the bravest and usually ventured furthest ahead, but he always waited to show her his latest find – a shimmering black beetle or a slow-plodding tortoise with a shell the colour of dark honey. Nipur stayed between Tigris and Nubia, often glancing over his shoulder to make sure she was still within sight. Scuto trotted close beside her and Ajax always took up the rear, eyes bulging, tongue flapping, little legs waddling. He was pathetically grateful whenever she carried him and would cover her face with hot kisses that made her giggle.

Suddenly she heard a bird's staccato warning cry and immediately she sensed that something was wrong. Up ahead, Tigris and Nipur stood motionless among the ancient twisted trunks of the olive trees. Beside her Scuto growled and she saw his hackles rise.

Nubia's heart beat faster as she moved cautiously forward. Then she followed the steady gaze of the two big black puppies and her blood ran cold.

On a low, horizontal branch of an olive tree, almost invisible in the dappled sunlight, crouched a black panther.

Lupus yawned. He had been watching the Patron receive his clients for almost two hours. There had been a steady stream of visitors: tenant farmers from the hills, craftsmen from Surrentum, even a magistrate from Neapolis. None of them had said or done anything suspicious. He longed to swim in the cold plunge of the baths or in the cool blue sea and he was just wondering if he should go when Felix's secretary said, 'Your last client of the day, sir.'

Lupus sighed but his eyes widened as he saw the person who stepped into the tablinum. Justus closed the double doors behind him, leaving the Patron and his client alone. And Lupus's jaw dropped when he saw what they began to do together.

Nubia did not take her eyes off the powerful panther crouched on the olive branch. He was alone and unchained. She could see the end of his tail twitching and his golden eyes flicking between Tigris and Nipur, both of whom stood gazing up at him and growling low in their throats.

Nubia always wore her cherrywood flute on a scarlet cord around her neck. Now she slowly pulled it out and began to play soft breathy notes. Instantly the dogs stopped growling. The panther's shoulders relaxed and his tail stopped twitching. He slowly turned his head and she felt a thrill as his steady golden gaze locked with hers.

'Oh there you are!' A woman ran into the clearing from between two olive trees and Nubia stopped playing. Voluptua's magnificent black curls were loose around her shoulders and she wore only an unbelted red silk undertunic. She glanced at Nubia and smiled. 'He ran away right in the middle of my coiffure. You're a very naughty boy!' This last was addressed to the panther, who regarded his mistress with golden eyes and then blinked. 'A very naughty boy to make me come out in public in such an immodest state.'

Nubia lowered her flute and softly called the dogs. When they were close beside her she said, 'Is he dangerous?'

'Oh, my dear, no!' Voluptua was fixing the red leash to the big cat's leather collar. 'He's very old, poor thing. I bought him from some Syrian beast-fighters who were badly mistreating him. He's been declawed and his teeth are so loose that he can only eat raw meat, ground up and beaten with an egg.' She glanced over her shoulder at Nubia and gave her another radiant smile. 'Oh, no! He's not dangerous. He couldn't even hurt the fish in the pond. He's just a big pussycat.'

'Even if the would-be murderer does intend to use another method,' said Flavia Gemina, 'there's no way we could guess how and when they might strike. I think we have to concentrate on poison.'

'I agree,' said Jonathan. 'My father says poison is a coward's recourse and often a woman's, too. The reason most people use poison is because they don't have to be in the room when the victim dies. If you push someone over a wall or knock them on the head or set your panther loose on them, well . . . you have to witness the consequences.'

'Yes, it must be poison.' Tranquillus pushed back his chair. He stretched and yawned, and then stood up.

'That's what I've been saying all along!' said Pulchra with a scowl.

'I know.' Flavia sighed.

A breeze flowed through the open library window and softly rustled the papyrus scrolls on the table. She closed her eyes for a moment and lifted her face to its cool caress. Even though it was nearly midday, she could hear a cock crowing exultantly somewhere outside in the shimmering heat.

'Edepol!' murmured Tranquillus, who had moved over to examine the scrolls on the shelves. 'He's got Ovid's *Art of Love*!'

Flavia looked up to see him pull the scroll slightly from its pigeonhole, so that it stuck out from the others. He glanced around guiltily, saw her watching and grinned. With his brown eyes and straight brown hair he was not bad-looking, she thought. But he was so *young*. She wanted a husband who was strong and masterful and brave. Like Felix. She sighed and turned her attention back to the twenty-third scroll of Pliny's *Natural History*. Expertly twisting her wrists, she scanned the lines passing before her. Suddenly a word caught her eye: ANTIDOTE.

'Eureka!' she cried. 'Admiral Pliny never lets you down. This is his universal antidote. Whoever eats this first thing in the morning will be immune to any poison all day long.'

'Is it called mithridatium?' asked Tranquillus, coming over to her.

'Yes!' Flavia looked up at him in surprise. 'How did you know?'

'Mithridates was a king who lived in fear of being poisoned, so he developed lots of antidotes and remedies, including a universal antidote which protects against any poison. Is the recipe there?' Tranquillus leaned over her shoulder.

Flavia nodded. '*Pound two walnuts,*' she read, '*two dried figs and twenty leaves of rue in a mortarium. Add a pinch of salt. Anyone who takes this on an empty stomach will be immune to poison for the whole day*. Do you think it really works?'

'No,' said Pulchra with a sigh. 'When mater was first ill pater called in all the physicians in Campania. Some of them prescribed universal antidotes like that one, but nothing helped. The elixir Jonathan's father sent was the best. But even that one only worked for a while. We don't want a universal antidote. We need a specific antidote.'

'And for that,' said Tranquillus, 'we need an expert on poisons.'

'Philodemus knows about poisons,' said Jonathan. 'He showed me half a dozen different poisonous plants on the way back from the hunt yesterday.'

Flavia's eyes grew wide. 'Do you think he's the culprit?'

Jonathan shrugged.

'I was thinking of a real expert on poisons,' said Tranquillus. 'Someone like Locusta.'

'Who's Locusta?' they asked.

'Only the most famous poisoner in the world,' said Tranquillus. 'They say three Emperors died because of her skills. She was one of Nero's most valuable assassins.'

'And how do you know about her?' asked Flavia suspiciously.

'Nero is one of my hobbies,' said Tranquillus. 'I want to be a biographer when I'm older.'

Jonathan stared at him. 'You want to be a biographer?'

Tranquillus nodded. 'I've already written one book. It's not exactly a biography, though; more like a collection of Greek swear words.'

Jonathan raised his eyebrows. 'That I'd like to see.'

'You know,' said Flavia thoughtfully, 'now that you mention it, I do remember reading the name Locusta somewhere recently. Maybe in Admiral Pliny's book.' She began twisting the scroll back to scan earlier passages.

'Locusta probably knows ten times more than any scroll,' said Tranquillus. He turned to Pulchra. 'I'll bet if we told her your mother's symptoms, she'd know what poison was being used straightaway.'

'And she would probably know the antidote, too!' said Pulchra.

'But how will we ever find her?' said Flavia.

'Simple,' said Tranquillus. 'She lives just the other side of the bay.'

'Euge!' breathed Pulchra. 'Pater promised to take us on an excursion. We could go tomorrow! Where does she live?'

'Baiae,' said Tranquillus triumphantly. 'As a reward for her services, Nero gave her a villa at Baiae.'

SCROLL X

'Flavia?' said Pulchra. 'Why are you crying this time?'

Flavia lifted her wet face from her pillow. Pulchra stood framed in the bedroom doorway.

'Because I can't go with you all to Baiae tomorrow. I want to go so much, but I can't.' Flavia began sobbing again.

'Oh dear,' remarked Tranquillus, stepping into the doorway. 'Blotched face and swollen eyes – not a good look for you, Flavia.'

'Why did you bring him here?' wailed Flavia, and buried her face in the pillow again.

'It's not her fault,' said Tranquillus. 'I followed her.'

'Go away!' Flavia's voice was muffled. 'I'm miserable.'

Pulchra sighed. 'Then why don't you stop wallowing in your misery and agree to come with us tomorrow?'

'Behold, we have returned!' said Nubia, coming into the room with four happy but tired dogs. Scuto came panting up to Flavia and she wrapped her arms around his hot, furry neck. The other three dogs went to their water bowl and lapped thirstily.

'Panther is a big pussycat,' announced Nubia.

'What about the panther?' said Jonathan and Lupus, coming into the bedroom with Lupus.

'Why are you all in here?' cried Flavia. 'Go away!'

'You told us to meet back here at midday,' said Jonathan.

'We're not leaving you alone until you've told us why you can't come,' said Pulchra, sitting on the side of Flavia's bed.

Flavia released Scuto and wiped her nose on her arm.

Tranquillus winced. 'My dear girl,' he said, 'if you're going to marry me you must learn to use a handkerchief.'

'I'm not your dear girl,' snapped Flavia, 'and I'm not going to marry you!' But she accepted his handkerchief and blew her nose.

'Flavia,' said Pulchra, scooping up Ajax and kissing his nose. 'Why can't you come with us to Baiae tomorrow?'

'Because I promised pater,' said Flavia in a small voice.

'Excuse me?' said Jonathan, sitting on Nubia's bed. 'Your father specifically made you promise him that you wouldn't go to Baiae?'

'Yes.'

'You can't blame him,' said Tranquillus to Jonathan. 'Baiae does have an extremely bad reputation. They say no maiden who goes there ever comes back the same, if you know what I mean.'

'That's not true,' said Pulchra. 'I've been there and I'm still the same.'

Lupus shrugged, then beckoned Flavia with a flick of his wrist, as if to say: *Why don't you come anyway?*

'Yes,' agreed Pulchra. 'Just don't tell him.'

'That would be wrong,' said Jonathan. 'Especially if she promised.'

'Jonathan's right,' said Tranquillus. 'A Roman woman should obey her father. And her husband,' he added.

YOU'VE BROKEN PROMISES TO YOUR FATHER BEFORE, Lupus wrote on his wax tablet.

'Yes, but this time I took a vow,' said Flavia. 'If I break my vow, then the gods might punish me. Or – even worse – they might punish pater.' Flavia made the sign against evil. 'But I want to go so much.'

Tranquillus rolled his eyes. 'Don't start crying again. I'll take extremely thorough notes and when you read them it will be just as if you'd interviewed her yourself.'

'That's right,' said Jonathan. 'I'm going to tell Locusta all Polla's symptoms and ask her what poison was being used and what the antidote is.'

'I will use my senses to see if she is telling the truth,' said Nubia.

AND I WILL DRAW HER, wrote Lupus, SO YOU CAN SEE WHAT SHE LOOKS LIKE.

'Also,' said Pulchra, 'if we're all at Baiae tomorrow, the villa will be practically empty. You could look for clues while we're all out.'

Flavia sniffed and looked round at their encouraging faces.

'That's better,' said Tranquillus. 'You almost smiled. Don't worry. We'll tell you every detail of what happens. And I know the gods will honour the fact that you kept your vow.'

*

After lunch, Jonathan rested on one of the smooth marble slabs in the tepidarium. The bath-slave had finished massaging his shoulders, back and thighs and he felt more relaxed than he had in days. As he lay there, halfway between sleep and wakefulness, he thought about the previous day's hunt and Felix's words of approval. He was beginning to understand why Flavia was under Felix's spell.

'What?' he mumbled, and opened his eyes. 'What is it, Lupus?'

Lupus was still damp from the cold plunge, but he was dressed and beckoning excitedly.

Jonathan sighed and pushed himself off the bench and slipped on the tunic that Lupus extended. Then he followed his friend back into the changing-room of the baths.

The domed room was full of men. Felix stood in the centre, laughing. A red and gold rooster with blue tail feathers struggled in his arms. Jonathan saw that the circular marble floor had been sprinkled with sawdust.

Felix's bearded secretary Justus was making notes on a wax tablet as men shouted out their bets. There must have been thirty or forty of them, crowding into the cylindrical room.

'Jonathan. Lupus.' Felix looked up from his struggling cockerel. 'Come stand on the bench behind me. You'll get a better view from there.'

The men grinned down at the boys and parted to let them through.

'First time?' said Felix to Jonathan, and raised an eyebrow at Jonathan's nod. 'You'll never be the same.'

Jonathan and Lupus stepped onto the bench behind

the Patron. Tranquillus was already up there and he grinned at them and gave them a thumbs-up. Jonathan looked around. From here he could see over the men's shoulders and he noticed Flaccus and Vopiscus standing on the other side of the apodyterium. Vopiscus nodded at Jonathan and then turned to say something to Flaccus, whose smile faded when he caught sight of the three boys.

Jonathan felt a twinge of guilt. He noticed Philodemus was absent and he thought he could guess why. He had often heard his father condemn cock-fighting as a barbaric and decadent sport. But how could he leave without insulting his host? Besides, he was here to keep an eye on the suspects.

The shouts grew in volume as Jason, one of Felix's right-hand men, came into the domed room with a pure white rooster. The men were increasing their wagers, making rude jokes and laughing.

'These are the only living creatures,' said a voice in Jonathan's ear, 'who crow for joy but fight to the death in utter silence.' Vopiscus had come up onto the bench to stand beside the boys. Flaccus remained on the other side of the room.

'Felix's bird is a Rhodian,' added Vopiscus. 'They say he needs at least five hens to keep him satisfied.'

Jonathan nodded and shifted slightly; Vopiscus was standing uncomfortably close to him.

Suddenly the domed room grew quiet. At a sign from the scribe, Felix and Jason stepped forward to let their birds assess each other. The cocks struggled in their owners' arms but were kept just far enough from each other to do no damage.

'They do that to get the cockerels in a fighting fury, don't they?' Tranquillus said to Vopiscus.

Vopiscus nodded. 'Now watch carefully for the referee to give the signal. The first bird released has the advantage.'

Felix and Jason were crouched opposite one another, holding their cockerels behind lines drawn in the sawdust. They were about six feet apart.

'Pugnate!' cried Justus and the air was suddenly full of flapping wings. Felix's blue-tailed Rhodian must have been released first, for he flew up above the white bird and brought his heel down, instantly piercing his opponent's right wing with the sharp bone projecting from the back of his leg. But the spur was stuck and the two birds flapped wildly, unable to detach from one another.

'Pax!' cried Justus. Felix and Jason moved quickly forward to free their birds from one another. After a few seconds' pause, Justus cried 'Pugnate!' again and this time the white had the advantage.

Jonathan watched in fascination as the cockerels beat their powerful wings and used beak and spurs to attack each other. There was no forcing them to fight; he could tell they wanted it with every fibre of their being. Soon the sawdust was spotted with blood and feathers. Felix's soldiers were yelling and Lupus was making a wild howling sound. Jonathan realised that his own throat was hoarse from shouting, too.

Suddenly it was over. The white cock was dead, his neck broken by a powerful blow from the Rhodian's thigh. Jason held his dead bird up by its feet, and the men cheered the vanquished warrior. Then Justus handed a small palm branch to Felix and the men roared their approval.

'What reward does the bird get?' asked Jonathan.

Vopiscus shrugged. 'A handful of barley and access to his hens. But he doesn't do it for the reward. He fights for the pure joy of it.'

Jonathan nodded. His heart was beating hard and in spite of himself he was filled with a strange euphoria. The colours around him seemed brighter and he felt a deep surge of affection for all the men around him, even the ugly, brutish ones. By Hercules, it was good to be alive!

Felix was holding the victor, stroking it and kissing it and murmuring into its ear, not minding that his cheek and tunic were smeared with the cockerel's blood. For the second time that afternoon, Jonathan understood Flavia's feelings for the Patron, and as he looked around at the men's faces, he saw he was not alone.

SCROLL XI

Nubia lay naked on a rock, as happy as a lizard in the sun. She and Flavia and Pulchra and the three widows had left their clothes in the shade of the Temple of Neptune and had swum out to the smallest of the three rocks in the sea behind it. Pulchra called these tiny islands the Sirens' rocks.

When they had gone swimming the first day, they had paddled modestly around the secret cove in their tunics. But today Pulchra had boldly shed all her clothes and encouraged the others to do the same.

Voluptua and Annia Serena immediately followed her example, but Nubia, Flavia and Claudia hesitated.

'Don't worry,' Pulchra laughed, treading water. 'We're going to swim to the littlest rock. Nobody can see us from the villa. The Temple of Neptune and the other rocks hide us. Come on!'

Nubia had only ever swum in her tunic before, and although she was used to being naked in the baths, the thought of stripping off outside frightened her. Just over a year ago, she had been led through the streets of Ostia wearing only a chain round her neck, a price tag, and chalk dust on her feet. Her face flushed as she remembered the terrible humiliation of being sold as a slave.

But now she was among friends, so when Flavia and Claudia slipped off their tunics, Nubia took a deep breath and followed suit. She was not a slave any more.

As soon as Nubia entered the water she was converted. It was glorious to swim in the nude.

There were three roughly cube-shaped rocks behind the temple: one medium-sized, the next big and tall and the last very low and flat. When they arrived at the furthest rock they discovered linen towels and cushions already laid out by slaves. On the middle rock, within touching distance, were parasols, a picnic basket and some musical instruments. Wedged in the cool water between the two rocks was a small amphora of watered wine with a copper beaker attached to its neck by a silk cord.

Now, lying on a linen bath-towel, Nubia felt warmed to her very core by the golden sunshine.

'Oh,' sighed Flavia from the shade of a parasol. 'That cool breeze feels wonderful, doesn't it?'

'Mmmm,' purred Voluptua, who had managed to keep her elaborate hairdo dry. She had tried to coax her panther into the water but he had refused, so they had left him tied to a pillar of Neptune's temple, dozing in the shade.

Claudia – the one Flavia called the tawny beauty – lay beneath a parasol, her eyes closed. She had been very quiet and Nubia wondered if it had anything to do with her aborted confession at the dinner party the night before. Flavia had reported the events of the evening in detail.

'So ladies,' giggled Pulchra, who was lying between Nubia and Flavia. 'What do you think of the bachelors?'

'They're all very sweet,' said Annia Serena. 'But I prefer my men older and more mature.'

'Me, too,' said Flavia, and although Nubia knew she was perfectly serious, the others laughed.

'I like all three of them,' said Voluptua in her low, husky voice. 'Especially Vopiscus and Flaccus.'

'You only like the size of their money-pouches,' said Annia Serena.

'Not at all.' Voluptua stretched luxuriously. 'Still, I wonder which one of the two is richer?'

'Vopiscus,' said Pulchra quickly. 'I'm sure Vopiscus is far richer than Flaccus.'

'But Flaccus is much more handsome,' said Annia Serena. 'Nice hair, nice voice, wonderful body.'

'I thought you liked your men older and more mature,' said Pulchra.

'I like the way Vopiscus looks at me,' said Voluptua.

Annia Serena gave an unladylike snort. 'Don't you mean the way he *leers* at you?'

Nubia let their voices float away in the distance. The depilatory the previous day had left her skin sleek and smooth. After a swim in the sea, the hot sun on her naked body made her feel deliciously heavy and relaxed.

The handsome face of her tutor Aristo swam up into her mind's eye, but she didn't want to think about him. That would just make her sad and spoil the beauty of the moment. So she pushed his image away and tried to make her mind as still and blank as a smooth grey pebble.

For a moment she achieved it. Her mind was perfectly calm and she was only aware of her breath coming and going as she lay on her soft linen towel in the hot sunshine.

Then another image blossomed in her mind. A beautiful dark stallion with a pale gold mane and tail. He was galloping along the wet sand where the water met the beach, full of joy and power and life. His presence was so strong and so clear that she sat up and shaded her eyes and looked towards the crescent beach that lay to the south. But they were too close to the water here; a low rocky promontory blocked her view.

'What is it, Nubia?' murmured Flavia. 'Are you hungry?'

'No,' said Nubia, 'but is there flute? I left mine with clothes at temple.'

'No flute,' said Pulchra, who had been combing out her damp hair in the shade of the parasol. 'But there's this.' She stood up, reached over to the big rock and handed a double aulos back down. 'Here you are.'

Nubia had only played the double aulos a few times but she practised her own flute daily, so it was not difficult to make a sound. This double pipe made a strange buzzy noise and the vibrating reed tickled her lip. When she had made friends with it, she began to play the joyful feeling of the stallion running on sand. As she played, the image became strong in her head again.

When she finished the song, she opened her eyes to

see Flavia and Pulchra and the three women staring at her in amazement.

'Oh,' said Claudia. 'That was wonderful. It made me feel so free and happy.' And Nubia saw that her cheeks were wet with tears.

'Jonathan! Lupus!' cried a boy's voice. 'Come quickly!'

Jonathan looked up from searching Tigris's fur for ticks as the light in the bedroom dimmed. Tranquillus was standing in the bright doorway.

On the other bed Lupus sat bolt upright and rubbed his eyes. He had fallen asleep, drugged by the ferocious heat of late afternoon.

'What is it, Tranquillus?' said Jonathan. 'Have you discovered something?'

'Yes! There are naked women on a rock out there!'

'What?'

'Women! Naked! Nude! No clothes!' Tranquillus's high voice cracked with excitement. 'Come on!'

Lupus was off his bed, instantly awake.

'Where?'

'The library. I was reading . . . um . . . a scroll, and I could see them all out on a rock. You can only see them from the library window,' he added over his shoulder. 'Unless . . .' He stopped dead.

In his eagerness to follow, Lupus bumped into Tranquillus's back. 'Unless' – Tranquillus turned around – 'we get a boat and go out there. I think there's a little rowing boat down in that cave by the yacht.'

'We can't do that,' said Jonathan. 'We can't spy on naked women.'

'Of course we can! We're supposed to be keeping an eye out for suspicious behaviour.'

'Lying naked on a rock isn't suspicious,' said Jonathan, folding his arms. 'It's sunbathing.'

'I think it's suspicious. Don't you Lupus?'

Lupus nodded enthusiastically.

'You just want to see naked women,' said Jonathan.

'Well, yes,' said Tranquillus. 'Especially Voluptua. Don't you?'

Lupus nodded so vigorously that Jonathan couldn't help grinning. 'OK,' he said with a shrug. 'Let's go investigate the naked women.'

Nubia and Flavia were playing Slave Song on double aulos and tambourine, and Pulchra was attempting to accompany them on the lyre when Annia Serena suddenly uttered a piercing scream.

'Boys!' she cried. 'I can smell boys!'

Flavia hastily pulled one of the yellow towels around her body and scanned the dazzling water.

'I can't see any boys,' she said after a moment.

'I didn't say I saw them,' said Annia Serena. 'I said I smelled them.'

Flavia and Pulchra exchanged a look and then giggled.

'Behold!' said Nubia, who had not bothered to cover herself but was still sitting straight-backed and cross-legged with her double aulos in her hands. 'There they are. They have run aground on that boulder.'

Pulchra squealed and flipped up the parasol as a shield for her modesty. Then she laughed. 'Silly boys!' she called out over the rim of her parasol. 'Why do you think we swam out here instead of taking a boat?' She turned to the others, 'Actually, you can get a boat out here but you have to go carefully or you run aground.'

'How do we get back?' Flavia heard Jonathan call.

'You'll have to swim!' she bellowed.

And Pulchra added with a giggle. 'Just make sure you swim away from us and not toward us!'

The next morning before dawn, Flavia took the four dogs for a long walk up the mountainside. She didn't want to be there when her friends set sail for Baiae with Felix.

It was already warm and the pale lemon sky in the east promised another scorching day. By the time she reached the small shrine of Dionysus up among the vineyards, the sun had risen above the Milky Mountains. Flavia turned and looked back down over the bay. It was the perfect day for sailing and there were so many boats on the water that it took her some time to find Felix's yacht, crawling like a many-legged insect across the wrinkled blue silk of the sea.

Flavia allowed a noble tear of disappointment to slip down her cheek, then she looked at the dogs. Scuto was urgently sniffing the base of a yew tree, Tigris and Nipur were wrestling, and Ajax sat panting at her feet, gazing up at her imploringly.

'Come on, boys,' said Flavia, scooping up Ajax. 'Let's go back to the villa for breakfast. After that you'll have to wait quietly in Jonathan and Lupus's room. I have some serious investigating to do. And I know just where to start.' She kissed Ajax's nose. 'Felix's bedroom.'

SCROLL XII

Back in her own bedroom, Flavia took care to change into her long dark blue tunic and pin up her hair. If a slave found her nosing around, her best defence would be confidence, and unless she looked neat she would not be confident. She used her new make-up box to grind a little ochre and add some colour to her lips and cheeks. She put in the pearl-and-sapphire earrings her father had given her for her birthday, but she left the gold bangles on the table. They jingled slightly when she moved and she wanted to be absolutely silent. For this reason she wore neither her new cork-heeled sandals or her flat-soled ones, but went barefoot instead. In this heat, nobody would question that.

She padded silently along the breeze-cooled colonnade and climbed the stairs to the upper level of the villa, then doubled back along the bigger colonnade that led to Polla's suite. She passed Polla's yellow triclinium and found the wicker chairs in their usual place outside Polla's dressing room. The lounge-chair was empty but the gold and sapphire cup sat on the little wicker table beside it. Flavia stopped and touched the wine cup: cool and beaded with droplets. She sniffed: well-watered wine, probably Surrentinum. She looked: half full. Someone had been here only moments before. Could it be Polla? Flavia thought she was still confined to her bed since her collapse two nights before.

Flavia moved quickly past Polla's suite of rooms and through the atrium to the corridor where she had first bumped into Felix. Maybe he had been coming from his room that day. Sure enough, the corridor led to only one room, a medium-sized bedroom.

The room was simple but luxurious, with frescoes of cockerels fighting on the walls. She knew at once that it was his. There were two small arched windows here – both with views of the villa's main entrance and the secret cove – and a light well, open to the sky. The skylight could probably be covered over in stormy weather, but now it caught a deliciously cool breeze and funnelled it down into the room.

Despite the breeze, Flavia could smell Felix's distinctive musky citron scent. Against one wall was a wide low bed with a lemon-yellow cover. At its foot was the usual cedarwood chest. In the wall on the opposite side of the room was a long low niche with his togas and cloaks hanging from pegs. The cloaks ranged in colour from dove grey to blue to black. Near the bed, beneath the skylight, was a writing table and an elegant chair of wood and ivory. Beside the table stood a bronze lamp-stand with at least a dozen oil-lamps. A tortoiseshell lyre had been set on the mosaic floor, leaning against the writing-table, and she recognised it as his.

Flavia moved closer and examined the objects on the surface of the table.

There were several bronze quills here, a little inkpot of pale blue glass and some sheets of papyrus with lines of Greek written in black ink. She noticed that several words had been scratched out and new ones written above. It was a poem. Felix was writing a poem in Greek. She leaned forward and her eye caught the phrase *'sirens on their rocks'*.

Suddenly she heard the soft slap of sandals in the corridor outside, and her heart jumped. Someone was coming!

Flavia looked around. Nowhere to hide. Unless . . .

She ran to the hanging clothes in the niche. She could stand behind the long hooded cloak but her feet would be visible at the bottom. Thinking quickly, she moved a pair of his grey, fur-lined boots beneath the cloak and stepped into them. The niche was only a little taller than she was, so nobody would suspect an adult could be hiding here. If anyone looked this way she hoped they would only see a cloak with boots underneath.

She heard the footsteps move into the room. A strong scent of saffron and cinnamon suddenly filled her head. It was maddeningly familiar, but she couldn't remember who wore it.

If she could just see who it was. There! An arm-slit in the cloak. She moved her head carefully until she could see through the slit. It was a woman wearing a filmy blue headscarf which obscured her face. Who was it? That scent was so familiar . . . The woman went to the box at the end of the bed and knelt and opened it. She pulled out one of Felix's tunics and held it up. It was a cream tunic with the two narrow red stripes that showed he was of the equestrian class. For a moment the woman examined the tunic.

Then she began to sniff it.

Flavia's eyes grew wide, then wider still as the woman's headscarf slipped back to reveal her face. Of course! The woman was Annia Serena, the woolly-haired blonde whose family had been killed by poisonous mushrooms. And her scent was the fabulously expensive blend called susinum.

Why are you here? Flavia wondered. *You're supposed to be in Baiae with the others.*

Flavia's jaw dropped as Annia Serena gathered the cream-coloured fabric of the Patron's tunic to her face and slowly inhaled, drinking in Felix's smell as if it were some heady wine or elixir. Her eyes were closed in ecstasy as she sank slowly back onto the bed, still embracing his tunic.

Abruptly she pushed the garment away, as someone might put down a beaker of wine they had drained. Now she was sniffing Felix's bed, nose down, rump in the air. She looked so much like Scuto on the trail of some exciting scent that Flavia had to bite her lip hard to keep from giggling.

But her desire to laugh died as Annia Serena suddenly lifted her head and sniffed the air.

'Who's here?' the woman whispered. She tested the air with her nose again, then rose from the bed and started towards the niche where Flavia was hiding.

SCROLL XIII

Flavia held her breath and closed her eyes as Annia Serena moved cautiously towards her hiding-place. What would she say? How could she explain her presence? It would be unbearably humiliating. *Help me, Castor and Pollux!* Flavia prayed silently.

'What are you doing in here?' A man's voice.

Annia Serena squealed and then pressed her hand to her heart.

'Oh, it's you, domina!' There was surprise in the man's Greek-accented voice. 'This is the Patron's bedroom. He doesn't permit visitors. I'm afraid you'll have to leave.'

'I'm sorry,' stammered Annia Serena. 'I didn't feel well and I went looking for one of the slave-girls to ask her to bring me a tonic. I must have taken the wrong turn. I think I'm still a little delirious.'

'Yes. I imagine so.'

Flavia suddenly matched the accented voice to the bearded face of Justus, Felix's secretary and scribe.

'I'll go now,' said Annia Serena.

'Let me escort you back to your room,' Justus said drily, 'lest you become delirious again.'

Flavia waited until the sound of their footsteps died away. Then she carefully stepped out of Felix's fur-lined boots and pushed aside his cloak. She tiptoed out of the room and back along the corridor to the atrium.

As she passed through the atrium into the breezy colonnade, she saw Polla stretched out on her wicker lounge-chair, her head turned to watch the retreating backs of Justus and Annia Serena. Flavia thought quickly. If she turned and ran, Polla might see her and it would look suspicious. Better to pretend she had been coming this way.

Flavia took a deep breath and began to stroll along the colonnade towards Polla. 'Salve, domina!' she said brightly, 'Are you feeling better? I thought you would still be resting in your room.'

Polla's head turned and her blue eyes widened. 'Flavia!' she murmured. 'I'm a little better this morning. I thought it would do me good to take some air. And the villa is so quiet today. Are you unwell, too?'

'A little,' lied Flavia. 'I felt sick in the night. But I feel better now. I only feel a little nauseous.'

'Oh dear. I hope it wasn't something you ate. Annia Serena didn't go because she gets terribly seasick, and apparently she's also unwell. Or perhaps it's just the heat. Come. Sit beside me and keep me company. I'll ask my girl to bring you some posca. That always makes me feel better when I've been ill. Parthenope!' She snapped her fingers.

The pretty, curly-haired slave-girl appeared a moment

later and Flavia swallowed. The Villa Limona was not deserted after all. She was lucky she had not been discovered in Felix's room.

'I begged my husband not to go to Baiae,' Polla murmured, after the slave-girl had gone, 'but Pulchra was determined and he gave in to her wishes, as usual.'

'Why didn't you want them to go?' asked Flavia, sitting on a yellow-cushioned wicker chair. 'Is it because Baiae is a glirarium of licentiousness?'

Polla arched one of her exquisite eyebrows. 'That's one way of describing it.' She took a tiny sip from her gemmed cup.

'What's a glirarium?' said Flavia, after a short pause.

Polla almost smiled. 'A glirarium is a kind of container for fattening dormice, until they can be eaten.'

'Oh,' said Flavia. She sipped her posca. 'And licentiousness?'

Polla sighed. 'The poet Propertius begged his girlfriend to *depart from corrupt Baiae, whose shores are so dangerous to virtuous girls and whose waters are tainted with crimes of love.* There is something about the air, so pure and sparkling, something about the tall, swaying palm trees, the sunshine, the natural hot springs, the golden beach and the blue waters of the sea and the lake. Such intoxicating beauty makes people forget all sense of right and wrong. They indulge their basest desires in the baths and on the beaches. That is what licentiousness means. Lust. A hunger for what is not yours by law or right.'

Flavia was still not exactly sure what Polla meant, so she remained silent.

'Let me illustrate it this way,' said Polla. Her voice was so faint that Flavia had to lean forward to hear her. 'Two nights ago at dinner, Vopiscus told us an anecdote doing the rounds at the moment. A beautiful and respectable Roman matron recently went to Baiae to take the waters. They say she arrived Penelope and departed Helen.'

'Penelope was the faithful wife of Odysseus,' said Flavia. Then her grey eyes widened. 'But Helen was unfaithful and left her husband to run away with a handsome young Trojan called Paris.'

'Precisely,' said Polla. 'The respectable Roman matron left her husband for a far younger man. I could tell you many other terrible things about Baiae: tales of drunkenness, seduction, even murder.'

'Murder?' said Flavia, pulling her wicker chair closer.

'Oh, yes,' breathed Polla. 'Baiae has had a tradition for murder ever since one of the most notorious crimes in Rome's history took place there. I can still remember the day I heard the news.'

'The news about what?' said Flavia.

'It was near Baiae,' said Polla, 'that the Emperor Nero murdered his own mother.'

Lupus sat beside Nubia in the shade of the small temple-like deckhouse of Felix's yacht. Straight ahead, he could see the palm trees and gilded domes fringing the small blue bay of Baiae.

On his right loomed Vesuvius. Even as close as this, he could see no trace of Herculaneum, the city buried at its foot. Lupus thought of his friends Clio and Vulcan, who had since moved to Rome with their family.

Over on his left was Misenum, where Rome's navy lay at anchor. He recognised the shape of the promontory and the three poplar trees that had marked the home of Admiral Pliny. Less than a year ago he had swum there to bring the admiral a vital message. But old Pliny had died in the eruption, along with thousands of others who had not been able to escape the tidal wave of white-hot ash.

On that terrible day in August the wind had been from the north-west. Today it was behind them, filling the yellow and white striped sail. Even so, the oarsmen were working hard. Lupus could hear the chant of the leader, and he watched the oars rise and fall in unison, pushing the ship forward in rhythmic surges. The harbour looked close, but Lupus guessed it would take them another half-hour to reach it. He hooked his arm around one of the wooden pillars that held the pitched canopy and leaned over the polished oak rail. Cobalt blue water hissed along the side of the ship, leaving a creamy trail behind them. It occurred to him that he had swum from very near this spot to the harbour at Misenum.

As if he had read Lupus's mind, Felix remarked, 'Nero's mother Agrippina swam to the shore from here the night he tried to kill her.' Lupus looked over his shoulder at Felix. The Patron was sitting on a cushioned bench in the shade with his guests around him. He had been holding court all morning.

'Nero tried to kill his own mother?' asked Jonathan, who was sitting on Felix's left.

'I know this story!' cried Tranquillus. 'Nero tried to have Agrippina murdered in a collapsing boat!'

'Oh, tell us about it, pater!' said Pulchra, who had squeezed herself between Jonathan and Flaccus.

'Yes, do tell,' purred Voluptua. She and her black panther had plenty of room to themselves at the end of one of the benches.

Felix looked around at them with his dark eyes. 'Nero and his mother had been to a dinner party in Baiae. He told his mother something was wrong with her own boat and urged her to take his new yacht to sail back to her villa near the Lucrine Lake, just there.' He pointed towards a distant ring of fluttering banners to the right of the blue bay they were entering. 'What she didn't know was that once they were well out to sea, the roof of his yacht was designed to collapse. It was his plan to kill her and make it look like an accident.'

'Why?' asked Jonathan. 'Why did Nero want to kill his own mother?'

'First,' said Felix, 'because she objected to his love affair with Acte, a beautiful but unsuitable freedwoman. Second, because she was becoming too influential and Nero didn't want to share his power with her.'

'Weren't there rumours that she even wanted to be his Empress?' said sleepy-eyed Vopiscus, who was lounging near Claudia. 'In more ways than one?'

It took a moment for Lupus to realise what Vopiscus meant.

'But she was his own *mother*!' cried Jonathan, and added, 'That's disgusting.'

'It is nefas,' said Flaccus.

'Quite,' said Felix.

'Tasteless, too,' drawled Vopiscus, 'though they say

Agrippina was still very beautiful, even at the age of forty.'

'What happened, pater?' asked Pulchra, her blue eyes wide and innocent.

'The plan went wrong,' said Felix. 'The awning of Nero's special yacht was not made of wood like this one' – here he gestured at the brightly painted roof above them. 'It was made of lead, designed to collapse when a certain lever was pulled and to crush anyone reclining underneath.'

'Oh! How awful!' cried Pulchra.

'Did it work?' asked Jonathan.

'No!' cried Tranquillus, leaping to his feet. 'One of the sailors pulled the lever and the roof did fall down but it only killed one of Agrippina's friends. Agrippina and her other companion – I forget the woman's name – fell into the water unharmed.'

Lupus mimed swimming and gave a questioning grunt.

'Yes, Lupus, they could swim,' said Felix, 'and the sailors heard a woman's voice in the dark water crying out, "Save me! I'm the mother of your emperor!" They took their oars, stretched them out . . . and beat her to death. Most of them were in on the plot, too, you see.'

'Oh!' gasped Pulchra, and Lupus saw her clutch Flaccus's muscular arm.

'But it wasn't Agrippina they killed,' continued Felix. 'It was Acerronia, Agrippina's companion. She realised what was happening and bravely claimed to be Nero's mother, in order to save her.'

'That's right!' said Tranquillus, his voice squeaking with excitement. 'Meanwhile, Agrippina swam to shore and some fishermen pulled her out of the water and took her to her villa.'

'So Agrippina didn't die after all?' asked Jonathan.

'On the contrary,' said Felix. 'When Nero's men told him about the botched assassination, he ordered them to go back and do it properly.'

Tranquillus nodded; he was still standing up and swaying a little with the movement of the boat. 'Just before dawn the men burst into Agrippina's bedroom. When she saw their resolute faces and the glinting knives, she tore open her tunic and—'

'Tranquillus!' said Felix sternly. 'There are women present, including my daughter. They don't need to know all the sordid details.' He looked around at them. 'Let's just say that Nero's men did what they had been commanded to do.'

Tranquillus sat down beside Felix again, apparently not offended by the Patron's rebuke, for he added, 'My father says that was when Nero started to go bad. The Kindly Ones caught him, you see. They caught Nero and they drove him mad.'

'Matricide,' breathed Flavia. 'The crime of Orestes.'

'The worst crime a human can commit,' said Polla Argentaria, leaning back on her couch in the upper colonnade of the Villa Limona. 'Nero was probably the most depraved man who ever walked this earth. After he murdered his mother he got worse and worse. I couldn't begin to tell you the horrible things he did. Finally, six years after Agrippina's murder, my husband and his friends decided to rid the empire of that monster.'

'He did?' breathed Flavia. 'I mean, they did? They planned to kill the Emperor?'

'Yes,' murmured Polla. 'For the good of Rome.'

'What happened? Did they succeed?'

'No,' said Polla. 'They were betrayed and their plot exposed. And that was when Nero commanded my husband to commit suicide.'

SCROLL XIV

'Felix?' gasped Flavia. 'Nero commanded Felix to kill himself?'

Polla had been resting with her eyes closed. Now she opened them and looked at Flavia. 'No. Not Felix,' she said softly, 'not him. Nero ordered the death of my first husband.'

'Your what?' said Flavia, and then, as understanding dawned, 'You've been married before?'

'Why, yes,' said Polla. 'Didn't you know? Has Pulchra never told you? My first husband was the greatest Latin poet to live since Virgil. He might have been greater than Virgil if his life had not ended at the age of twenty-five.'

'What was his name?' asked Flavia.

'Lucan,' said Polla. 'Marcus Annaeus Lucanus.'

'I've heard of him!' cried Flavia. 'I think pater has a long poem by him.'

'Probably his unfinished epic on the civil war. He was a genius. It was such a crime that his talent was snuffed out by that monster Nero.'

'Tell me what happened! Please.'

Polla sighed and took a sip from her gemmed cup. 'Both Lucan and his uncle Seneca were involved in the plot to assassinate Nero,' she said. 'Seneca had been Nero's tutor and was a great philosopher as well. A man called Piso was the leader. He and some other noblemen realised that Nero was insane and could destroy Rome. So they plotted to kill him. But they hesitated. They failed to seize the right moment and eventually they were all betrayed. Nero had them arrested and offered them a choice. They could suffer public execution, along with the loss of their homes and goods. Or they could go home, put their affairs in order and open their veins.'

'What does that mean: *open their veins*?' asked Flavia. 'I've heard that expression before but never understood it.'

'It means they had to cut their wrists and the back of their knees and let the life blood drain away from their bodies. A slow but noble way to die,' she murmured.

Flavia stared.

Polla leaned toward Flavia. 'When Seneca opened his veins his wife did, too. Later, Nero commanded his physicians to save her, and they bound up her wounds. But do you see? She was willing to die with her husband. I would have done the same for Lucan,' said Polla, leaning back again, 'but I wasn't with him when the death sentence from Nero came. They say my husband took the news calmly, sent for his physician and died reciting his own poetry.' She looked at Flavia. 'I was a poet, too, you know, and a patroness of poets. But since that day I have hardly written a single line.'

'You must have loved your first husband very much,' said Flavia, 'to be willing to die with him.'

'Did I love Lucan? No.' Polla smiled sadly. 'It was an

arranged marriage. I married him when I was fourteen, the same year Nero murdered Agrippina. Although Lucan was six years my senior, I always felt more like his mother than his wife. Still, he was clever and witty, and he made me laugh. No, I didn't love him, Flavia, but I liked him, and we were happy together.' She took a small sip. 'Whereas, although Felix and I are the same age, he has always been the strong one. Always masterful. Always in control.'

'Felix is the same age as you?' said Flavia.

'A little younger, in fact,' said Polla. 'By a month or two.'

'How did you meet him?' asked Flavia.

'Felix?' asked Polla.

Flavia nodded. He mouth was dry so she took a long drink of posca from her plain silver cup.

Polla Argentaria turned and gazed out through the columns towards the bright bay. 'I first met Felix when he came to Rome to attend Lucan's funeral. He was a distant cousin of mine, twenty years old, just back from two years in Athens where he'd been studying philosophy and rhetoric at the Academy. He walked into my garden and the moment I saw him, Cupid fired an arrow deep into my heart. Right up to the feathers,' she added.

Flavia felt a strange pang in her own heart. She could easily imagine Felix at the age of twenty, tanned and handsome, but already with his striking silver-grey hair. '*Aeneas stepped forward,*' quoted Flavia, '*brilliant in the clear light, with the face and shoulders of a god.*'

'Exactly,' breathed Polla, turning astonished blue eyes on Flavia. 'Exactly so. I was like Dido, the first time she sees Aeneas.' She lowered her gaze. 'I have loved him passionately from that moment until today. And that,' she said softly, '*that* is the great tragedy of my life.'

As Felix's yacht entered the port of Baiae, Lupus stood at the front of the shaded deckhouse to get the best view. They were now so close that he had to tip his head back to see the bronze statues on a dozen lofty columns. Some were even taller than the palm trees that lined the harbour.

'So, Tranquillus,' said Felix, as the ship slowed its speed and described a pulsing curve towards a vacant berth. 'Pulchra has just told me that you want to interview Locusta, the imperial poisoner.'

'Yes, Patron,' said Tranquillus. 'For research purposes.'

'That may be difficult. She was put to death ten years ago by the Emperor Galba.'

Pulchra gasped and turned to glare accusingly at Tranquillus.

'But my father said . . . I was sure that Locusta lived in Baiae.'

'She does,' said Felix. 'But it's not the Locusta you're thinking of,' he added. 'This one's her daughter. Why did you want to talk to her, anyway?'

'I hope to be a biographer some day and Nero is my particular subject of interest. Also poison,' he added, with a glance at Pulchra.

'Ah.' Felix gave a small nod of understanding. 'Then you're in luck. Locusta's daughter might well be able to tell you something about Nero, though I can't promise.

And they say she knows as much about poison as her mother did. Do you still want to see her?' The boat shuddered as it nudged the pier.

'Yes, please, sir.'

'Very well. It's short notice, but I should be able to arrange it. She owes me a favour or two. However, we can't all descend on her like crows on a freshly-ploughed field. I'll take a group to the baths and we'll met you and your party later at the oyster-beds of the Lucrine Lake, at the fourth hour past noon. Who's going with young Tranquillus, then?'

'Oh, pater!' cried Pulchra, who had been smoothing her pink silk tunic. 'Aren't you coming with us?'

'We can't all go, my little nightingale. There are twelve of us, plus the panther. Don't worry,' he said, seeing the expression of disappointment on her face. 'You can take Brassus as your bodyguard.'

Pulchra turned away from her father with a pout.

'I'll go with Pulchra,' said Jonathan.

'I also,' said Nubia.

'When you say the baths,' Claudia was examining her fingernail, 'do you mean the Baths of Nero?'

'I do,' said Felix.

'Then I'll go with the children.'

'Oooh!' said Voluptua, standing up and stretching luxuriously. 'The famous Baths of Nero. I think I'll go with you, Patron.'

'Us, too,' Vopiscus gave Flaccus and Philodemus a slow wink. 'Especially if we're going to *those* baths.'

'What about you, Lupus?' said Felix with a half-smile. 'Are you for Locusta or the baths?'

Lupus glanced at Jonathan. He had promised Flavia a

portrait of Locusta, but someone needed to stay with Felix and the others, to keep an eye out for suspicious behaviour. Jonathan gave him a tiny nod, as if to say: You go.

Lupus smiled, pointed at himself and then to Felix.

'As you wish,' said Felix. He turned to Tranquillus. 'Do you see that apricot-coloured building up on the hill? The one with the white-columned porch? Near the gilded dome of that bath-house?'

Lupus and the others turned to follow Felix's pointing finger.

'Yes,' said Tranquillus.

'That's Locusta's villa. Now look further to the right.' They all turned dutifully. 'Do you see those yellow and red banners fluttering in the breeze towards Puteoli, the other harbour?'

'Yes,' they said.

'Those ring the Lucrine Lake, with its famous oyster-beds. We'll meet you there at the fourth hour after noon. If you don't feel up to the walk, hire a couple of litters. Brassus has money. The entrance to the oyster-beds is clearly marked. And now,' he said, 'I'll dictate a quick note of introduction for you, Tranquillus, to make sure Locusta receives you and tells you everything you want to know.'

'Why is it a tragedy,' said Flavia to Polla Argentaria, 'that you love Felix?'

Polla was still gazing through the fluted columns towards the sea. It was almost noon, and a million spangles of golden sunlight danced on the blue-grey surface of the water.

'Felix is like a god,' she whispered, almost to herself. 'When he takes you in his arms, you forget that anything else exists. It is just you and him, alone in a universe of pleasure. It is like dying. It is like being born.'

'And that's bad?' Flavia's heart was thudding.

Polla turned and looked at Flavia. 'You've just turned eleven, haven't you?'

Flavia nodded.

'As old as Pulchra. Next year you two girls will be of marriageable age, though I hope you don't marry until you are at least sixteen.'

Flavia gasped. 'But that's so *old*.'

'No,' said Polla with a sad smile. 'It's very young. I thought I was old enough at fourteen but . . . I wish I'd waited. I wish I had savoured every drop of my childhood. One day you'll understand. But what I've told Pulchra many times before – and what I want to tell you now – is this: When you *do* decide to marry, don't choose the dangerous man, choose the safe one.'

'What do you mean?' asked Flavia.

'Many women are attracted to a man of power, mystery, excitement, even violence. I call this sort of man the dangerous man. He brings the woman something very powerful: passion. But he is a trap, a snare. He will catch you like a sparrow in bird-lime and drag you down. Down into misery.' She turned to look at Flavia and in the reflected light from the sea her fine skin was almost translucent. 'Do you understand?'

'I should marry a safe man,' said Flavia.

'Yes,' whispered Polla. 'A man of virtue – what the Greeks call *arete*. Marry a man who is kind, wise, gentle and just. A man with whom you have things in common. A man who shares your philosophy. A man you can laugh with. A man you can respect. With such a man you can raise fine children in love and security.'

'But what about passion?' said Flavia in a small voice. 'What if you want passion?'

'Then you will end up like Dido,' said Polla, 'because passion and pain invariably go hand in hand.'

SCROLL XV

Nubia felt a surge of bittersweet emotion as she gazed around the port of Baiae. In many ways it reminded her of her desert home: the vast blue sky, the tall green palm trees and the shimmering light.

But there was no water in the desert. And the people of her clan did not behave like the people here. She saw the boys staring to the right and she followed their gaze. Further along the coast she could see men and women bathing together on a golden beach. Their wet tunics clung to their bodies so that they might as well have been naked. Some of them were even lying together on towels and carpets. Nubia felt her face grow hot and she quickly turned back to the port.

Here she saw women wearing silken tunics in jewel-like colours and carrying matching parasols against the blazing sun. They wore gauzy scarves instead of modest woollen pallas, and many of them had cork-soled platform-shoes, like the ones Flavia and Pulchra had worn on Flavia's birthday. Almost all the women in Baiae had complicated hairstyles, with masses of tight curls piled like diadems above their foreheads, and the remaining hair pulled tightly back.

The women of Baiae reminded Nubia of the women

she had seen in the port of Pompeii, shortly before its destruction. Here in Baiae, as at Pompeii, the men seemed to be either young and handsome or old and rich; the latter proclaimed their wealth by the amount of jewellery they wore. Gilded sandals, heavy rings and gold-plated wrist-guards seemed to be particularly in fashion. Many of the men, both young and old, had fierce-looking dogs with spiked collars and leather leads.

But when Voluptua followed her black panther down the boarding plank, all heads in the port turned to admire her.

'We'll walk with you as far as Aphrodite Street,' said Felix to Tranquillus, 'then our ways part. Come, my little nightingale,' he said to Pulchra, 'take my arm.'

The massive bodyguard Lucius Brassus led the way, followed by Flaccus, Vopiscus and Philodemus, wearing their togas and walking in front of Felix as befitted clients with their patron. Then came Felix and Pulchra, with Nubia and the others taking up the rear. As they passed through the crowded square Nubia heard people whisper, 'Pollius Felix!' and 'The Patron!' and 'It's him!'

'Look at the cat!' said a dark-haired young woman in pink silk. And her blonde friend in aquamarine breathed, 'Is that his latest? Lucky creature.'

As they left the square and started down a street of expensive shops, one young woman in particular caught Nubia's eye. She stood with her slave-girl on the other side of the street, in front of a perfume shop. Her hair was a lovely bronze colour, streaked with natural gold highlights. Nubia could tell that her curls were natural, too. The woman's skin was flawless and

Nubia guessed she was not much older than Jonathan's sister Miriam. She was looking over her shoulder, staring openly at them, not hiding her interest behind a silken fan like the others. Her large brown eyes were alive with pleasure.

Nubia followed the direction of the young woman's gaze and saw that she was looking not at exotic Voluptua and her panther, nor at any of the younger men, but at Felix, who had linked arms with Pulchra and was talking over her head to sleepy-eyed Vopiscus.

The young woman stepped smiling off the pavement in order to cross the street.

Without breaking his stride or his conversation, Felix glanced at the approaching woman and gave a tiny, almost imperceptible shake of his head. Then he looked back at Vopiscus. For a moment Nubia wondered if she had imagined it. But the young woman stopped so abruptly that her slave-girl bumped into her, and Nubia saw an anguished expression on her lovely face as they passed her by.

'Who is that woman?' Nubia whispered to Claudia, who was walking beside her.

Claudia glanced over her shoulder, then shrugged, 'Another one of his conquests, I suppose,' she said, and added bitterly, 'poor thing.'

Before they turned the corner Nubia glanced back. The young woman and her slave-girl were still standing in the middle of the street, gazing after them.

Locusta's apricot-coloured villa had looked impressive from the harbour, but up close Jonathan could see the plaster was cracked and the paint was peeling. Broken marble stairs the colour of old teeth led up to a small porch and wooden double doors. Furry vines curled round the two columns which flanked the porch and a pile of dead brown leaves lay in one corner.

Tranquillus seemed undeterred by the general impression of decay. He resolutely stepped forward and gave the rusty door-knocker three cheerful bangs. Felix's huge bodyguard Lucius Brassus loomed behind him, breathing heavily through his mouth.

Presently a peephole grated open at waist level. Tranquillus bent and spoke into it, then passed through the papyrus letter which Felix had dictated onboard his yacht.

'This is going to be good,' said Tranquillus, grinning over his shoulder and rubbing his hands together. 'She's got a dwarf for a doorkeeper.'

Jonathan and Nubia exchanged a glance. He noticed she looked subdued and gave her a reassuring smile.

'Remind me what we're doing here,' said Claudia with a sigh.

'Finding out about poison,' said Tranquillus. Pulchra shot him an angry look but Claudia merely shrugged and said, 'That's all right, then.'

A moment later the door opened and they found themselves face to face with a short, sturdy woman in an unbelted green tunic. She was barefoot and her greying hair was short and spiky.

'Hello, friends of Publius Pollius Felix,' she said. 'Do please come in. Excuse my hair. It's far too hot for my wig today.' She gave them a gap-toothed grin and stood aside as they filed into a large, cool atrium. Jonathan noticed more dead leaves piled up against one wall and an oily film on the surface of the impluvium.

'Forgive the state of the place,' she said. 'I wasn't expecting visitors.'

'Are you Locusta?' asked Tranquillus.

'I am,' she replied, then turned and led them through the atrium, down a dim corridor and into a large garden courtyard. Unlike the rest of the house, the garden was immaculate and ordered, with a marble fountain bubbling at its centre. Shaded by a thickly-woven grapevine overhead, it was fragrant, lush and blessedly cool. On one side of this garden, in deep shade of the peristyle, sat a large maple table with half a dozen mismatched chairs around it. The dwarf was just setting down a seventh chair – a stool.

'Please sit.' Locusta gave them her gap-toothed grin again. 'My girl is just coming with some refreshment. 'Oh, my dear,' she said, as Pulchra claimed the most comfortable-looking chair. 'You're lovely.'

'Thank you,' said Pulchra, touching her hair to make sure the pins were still in place.

'You know,' said Locusta, 'you look exactly like your mother did when she was a girl.'

'How do you know my mother?' asked Pulchra sharply.

'My little plum, everyone knows the beautiful Polla Argentaria, wife of Lucan and the Patron.'

'Lucan?' said Jonathan with a frown. 'Who's Lucan?'

'Lucan the famous poet?' asked Tranquillus.

'Who else?' said Locusta, pulling back a wooden chair and settling her sturdy frame on it. 'Poor Marcus Annaeus Lucanus. They say that if he'd lived, he would now be as celebrated as Virgil. But if he'd lived,' she winked at Pulchra, 'you would never have been born.'

'What are you talking about?' said Jonathan, his head swivelling from one to the other. 'Who's Lucan?'

'He was mater's first husband,' snapped Pulchra. 'He and his friends tried to kill Nero but they got caught and had to slash their wrists.'

'Great Neptune's beard!' muttered Jonathan.

Tranquillus eagerly pulled out his wax tablet and began to make notes.

A moment later, another dwarf emerged from between the columns of the peristyle. This one was female and she carried a large brass tray with three silver jugs and seven copper beakers.

'Posca or wine?' asked Locusta brightly.

Brassus was the only one who wanted wine, so Locusta filled his beaker first. Suddenly she put down the jug and gazed up at the chinks of blue sky showing through the grape vine. 'Beware,' she whispered, 'Jupiter is in his ascendancy.' Then she looked cheerfully back at Jonathan. 'Drinking from copper will help your asthma,' she said, taking up another jug and adding a splash of vinegar to a copper beaker of water.

'How do you know I have asthma?' he said, taking the beaker.

'I can smell the ephedron in your neck pouch.' Locusta poured out another drink and handed it to Claudia. 'Help yourself to sweetmeats, my sweet,' she said as the male dwarf put a platter on the table.

Jonathan's stomach growled as he saw golden-brown dates, red pomegranates, green almonds and moist honeycakes.

'Oh, I'll have one of those,' he said, reaching for a honeycake. 'I didn't have any breakfast today. We left so early.'

The others helped themselves, too, all except for Brassus, who extended his beaker for a refill of wine, and Nubia, who sat with her hands folded in her lap.

'Nothing for you, my dark beauty?' said Locusta to Nubia. 'How about an almond-stuffed date?'

'No, thank you,' said Nubia.

'Are you sure you don't want anything?' Locusta stood and plucked a fig from a nearby branch. 'Not even a fresh fig? They're just coming into season.'

'No, thank you,' said Nubia again.

'I'll have it!' said Pulchra, snatching the fruit from Locusta's surprised hand. 'I adore figs.' She bit into the soft purple skin.

'These almonds are delicious,' said Tranquillus with his mouth full. 'I like them slightly bitter.'

'Ugh!' said Pulchra. 'That fig isn't delicious. It tastes foul.'

Tranquillus looked up from his wax-tablet, his stylus poised. 'Now Locusta,' he said, 'can you tell us anything useful about poisons?'

'Oh yes,' said Locusta, sitting down again and beaming around at them. 'I can tell you lots about poison. For example, I can tell you that each of you has just been poisoned by me.' She giggled. 'Well, all except for the African girl. She's the only sensible one among you!'

SCROLL XVI

'What?' Jonathan cried, his chest suddenly tight. 'You've poisoned us?'

'Edepol!' Tranquillus spat a mouthful of half-chewed almonds onto his plate.

'No!' gasped Claudia, her lovely face suddenly chalk white. 'You can't have done! It's a ghastly joke. Say it's a joke!'

Brassus blundered to his feet and stared at Locusta, breathing hard. Then he staggered, grasped at empty air and fell back. His shoulder struck one of the columns of the peristyle and he bounced off it, falling into the garden with a resounding thud.

Pulchra screamed and clutched Jonathan's arm.

'I'm afraid it's no joke.' Locusta nodded at the still form of the huge bodyguard. 'I'm doing what the Patron requested. He asked me to teach you about poison. And the first rule is this: if you go to the house of a master-poisoner, don't eat or drink anything she serves you!'

There was a moment of horrified silence. Then Tranquillus began to laugh hysterically.

Locusta beamed at him. 'That's the spirit,' she said. 'I like someone with a sense of humour. Because you have such a charming attitude I'll give you your antidote first.' She made a gesture and the female dwarf stepped forward with a tiny phial of yellow glass. 'Drink this,' she said, handing the little jar to Tranquillus. 'Quickly.'

'Give it to me!' cried Pulchra, snatching the phial from Tranquillus's hand and trying to undo the cork stopper with her fingernails.

'NO!!' Locusta's voice was so loud that Pulchra almost dropped the bottle.

'Each of you has tasted a different poison,' she said, her face hard for the first time. 'If you take the wrong mixture it might kill you instantly. Give it to the boy.'

Pulchra handed the tiny yellow bottle to Tranquillus and began to cry. 'Please give me my antidote,' she sobbed. 'I don't want to die.'

'Very well,' said Locusta coldly, 'though I would have expected more courage from the daughter of a Stoic.'

She gestured to the female dwarf. The little woman stepped forward and handed Locusta a white feather.

'What's this?' Pulchra stared at the feather in disbelief. 'Where's my antidote?'

'Your fig contained oleander,' said Locusta. 'For that, there is no antidote.'

'Then I'm going to die!' wailed Pulchra.

'No,' said Locusta calmly. 'Go to my latrines – they're just over there – and stick this feather down your throat to make yourself sick. Vomit until you cannot vomit any more. Then come back here and I'll give you another cup of posca to rinse the taste from your mouth.'

'You evil witch!' screamed Pulchra. 'I'll tell my father and he'll have you crucified!'

'You won't be around to tell him anything,' said Locusta, 'unless you vomit immediately. Take it!'

Pulchra snatched the feather from Locusta's fingers and ran sobbing for the latrines.

'Edepol!' said Tranquillus, looking distinctly green, 'I think I'm going to vomit, too.'

'Follow the girl, then,' Locusta said briskly. 'There are three seats in the latrines.'

After he had gone, she made a sign to her little slaves. The male dwarf handed Jonathan and Claudia a buttermilk-coloured pastille each. 'You both had the honeycakes, didn't you?' said Locusta.

Jonathan nodded. He felt dizzy and slightly nauseous.

'Don't worry. You had the mildest poison. Eat that pastille. Wash it down with plenty of posca. I doubt if you'll even have to vomit. Oh, and if your legs feel heavy later, just keep moving until it passes.'

'I had two honeycakes,' admitted Jonathan, when he had chewed and swallowed the tablet.

'Better give him another one, Nanus,' said Locusta to the dwarf.

The little man gave Jonathan a second pastille and a wink.

Jonathan returned a queasy smile.

'Oh, that's better!' said Tranquillus, coming back to the table. 'But poor Pulchra is still being sick as a dog in there. Thanks,' he said, as Locusta handed him his posca. He had just raised the copper beaker to his lips, when he stopped and then extended it towards Locusta. 'You drink first.'

'Good!' she clapped her hands. 'You're learning fast. I like that. But that test wouldn't prove anything. I take a little poison each day and over the years I have built up my resistance to almost every poison known to man. Just like Mithridates. I could drink a goblet full of toad venom and not twitch an eyelid. Go ahead! Drink it.' She flapped her hand. 'It's just vinegar in water.'

Tranquillus drained the beaker and wiped his mouth with the back of his hand. 'How did you poison the fig?' he asked, sitting down. 'We all saw you pull it right off the tree.'

'Very simple,' she said. 'Just before I let you in, I used a syringe to inject the poison into the fig, while it was still on the tree. They say that's how Livia poisoned Augustus. You can also dip hard fruit like apples and pears in poisoned wax. People rarely notice because fruit is often dipped in wax to preserve it over the winter.'

'Fascinating,' said Tranquillus, scribbling on his wax tablet.

'Oh, and another interesting fact,' said Locusta, obviously pleased with Tranquillus's interest. 'The method Agrippina used to kill her husband Claudius was not mushrooms, as most people think.'

'It wasn't?'

'No. He threw them up. The poison that killed him was applied to the tip of the feather he used to make himself vomit.'

'Clever!' exclaimed Tranquillus and then looked up in alarm, his stylus frozen in mid-word.

'Don't worry,' said Locusta. 'The girl's feather wasn't poisoned.'

'What was in the honeycakes?' asked Jonathan.

'Hemlock,' said Locusta. 'Noblest and gentlest of all the poisons.'

'That's what they made Socrates drink, wasn't it?' said Jonathan. 'It makes you go cold and heavy from the feet up. My father's a doctor,' he explained when she raised her eyebrows questioningly at him.

'Excuse me,' said Claudia, rising from her chair. She was still deathly pale. 'I'll be right back.'

'Amazing: the power of the mind over the body,' said Locusta, watching the young woman move unsteadily through the garden.

'What do you mean?' asked Tranquillus.

'Those honeycakes didn't have much hemlock in them,' said Locusta. 'And it wouldn't begin to take effect for at least an hour anyway. It's her fear that has driven her to the latrines.'

'What about him?' said Jonathan, pointing at the massive form of Lucius Brassus, still lying on the ground.

Locusta chuckled. 'I put a sleeping potion in his wine. Listen closely,' she said. 'You can hear him snoring.'

They were all quiet for a moment and above the splashing of the fountain Jonathan could hear Brassus breathing.

'I think you are a bad woman to poison us,' said Nubia quietly. 'We are your guests.'

'What is your name?' Locusta turned to Nubia with a smile.

'Nubia. My name is Nubia.'

'That's not your real name, is it?'

Nubia looked surprised, then flustered. 'No.'

'What is your real name?'

Nubia did not reply.

'Why are you angry with me, Nubia?' Locusta leaned back in her chair. 'You're safe. You did well to refuse my food. You passed the test.'

'You did a bad thing to my friends.'

'I don't mind,' said Tranquillus.

'I do,' said Jonathan. 'Especially for Pulchra's sake.'

'Tell me, Nubia,' said Locusta. 'How I can make it up to you?'

Nubia glanced at Jonathan; Claudia was still in the latrines with Pulchra. He gave her a shrug, and then a nod.

'Help us please,' said Nubia, 'to find out who is trying to poison mother of Pulchra.'

As Lupus followed Felix and the others into the apodyterium of the Baths of Nero, his jaw dropped.

It was not the opulence of the large changing-room, with its golden tiles, erotic frescoes and marble niches that made him stare.

It was the fact that for the first time in his life he saw men and women undressing together at the baths. And most of them were as naked as the day they had been born.

'Ah!' Locusta smiled and closed her eyes. 'So that's why you're asking me about poison. Someone wants to kill the girl's mother.'

'Yes,' said Nubia.

'And you suspect poison?'

Jonathan nodded.

'It makes perfect sense,' murmured Locusta. 'Poison is easy to administer and often confused for real diseases. You can kill someone without anyone realising it was murder. What are her symptoms?'

Tranquillus consulted his wax tablet. 'In the past she complained of heaviness and coldness in her legs, of dizziness, drowsiness and blurred vision. Sometimes she was blue around the mouth.'

Locusta nodded. 'Any ideas, doctor's boy?' she said, turning her bright eyes on Jonathan.

He hung his head and nodded. 'I should have guessed before,' he said. 'Hemlock. The poisoner is using hemlock.'

'Almost certainly,' said Locusta, 'And that tells me that the poisoner is not very knowledgeable. Hemlock must be administered in the proper dose to be fatal. If you take it in small regular doses you just build up a resistance to it.'

'Like you've built up a resistance to the poisons you take every day?' Tranquillus looked up eagerly. 'Pulchra's mother has become immune to hemlock!'

'Probably. You know, hemlock is a very unreliable poison. It loses its effectiveness if it's left to sit too long. When Nero ordered Seneca to take his own life, Seneca drank a phial of hemlock which he had been saving for just such an occasion.'

'Seneca the Stoic philosopher?' asked Jonathan. 'I thought he cut his wrists.'

'He did,' said Locusta, 'but only because the hemlock he drank had absolutely no effect on him. Some say it was because he was in such good physical shape from all those cold baths and his strict vegetarian diet. But I suspect the hemlock was past its best.'

'But if Pulchra's mother has built up a resistance to hemlock,' said Jonathan, 'then why did she become so ill two nights ago?'

'That I don't know,' said Locusta. 'Maybe the would-be murderer has increased the dose. Or even changed poisons. Were there any new symptoms?'

'Her stomach hurt,' said Pulchra, coming up to the table. Some of her honey-coloured hair had come unpinned and hung in damp tendrils around her face. 'Mater clutched her stomach and said, "Oh it hurts," and then she fainted.' Pulchra looked down at the prostrate form of Lucius Brassus. 'Is he dead?' she asked in a small voice.

'No, my little plum, just sleeping. Sit down and drink a beaker of posca. Vinegar is always good for cleansing poison from your body.'

'So what do you think the new poison is?' asked Tranquillus. 'Which poison can give you stomach-ache?'

'Almost all of them,' said Locusta with a sigh. 'Did your mother have any other symptoms?'

They all looked at Pulchra. She shook her head. 'Just that she fainted.'

'Did she notice a taste of sharpness? Bitterness? Practically every poison tastes foul. That's always your first warning.'

'I don't know,' said Pulchra, carefully setting down her empty beaker.

'When you go back home,' said Locusta, 'ask your mother how she felt two days ago, the day she complained of stomach cramps. Then send me a detailed list of all her new symptoms. Oh, and tell me the colour of her stool.'

'Her stool?' said Pulchra.

Jonathan whispered in her ear.

'That's disgusting!' Pulchra glared at Locusta.

'My little plum, you don't have to do it yourself. Ask her slave-girl to look.'

'Just for my records,' said Tranquillus, his stylus poised, 'what is the worst poison of all? I mean the most deadly?'

'Love,' said Locusta without hesitation. 'Love is the worst poison. Love has driven more men to murder than hate or greed ever did. And for love there is no known antidote.'

Lupus lay in a private room on a marble slab. A bath-slave had covered his body with grey mud and then wrapped him in a linen towel. Apparently this was one of the specialties at the Baths of Nero, and Felix had paid for all of them to have a session. At first it had felt strange, but soon he began to enjoy squirming like a caterpillar in a squishy cocoon. The mud was slippery and warm and delightfully sensuous as it squelched between his fingers and toes.

After about half an hour, the bath-slave unwrapped Lupus and helped him climb down off the marble slab. Lupus stood over a marble drain while the slave sluiced him down with bucket after bucket of hot water until all the mud had melted away.

'Massage?' asked the bath-slave, gesturing back towards the marble slab, now clean and dry.

Lupus nodded eagerly. In baths as opulent as these, the massages should be wonderful.

'Which oil, sir?' asked the slave. 'Saffron, lemon, cinnamon or myrtle?'

Lupus thought about it. Saffron was the best, but it was also the most expensive. Still, the Patron was paying . . .

Lupus held up one finger.

'Saffron?' said the slave. 'The number one oil?'

Lupus nodded.

The slave smiled. 'An excellent choice, sir.'

Lupus was halfway through a full-body massage when the door to his cubicle opened and Vopiscus's red and sweating face peeped round it. For once he didn't look sleepy.

'Where's Flaccus?' he cried. And when Lupus jerked his head to say 'next cubicle' Vopiscus disappeared. A moment later he was back, a towel wrapped round his waist. 'They won't come so you may as well,' said Vopiscus with a vulpine grin. 'You can count this as part of your education.'

SCROLL XVII

'Oh, pater, it was horrible!' cried Pulchra, throwing herself into Felix's arms.

'Hello, my little nightingale!' Felix laughed and kissed the top of Pulchra's head.

He and his party had arrived at the Lucrine Lake slightly late, looking relaxed and cool after their afternoon at the baths. The others had been waiting in the shade of several tall umbrella pines by the entrance to the oyster-beds. Every half hour Pulchra had to go behind the bushes. Each time she had demanded that Nubia keep watch.

'Oh, pater!' Pulchra burst into fresh tears and sobbed in her father's arms.

'What?' Felix's smile faded as he held his daughter at arm's length. 'My dear, you look terrible. Your face is blotched and your hair is coming unpinned. What's the matter?'

'Locusta tried to poison us!' wailed Pulchra.

'Is this true?' Felix looked sharply at Brassus, who hung his big head and nodded. Nubia could tell he was deeply ashamed that he had not protected them.

Tranquillus stepped forward. 'Locusta had all the

antidotes, Patron, so we were never in any real danger. And we did learn a lot about poisons.'

'By Jupiter!' muttered Felix. 'That venefica! Don't worry, my dear,' he patted Pulchra's back. 'We'll take the yacht to Limon and stay there until you've recovered. Brassus, hire a horse and ride over to Limon. Tell Phileros to prepare the villa for a dozen guests.'

Brassus lifted his head. 'Yes, Patron!' he said, eyes shining. 'I'll go right away.'

'And get him to send a pigeon to my wife informing her that we're fine but won't be returning tonight.'

'We're not going back to the Villa Limona today?' said Jonathan.

'Not until my little nightingale is feeling better,' said Felix, giving Pulchra a paternal squeeze round the shoulders.

'Flavia will be most unhappy if we do not return tonight,' said Nubia softly to Jonathan.

'You can say that again,' he muttered.

Flavia Gemina to her beloved pater M. Flavius Geminus.

Greetings, pater! I hope you are well. It is late afternoon and at last the air is growing cooler. I am sitting on a cushioned marble bench in the library of the Villa Limona. It is very beautiful up here, with coloured marble everywhere and bronze busts of Epicurus and Athena and a view of the whole Bay of Neapolis. I can feel a cooling sea breeze and I can smell jasmine and I can hear pigeons cooing. You would be very proud of me. Why? This morning everyone went on an excursion to Baiae! Their reason for going wasn't just pleasure. We are investigating a Mystery and an important clue was to be found in that glirarium of licentiousness. But I was faithful to my vow and remained here. I hope you are proud of me. Pulchra's mother stayed behind, too, and she told me a tragic tale. She used to be married to a poet called Lucan. I think you have one of his epic poems in your collection. After Nero had his mother murdered, Lucan and some other good men plotted to kill that evil despot. But Nero discovered their plot and forced them to open their veins. I'm sure you must know all this, pater, so why have you never told me this fascinating story? Anyway, I am glad I stayed here at the Villa Limona, because I have a feeling that what Polla told me is somehow linked to the Mystery. I must go now, because everyone will be back soon. I hope you are feeling better. Remember to take your tonic, dear pater! Farewell. Cura ut valeas.

Lupus was bursting to tell the others his news, but he did not have a chance until they arrived at Limon later that afternoon.

The Patron's second Neapolitan property was an estate on the lower slopes of the hills between the Lucrine Lake and Puteoli, with views right across the Bay of Neapolis to Surrentum and the Cape of Hercules. It was a working farm – with ancient vineyards and infant lemon groves – and although it was not as luxurious as the Villa Limona, there were enough beds for everyone. There was even a small baths complex attached to the farmhouse.

The bailiff's wife had taken Pulchra off to these baths as soon as they arrived. Nubia had gone too, because Pulchra would not let go of her hand.

After a short tour of the villa, a grizzled old farm-slave showed Lupus, Jonathan and Tranquillus the room they were to share. It had a low double bed and someone had recently brought in a narrow pallet.

'You two share the big bed,' said Tranquillus. 'I'll take this one.' He dropped his writing case onto the pallet.

Lupus shrugged. He had more important concerns than who would sleep where.

WHAT NEWS? he wrote on his wax tablet.

He had heard about their adventures at Locusta's while they were on Felix's yacht. But he knew they had things to tell him that couldn't be related in front of the others.

'We think the poisoner has been using hemlock on Polla.' Jonathan sat on the edge of the big bed, took off his sandals and massaged his feet. 'But they used it in such small doses that instead of killing Polla they helped her built up a resistance to it. It seems the would-be murderer realised this and is now using a new poison, but we don't know which one, only that it wasn't strong enough to kill her in one dose. The only symptoms Pulchra noticed were stomach-ache and fainting. Locusta said that could mean almost anything.'

'Felix has carrier-pigeons that go back and forth between here and the Villa Limona,' said Tranquillus, lying back on his pallet. 'When we get back we'll send a more detailed list of the latest symptoms. A messenger can take it to Locusta, and once she has that information she can quickly send a reply to tell us what poison is being used. What about you, Lupus?' He closed his eyes. 'Anything to report?'

Lupus nodded vigorously and wrote on his tablet.

'Men and women share the same changing-room?' yelped Jonathan, reading over Lupus's shoulder.

Tranquillus was off his bed like a stone from the sling.

'You saw naked women?' he cried, staring at Lupus's wax tablet. 'At the Baths of Nero?'

Lupus grinned and nodded proudly. LOTS OF THEM he wrote.

Tranquillus stared at Lupus in awe. 'Even Voluptua?' he whispered.

Lupus nodded.

'Is she very beautiful?'

Lupus nodded enthusiastically and then wrote:

SHE AND FELIX WENT INTO A ROOM FOR A MUD BATH AND LEFT THE PANTHER OUTSIDE AS A WATCHDOG.

Jonathan stared at Lupus. 'Felix and Voluptua?' he said. 'Alone together in a private room of the baths?'

Lupus nodded and chuckled.

THEY THOUGHT NOBODY NOTICED BUT VOPISCUS SPOTTED THEM. WE TRIED TO LOOK THROUGH A CRACK IN THE DOOR BUT THE PANTHER WOULDN'T LET US.

'Edepol!' breathed Tranquillus.

Jonathan shook his head in disbelief. 'This puts a whole new light on things. Oh, hello, Nubia!' he said. 'How's Pulchra?'

'She is resting in our bedroom with an infusion of chicory,' said Nubia. 'Now I know what a clyster is,' she added, coming to sit on the bed beside them.

'Oh dear,' said Jonathan. 'Did you have to administer it?'

'No. But I had to hold her hand while she sat on latrines. Bailiff's wife said it was like Jove's thunder.'

'Oh!' Jonathan winced.

'Wait until you hear *our* news,' said Tranquillus. 'Felix and Voluptua are lovers!'

'Yes,' said Nubia calmly. 'I know.'

'And they went into a private room of the – How do you know?' Tranquillus interrupted himself.

'I can tell by how they are together,' said Nubia. 'On the boat coming here from Baiae they pretend to be distant from each other, but they give each other honey-looks when they think no person is looking.'

'Honey-looks?' said Jonathan.

'You know. When the man looks at woman as if to say "Only I can make you happy" and the woman looks back to say "Yes I know". Felix and slave-girls are lovers also,' added Nubia.

'What?' cried Jonathan and Tranquillus together.

SHE'S RIGHT, wrote Lupus. YESTERDAY I SAW FELIX AND POLLA'S SLAVE-GIRL ALONE TOGETHER IN HIS STUDY.

'Parthenope,' said Nubia.

'The pretty one with dark curly hair?' said Tranquillus.

Lupus and Nubia both nodded.

'What were they doing?' asked Tranquillus. 'Honey-looks? Kissing?'

Lupus glanced at Nubia and grinned. VERY KISSING he wrote on his tablet.

Jonathan looked at Nubia. 'You said slave-girls. As in more than one.'

'Ligea, too,' she said. 'Nurse-maid of little girls. And maybe Leucosia.'

The boys stared at her.

'Well,' said Tranquillus after a moment, 'lots of masters sleep with their slave-girls. It's allowed.'

'Also, a beautiful young girl we pass on the street today,' added Nubia. 'And I think that once before – but not now – Felix and Claudia are lovers, too.'

'Edepol!' breathed Tranquillus. 'I want to be Felix when I grow up.'

Lupus guffawed.

'No, you don't,' said Jonathan. 'That's nefas.'

'I suppose,' said Tranquillus. 'But still . . .'

'Poor Pulchra,' said Nubia.

DOES SHE KNOW? wrote Lupus.

'No,' said Nubia. 'She thinks her father is like unto a god.'

'If Felix is like one of the gods,' said Jonathan drily, 'then it must be Jupiter. Wait until Flavia hears this,' he added. 'She'll be devastated.'

'Why will Flavia be devastated?' said Tranquillus. He looked at each of their faces in turn and then understanding dawned. 'Great Juno's beard! Don't tell me she's his lover, too!' he yelped.

'No!' said Jonathan and Nubia together.

BUT SHE'S IN LOVE WITH HIM wrote Lupus.

'My future wife loves that satyr?'

'Her and half the women in Campania it seems,' muttered Jonathan.

Suddenly a thought struck Lupus. He rubbed out what he had just written to make room for a fresh message:

THE PERSON TRYING TO KILL POLLA MUST BE A WOMAN WHO WANTS TO MARRY FELIX!

Flavia was lying beside Felix in the sunshine. They had just swum to the furthest Sirens' rock. Their soaking tunics were plastered against their bodies and they were both breathing hard.

'I can't stay out here too long,' said Flavia presently, her eyes still closed against the heat and brilliance of the sun. 'I'll turn brown as a field-slave if I do.'

She felt the sudden delicious coolness of shade on her face, like a caress, and opened her eyes to see him leaning over her. He was so close she could see the tiny droplets of water on his eyelashes.

'It doesn't matter,' Felix whispered. 'You're beautiful.'

'I am?' said Flavia.

He nodded. 'I love you, Flavia. I have never loved anyone the way I love you. And when my wife is dead I will marry you, just as I promised.'

Then he lowered his head to kiss her.

SCROLL XVIII

'Flavia?' said a female voice. 'Flavia?'

'What?' Flavia's eyes jerked open and she sat up.

A curly-haired slave-girl stood framed in her bedroom doorway, the pale sky of evening behind her.

After a fruitless exploration of the villa, Flavia had returned to her room at the hottest time of the day to rest. Now, at the foot of the bed the four dogs raised their heads and thumped their tails, causing the scroll of Seneca's letters to drop onto the floor and slowly unroll. Flavia wiped her mouth and squinted at the girl in the doorway.

'Oh, hello, um . . . Parthenope,' said Flavia. 'I was just . . . reading Seneca's letters . . . I must have . . .'

The girl smiled. 'My mistress Polla Argentaria invites you to dine with her. May I take you there now?'

'Polla's eating again?'

'Yes, she's breaking her fast.'

'Will Felix be there, too?' said Flavia, automatically touching her hair to make sure it hadn't come unpinned. 'I mean, will your master be there? And the others?'

'My mistress has just received a message by carrier-pigeon,' said Parthenope. 'They will not be home tonight. The only other guest will be Annia Serena.'

Now Flavia was wide awake. If Annia Serena was the poisoner, then this would be her chance to strike.

'So, Flavia,' said Polla Argentaria, daintily nibbling a radish to break her fast. 'Parthenope tells me you're reading Seneca.'

Flavia, Polla and Annia Serena were dining together in Polla's lemon-yellow triclinium. Although each reclined on a separate couch, the couches had been moved forward so that they all shared salad from a single table in the centre of the room. Two slave-girls attended them: Parthenope and Leucosia.

'I've been trying to read his letters,' said Flavia, dipping a spring onion in a little bowl of honey-and-garum salad dressing, 'but they always put me to sleep.' She started to put the onion in her mouth, then froze. What if Annia Serena had put the poison in the garum?

On the couch opposite, Annia Serena gave a bleat of laughter. 'Seneca puts me to sleep, too. I think he's a terrible old bore.'

'Parthenope,' said Flavia. 'Taste my onion?'

'That's because you're an Epicurean, my dear Serena, and not a Stoic,' said Polla mildly.

Parthenope came forward and neatly bit off the garum-coated tip of the onion. For a brief moment her hazel eyes locked with Flavia's, then she went back to her place at the foot of the couch. Flavia put down her uneaten onion. 'I don't really understand what those two words mean,' she said, waiting to see how

Parthenope would react to the fish sauce. 'Stoic and Epicurean, I mean.'

'In the world today,' said Polla, 'there are two main philosophical schools: the Stoics and the Epicureans. To put it very simply, Epicureans believe that this life is all we have and that we should enjoy it to the maximum. Many are therefore devoted to sensual pleasure and often renounce a public career in favour of living a quiet life of leisure outside Rome. *Otium versus negotium.* Leisure rather than business.'

'A broad but accurate definition,' said Annia Serena, taking a piece of fried lettuce. 'Now let me see if I can describe the philosophy you favour.' She turned to Flavia. 'Stoics,' she said, 'believe that humans should be indifferent to pleasure and pain, should never give way to passion and should devote themselves to seeking the summum bonum – the highest good – which consists of these four principles: wisdom, self-control, justice and courage.' Annia Serena dipped her lettuce in the fish-sauce and ate it.

Flavia breathed a sigh of relief: The garum was not poisoned.

'Of course it's not that simple,' said Polla. 'Some Epicureans, like my husband, also seek the highest good.'

'Felix is an Epicurean?' asked Flavia, sitting up straight on her couch.

'What else could he be?' said Annia Serena, licking honeyed fish-sauce from her fingers, 'Devoted as he is to—' She stopped abruptly, and glanced nervously at Polla.

'So,' said Flavia to Polla, 'Felix is an Epicurean, but you're a Stoic?'

'Precisely. But in fact our two philosophies are not really so very different. Epicurus himself defined pleasure simply as *ataraxia*: "freedom from passion" or "peace of mind". Many Epicureans are quite restrained.'

'But Polla,' said Annia Serena, 'don't you find Seneca terribly obsessed with death and suicide?'

'Yes!' cried Flavia. 'Just this afternoon I was reading a letter in which he praises a barbarian from Germania who stuffed a sponge-stick down his own throat rather than fight wild beasts in the arena. I don't understand why that was good. Isn't it braver to face a tiger in the amphitheatre than to choke yourself in the latrines?'

Polla smiled patiently. 'What Seneca was saying in that passage is that even a barbarian thought it better to choose his own death than to die entertaining his conquerors. Even though he was a slave, he was free to control his own destiny.'

'But he might have killed the tiger and received a bag of gold!' cried Flavia.

'Aha!' Annia Serena's woolly yellow curls bobbed in triumph. 'She's an Epicurean at heart.'

'Let me tell you another story,' said Polla. 'About a woman Stoic named Arria.'

'Oh, not Arria!' Annia Serena rolled her eyes.

Polla ignored her. 'Arria was married to a good and wise man named Paetus who, like my first husband, was involved in a plot to get rid of a corrupt emperor, in this case Claudius. But – like Nero – Claudius discovered the plot against him. And like Nero, Claudius ordered the conspirators to take their own lives, or suffer a humiliating public execution. But Paetus hesitated to fall on his sword, fearing the pain of the wound almost more than death itself.' For once, Polla's voice was strong and clear.

She continued: 'Paetus's wife Arria took a knife, plunged it into her own chest, pulled it out and handed it to her husband with these words: *Paete, non dolet.* "It does not hurt, Paetus." Wasn't that a glorious deed?'

'Did she die?' asked Flavia.

'Of course,' said Polla. 'She and her husband both died, but they gained a kind of immortality by their noble words and action!'

'I think Arria was mad,' said Annia Serena. She turned to Flavia. 'Before the famous it-does-not-hurt incident, Arria's grown-up children suspected she might commit suicide, so they removed all the knives and sharp objects from her household. At a dinner party with them one evening, she suddenly got off her couch, put her head down and rammed the wall as hard as she could.'

'Great Juno's peacock!' cried Flavia. 'What happened?'

'She knocked herself unconscious, of course. When she revived, her family asked her why she had dashed her head against a wall. She replied that if she wanted to find a way of ending her life, she could do it with whatever lay to hand.'

'Wasn't that sublime?' said Polla, and Flavia noticed a pink flush on her pale cheeks.

Annia Serena sighed and rolled her eyes. 'Wasn't that stupid?'

Luckily, Flavia was saved from having to answer by the arrival of the prima mensa: hare with quince and raisins in a cumin sauce.

*

'So, Jonathan,' said Publius Pollius Felix, tipping his head back to let a raw oyster slip down his throat. 'Pulchra tells me you've been reading Seneca's letters.'

Jonathan was reclining between Lupus and Tranquillus in the small garden triclinium of the farmhouse at Limon. Nubia was having supper in Pulchra's room and Voluptua and Claudia were dining alone in their separate rooms, leaving the men and boys to dine together.

'Yes,' said Jonathan. 'I admire Seneca very much.'

'Me, too,' said Tranquillus.

Lupus was intent on freeing an oyster from its shell with the sharp end of his spoon, but he nodded absently.

'Excellent,' murmured Flaccus in his deep voice. 'It's good to know you boys are reading the right sort of thing.'

Vopiscus snorted. 'Seneca's letters are just collections of quotable mottoes,' he said. 'Reading them is like eating a meal of nothing but garum.'

'You say that because you're an Epicurean, not a Stoic,' said Flaccus, squeezing lemon onto his oysters. He grinned. 'You Epicureans seek the highest good, with its four principles: women, food, games and the baths.'

Lupus guffawed and Tranquillus giggled.

'Be careful what you say, Flaccus,' said Vopiscus lazily. 'You're enjoying the hospitality of an Epicurean tonight.'

'You're an Epicurean?' said Jonathan to Felix, who was reclining alone on the central couch. 'I thought you were a Stoic.'

Felix smiled. 'My dear boy, whatever gave you that impression?'

'Locusta called Pulchra the daughter of a Stoic.'

'And so she is,' said Felix, with an amused smile.

'Polla Argentaria is the Stoic in the family,' explained Flaccus.

'So you're an Epicurean, but you married a Stoic?'

Felix nodded. 'Our two philosophies are not really so different. Seneca often quotes Epicurus.' Felix tipped another oyster down his throat. Then he wiped his mouth with a napkin and said, 'Is the food not to your liking, Philodemus? You haven't touched a thing.'

'I am appalled,' said Philodemus, raising his liquid brown eyes to look at Felix. 'Disgusted and appalled by what I have seen and heard today.'

Everyone stared at Philodemus, who was trembling with emotion. Lupus froze with an oyster poised above his open mouth.

'An hour ago,' said Philodemus to Felix, 'I asked Claudia Casta to marry me.

'She wept and asked me to hear a confession first. She told me that you seduced her when she was only a girl, not much older than your own daughter is now.'

'What?' cried Flaccus.

'I shared some of my philosophy with her,' continued Philodemus, 'and I believe it brought her a small amount of comfort. She has asked me to take her back to her villa in Pausilypon immediately.'

Flaccus twisted on his elbow to look at Felix. 'Is that true? Did you seduce Claudia?'

'Of course not,' said Felix coldly.

'I do not believe in any of your philosophies,' said Philodemus, sliding awkwardly off his couch. 'But at least Seneca said some wise things.' He turned his dark eyes on the boys. 'Seneca told his young friend Lucilius to *stop up your ears with something stronger than wax.* And another philosopher says this: *My son, if sinners entice you, do not give in to them.* I suggest you follow my example and leave this company, before you are corrupted.' He turned stiffly back to Felix. 'I thank you, sir,' he said, 'for your hospitality. Please give my apologies, and Claudia's, to your wife. Goodbye.'

He strode out of the room, jostling one of the tables and causing the ceramic bowls to clink.

Jonathan looked around at the stunned faces and saw Lupus slowly lower his oyster to the table.

Vopiscus was the first to recover. 'Don't mind Philodemus,' he said contemptuously. 'He used to be a rich Epicurean. But since his inheritance was buried under the mud from that volcano he's become a Jew. Or a Christian. One of those strange eastern philosophies. And if anyone is more tedious than the Stoics, they are.'

SCROLL XIX

Flavia Gemina to her adored pater M. Flavius Geminus.

Greetings, pater! I hope you are well and surviving the heat. Is it as hot there as it is here? At the moment Nubia and I are sitting in Pulchra's bedroom and her slave-girl Leda is fanning us with a large ostrich-feather fan. Pulchra got a stomach upset in Baiae, along with Lupus and all the men. Pulchra accidentally ate some poison but the others blame their misfortune on bad oysters. Pulchra says that Philodemus (the one who reminded me of an eager hunting-dog) and Claudia (the tawny beauty) were so badly affected that they went straight back to Neapolis and won't be returning. Only Jonathan escaped, because he doesn't like oysters, and also Nubia and Voluptua, who dined in their rooms on leek soup and cold chicken. (Voluptua's panther is fine, too; he always eats raw ground-up meat with an egg beaten into it.)

It was almost comical. Felix's yacht came in this afternoon, two days later than expected. Justus and Annia Serena and I were standing there on the docking platform waiting to greet them, but all the men just ran right past us, their faces very pale and intent as they headed for the latrines. Jonathan says it's bad, but nothing compared to yesterday and the day before when it sounded like Tartarus in the latrines, with rumblings and groans and coughs and curses. Poor Lupus. Poor Felix. Poor Flaccus. Poor Tranquillus.

Oh pater! I forgot to tell you in my last letter that I met the boy you want me to marry! At first I didn't like him, but now I think I might. He has been helping us with our Mystery and I must say he is quite clever and funny. But I haven't seen him for two days because he went to that glirarium of licentiousness and he's still suffering the penalty.

For the past two days – while the others were in Baiae – I have been reading, walking in the gardens and taking the dogs exploring. You will never guess what the dogs found this morning! An ancient wooden shrine of Hercules just over the hill by a sandy crescent beach. It is half hidden by olive trees and I don't think it's been used as a shrine in ages. But someone has been staying there. I could tell because there was a carpet and blanket and cushions and even an amphora of wine in the corner with two beakers. I can't wait to show the others tomorrow morning. We could take some more beakers and also olives and salted chickpeas and maybe some scrolls, and make it our secret den. I just hope it's not the Lair of Pirates!

Well, I must finish now. Pulchra is demanding that I read something to her. It is a choice between Seneca's letters, Pliny's Natural History *or scroll four of the* Aeneid, *all in my room nearby. I think you know which one I will choose. Don't forget to take your tonic and apply the balm, dearest pater! Farewell.*

P.S. Pulchra wants me to tell you that if her father and the other men are recovered they are going to do something amazing tomorrow night, to celebrate the festival of Fors Fortuna.

P.P.S. She won't tell me what.

Midsummer's day dawned clear and bright, promising to be the hottest day of the year so far. While it was still relatively cool, Flavia led her friends through the dappled olive groves to the small wooden shrine which she and the dogs had discovered the previous day.

Lupus and Tranquillus were with them, both looking paler and thinner than they had three days previously. Tranquillus held Ajax's gilded lead because Pulchra was spending the morning with her mother.

'See?' said Flavia, leading them through two wooden columns into the dim shrine. 'There's a carpet and cushions and everything. Don't let the dogs in,' she added. 'They can keep guard in the portico.'

'Stay, Tigris! Good dog,' said Jonathan and looked around. 'It's not far from the beach. Maybe fishermen sleep here.'

'Look up,' said Flavia. 'See the garland of roses I hung from the rafters? That means that everything we say here is *sub rosa*, in confidence. Wave to Hercules,' she added, indicating the painted wooden statue of the demigod. 'I had to stand him upright and give him a good dusting,' she added.

They all turned and dutifully greeted the ancient cult statue.

'Now.' She sat on one of the cushions. 'Tell me what

you learned in Baiae. Pulchra says Locusta tried to poison you. Is that true?'

'Yes,' said Tranquillus, sitting beside her, 'but she gave us the antidotes.' He shook his head. 'Those bad oysters were far worse than her poison. I felt like dying.'

Lupus nodded his agreement, then pointed to his mouth, shook his head and waved his forefinger back and forth, as if to say: *never again.*

'Oh, Lupus,' said Nubia. 'That is sad. Oysters were being your favourite food.'

He shrugged.

'We think the poisoner was using hemlock,' said Jonathan. 'But they used it in such small doses that Polla built up an immunity to it.'

'Hemlock,' breathed Flavia. 'The poison they made Socrates drink.'

'Exactly,' said Tranquillus. 'Listen to this.' He flipped open his wax tablet and read:

'The jailer pinched his foot quite hard and asked if he felt anything. "No," replied Socrates. Later the man pinched his thighs, showing how he was growing cold and numb. "When it reaches his heart," said the jailer, "He will die."'

'That's from Plato,' explained Tranquillus. 'I translated it myself this morning.'

Jonathan nodded. 'Even after Locusta's antidote it felt as though I was wearing sandals made of lead. But Pulchra's mother didn't mention heaviness of limbs on the night of your birthday. So we think the poisoner is using something else now.'

'What? What poison are they using?'

'We don't know,' said Tranquillus. 'That's why Pulchra is with her mother this morning. She's going to find out more about the symptoms.'

'What else did you discover?' asked Flavia.

'Lupus has a theory,' said Jonathan. 'Show her, Lupus.'

Lupus opened his wax tablet with a flick of his wrist. It was dim in the shrine and Flavia had to lean forward to read the message etched in the beeswax.

THE PERSON TRYING TO KILL POLLA MUST BE A WOMAN WHO WANTS TO MARRY FELIX!

'I'm surprised you didn't think of that motive right away, Flavia,' said Jonathan.

'Well,' she replied, feeling her face grow warm. 'I admit that could be a motive. But there must be others.'

'Can you think of one?' said Jonathan.

Flavia considered for a moment. 'While you were gone,' she said, 'I found out that Polla Argentaria used to be married to the poet Lucan, who tried to kill Nero. Maybe the person trying to kill her is a relative or friend of Nero who wants revenge. Maybe Annia Serena. Her father was a supporter of Nero.'

'But that was fifteen years ago,' said Tranquillus, 'and Nero's been dead for over ten years. Also, Polla wasn't associated with the conspiracy, apart from being Lucan's wife.'

'Do you have a better theory?' snapped Flavia.

'As a matter of fact I do,' said Tranquillus. 'I think the would-be murderer is Felix himself.'

'What?' gasped Flavia. 'Why would Felix want to murder his own wife?'

'Because maybe he is wanting to marry someone else,' said Nubia.

Flavia stood up and turned to face the wooden statue of Hercules, so they wouldn't see her pink cheeks. 'If Felix wanted to marry someone else, he could just divorce Polla Argentaria,' she said.

'But then he'd have to give back her dowry,' said Tranquillus. 'While we were in Limon the bailiff kept referring to "Polla's villa". What if the Villa Limona – or the land it's built on – really belongs to her? If Felix divorced her, he might have to give it up.'

'And you know how much he loves that villa,' said Jonathan quietly.

'So you think Felix is trying to kill Polla?' said Flavia. 'Because he loves someone else and wants to re-marry and keep the Villa Limona?'

She turned to see the four of them nodding.

'No. I refuse to believe it. Last year some people accused him of a crime, but he was innocent. Remember how he came to our rescue? And remember how he rode all the way to Ostia last December to get Doctor Mordecai's elixir for Polla? No. Felix is brave and good and noble. And he wants to find the poisoner just as much as we do.'

She saw Nubia and Jonathan exchange a glance.

'Flavia,' said Jonathan. 'You're an excellent detective. Except when you're emotionally involved. Are you sure you aren't a little biased towards Felix?'

'Of course not,' said Flavia, and hurried on: 'Maybe Lupus's theory is right after all. Maybe the poisoner is a woman who wants to get rid of Polla so she can marry Felix. That means the culprit must be either Annia Serena or Voluptua, because Claudia is out of the picture. Nubia and I will try to get some more information from those two. I'll take Serena. Nubia, you take Voluptua. You boys see if you can identify the poison Polla took a few days ago. Pulchra should have a good list of her mother's symptoms by now. Come on, let's go!'

SCROLL XX

Flavia did not find Annia Serena in the baths; only the little girls were there, splashing and squealing in the cold-plunge of the domed frigidarium with their Egyptian nurse-maid.

She did not find Serena in the shady garden, but she nodded with approval to see Nubia quietly stroking the panther and listening to Voluptua and Vopiscus chat as they played a board game.

She did not find Serena up in the library, where Pulchra and the three boys looked up from their scrolls and sighed and shook their heads.

Finally she went to Felix's tablinum. Although the household would be celebrating the festival of Fors Fortuna later that evening, it was not strictly a festival day so he might be receiving clients.

'Annia Serena?' said Felix's scribe. 'I haven't seen her today.'

'Is your master still here?' said Flavia, looking beyond Justus at the closed double doors of Felix's tablinum.

'No, I'm sorry. He just saw the last of his clients. You might try the mistress's suite.'

But neither Annia Serena or Felix were with Polla

Argentaria, who was dozing peacefully on her wicker couch. Flavia went to the herb garden to think.

She was standing before his statue, trying to make sense of the thoughts and feelings which crowded her mind, when she heard a child crying. In the shimmering olive groves the cicadas were throbbing so loudly that she almost missed it. Then it came again, and she followed it around the corner to some tubs of pomegranate bushes beneath the shade of a yellow canvas awning. Moving closer, she found a small wooden door she had never noticed before. It was slightly ajar, and from here she could hear the sobbing more clearly. Hesitantly, she pushed open the door and started down the stone steps. A crowd of tiny silent flies circled here in the coolness.

As she ducked through the flies and descended the steps, the air became cooler. These stairs must lead to the underground storage area of the villa. The light was dim down here and her fingertips on the rough stone wall helped her find her way down to the packed earth floor.

She was about to call out to Pollina or Pollinilla, when she remembered they were up in the baths. Then she caught a whiff of the expensive cinnamon-saffron scent of susinum. She frowned. 'Annia Serena?'

Now the sound was coming again, a rhythmic whimpering interspersed with little sobs, now louder, now softer. And then silence.

As Flavia turned a corner she saw something like a huge marble block looming in the murky half light. The air was strangely cool around it, so Flavia reached out to touch it. Ice! It was a massive block of ice, twice as tall and wide as she was.

Then the sobbing started again, louder and more urgent, just the other side of the ice block. The smell of saffron and cinnamon was stronger now, mixed with the faint scent of musky citron. Suddenly she realised what she was hearing.

It wasn't a child crying with pain.

It was a woman crying with pleasure.

Her cheeks burning with embarrassment, Flavia turned and stumbled back up the dim stairs and out into the blazing heat of midsummer.

'Beach banquet! Beach banquet!' screamed Pollinilla, rushing into Flavia's bedroom. 'We're going to have the beach banquet tonight!'

Pulchra followed her youngest sister into the bedroom. 'Pollinilla,' she said, 'be a good girl and don't bother Flavia and Nubia. They're trying to nap.'

'It's all right,' said Flavia, stretching. 'We were just getting up.'

'What is beach banquet?' asked Nubia, sitting up on her bed.

'Remember the Green Grotto where the pirates held us prisoner last August?'

Flavia and Nubia nodded.

'Right next to it is a crescent beach. It's the only beach for miles around. Everyone else calls it the Bay of Pollius but I call it the Pirate Beach. Each summer when the weather gets unbearably hot, the slaves take couches and tables and food down there and we all have a banquet together. The rule is you have to run into the water between each course.'

'Oh, what fun!' said Flavia with a yawn.

'What fun!' screamed Pollinilla, twirling around the room and causing the dogs to retreat beneath the beds. 'What fun! What fun!'

'We usually go in July or August, when the dog-star has risen, but this year it's hot enough to do at our midsummer bonfire for the festival of Fors Fortuna.'

'Bonfire? I thought that festival was celebrated with garlanded barges and a statue of Fortuna.'

'In Rome it is,' said Polla. 'But our household celebrates it with a midsummer bonfire. It's something pater's family always did in Greece. The bravest men soak themselves in seawater and either run or ride horses through fire.'

'What fun!'

'Horses go through the fire?' asked Nubia in alarm. 'Does this not frighten them?'

'No, Nubia, the horses don't mind,' said Pulchra.

'By the way, Pulchra,' said Flavia, glancing at the twirling Pollinilla, 'did you get a message to you-know-who about you-know-what?'

Pulchra nodded. 'I sent the list of symptoms a few hours ago and we just had a pigeon back from Limon.'

'*What did Locusta say?*' asked Flavia in halting Greek, so Pollinilla wouldn't understand. '*What poison?*'

Pulchra replied in the same language. '*Locusta said the symptoms didn't match those for any poison she knew.*'

'Oh, no! How frustrating! We'll have to ask her again,' said Flavia in Latin.

'We can't,' said Pulchra in Greek, and looked away. *'Locusta's dead.'*

'What fun! What fun!' cried Pollinilla, falling dizzily onto Nubia's bed.

Flavia stared at Pulchra.

'As soon as the pigeon arrived at Limon,' said Pulchra, *'one of pater's men took my message to Locusta in Baiae. He showed her the list and she wrote her reply. But when she was going to the door to see him out she slipped on the front steps and broke her neck.'*

'What fun! What fun!' cried Pollinilla, jumping up and down on Nubia's bed.

'Don't look at me like that, Flavia,' said Pulchra, reverting to Latin. 'Pater says he's certain it was just a tragic accident.'

Flavia's bedroom smelt of unguents, ochre and singed hair.

Pulchra's slave-girl had spent almost an hour giving her a coiffure of the latest fashion. Leda had pulled Flavia's light-brown hair back into a painfully tight bun, then used a heated bronze rod to make lots of soft little curls in front, with a dangling ringlet on either side.

Flavia had put on all the jewellery she possessed and her long dark blue summer tunic.

Best of all was the make-up. Pulchra had applied a face-cream made of olive-oil blended with beeswax and lemon water. Then she had lightly dusted Flavia's face with fine chalk powder, to make it look fashionably pale. A subtle smudging of red-ochre powder – ground on the slate palette – restored some colour to her cheeks. Then Pulchra applied a lip-salve of beeswax blended with ochre to make Flavia's lips look pink and moist. But Flavia was most pleased with her eyes. Pulchra had used a crescent-shaped copper tool to outline them in black. Then she had ground some azurite powder and mixed it with castor oil to make Flavia's upper lids shimmery blue.

Flavia looked at herself in the mirror, turning her head to make her ringlets swing. Satisfied, she swivelled on her stool and leaned forward to strap on her platform shoes.

A few moments later she was tottering along the colonnade in the direction of the landing platform and the garlanded yacht, which would take them to the banquet.

When she reached the boys' room she stopped and gripped the folding lattice-work screen, which had been pulled across. 'I'm sorry, boys,' she said to the dogs, 'but Voluptua's panther has been invited and I don't think you'd get on with him. I'll take you for a walk later.'

She ignored their reproachful looks and hurried down the stairs leading to the fish-pond. As she passed the bath-house she twirled the blue parasol Pulchra had loaned her, and tried swinging her hips a little, the way Leucosia the slave-girl did. But it made her stagger and she almost fell off her cork-heeled shoes. Suddenly a muscular arm blocked her way and she looked up to see Flaccus glaring down at her.

'Where do you think you're going?' he said, his hand pressing the curved plaster wall of the bath-house beside her. He looked very handsome in a sky-blue tunic bordered with gold thread.

'To the beach banquet,' she said.

'Looking like that?'

'Looking like what?'

'Looking so grown up. As if you're sixteen years old, with all that dark stuff around your eyes—'

'Thank you,' she said, twirling her parasol. 'It's kohl—'

'—and the colour on your mouth and cheeks . . . Take it off.'

'What do you mean?'

'Go back to your room and take it off.'

'Who do you think you are?' she cried. 'You're not my pater!'

He leaned closer, his face still grim. 'And if your father were here? What would he say?'

She had no answer.

'Flavia,' he said, in a gentler tone of voice, 'please take it off. At least some of it. For me?'

'I don't know why I should.' She glared defiantly at him, but something about his expression made her gaze waver. 'All right. Some of it.' She lowered her parasol and scowled down at her feet. 'But I don't see why I should.'

'Thank you,' he said, and lowered his arm.

'I'll miss the boat.'

'I'll tell them to come back for us. Annia Serena's not ready either. I was just coming to fetch her. We'll both wait for you down at the landing platform.'

Flavia sighed and as she turned to go back to her room he said, 'Flavia?'

'Yes?' She kept her back to him and rolled her eyes.

'Tomorrow I'm leaving, and in case I don't get a chance to say a proper goodbye, well: Goodbye.'

'You're going?' she turned to stare at him. 'Why?'

'When I was in Halicarnassus last month I hired some agents to make discreet inquiries about the illegal slave-trade. One of my agents has just sent me a letter. He's tracked down Magnus. I'm going back there to see if he can lead us to the mastermind behind the operation.'

'Oh, Flaccus, that's wonderful! Will you tell me what you find? Will you write to me?'

He smiled and nodded. 'I promise if I find anything I'll let you know.' He looked at her for a moment and his smile faded. 'By Hercules, you look so grown up.'

'Thank you!' she said, giving him a radiant smile and flipping up her parasol again.

'Flavia. Magnus isn't the only reason I'm leaving the Villa Limona. Philodemus was right.'

'Why? What did Philodemus say?'

Flaccus leaned so close that she could smell the faint scent of mastic on his breath. 'This place isn't good for us. It's corrupt. It's like a piece of fruit that looks beautiful on the outside. But when you bite into it you find worms and rotten pulp. Why don't you take Nubia and the boys and go back home to Ostia?'

'Oh, I can't possibly do that! I have a mystery to solve. But I'll be careful. I'm a big girl.'

'No,' he said softly, 'you're not a big girl. But one day you will be, and I'd like to know you then. Now take that stuff off your face and I'll see you down at the boat.'

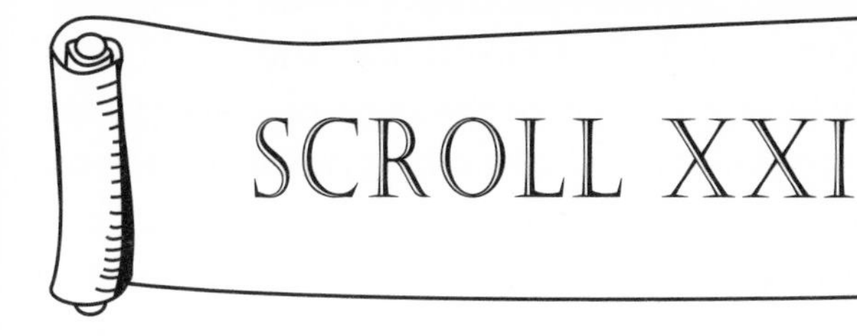

SCROLL XXI

'There's a sight you don't see every day,' murmured Jonathan. 'Three sea-nymphs emerging from the sea.' Dark-skinned Nubia, wearing a mustard-yellow tunic, was flanked by raven-haired Voluptua in ruby red and Polla Argentaria in ice blue. Their hair and faces were dry but from the neck down they were soaking wet.

Without taking his eyes from them he said, 'Do I have to get my clothes wet, too?' It was evening on the hottest and longest day of the year. He and Pulchra were standing on the sand of a crescent beach near the Villa Limona. Sheer limestone cliffs loomed dramatically behind them to the south and to the north terraced steps mounted the hillside. The terraces were covered with dark green vine-rows on the higher levels and silvery olive-groves on the lower.

At the foot of one of these terraces, just where the beach began, stood a shaggy blue-grey pine tree with five low dining couches arranged in a semi-circle beneath it. Turning, Jonathan saw that the three sea-nymphs were making for that. Then he noticed his boar, turning slowly on a portable spit and attended by two long-haired boys in yellow tunics.

'Of course you have to get your clothes wet!' Pulchra

laughed and showed her dimples. 'It's what we always do. Come on! Don't be a coward!' She caught his hand and pulled him into the water. Pollina and Pollinilla ran after them, even though their pink tunics were already wet from a previous soaking.

'Master of the Universe!' Jonathan exclaimed. 'The water's as warm as milk!' His best cream linen tunic ballooned up beneath his chin as the water reached his waist and the little girls screamed with laughter.

'Duck down to get it wet,' Pulchra said with a giggle, 'then it won't puff up.'

Jonathan sank down as far as his neck in the blood-warm water and then stood up.

'I have to admit,' he said, 'it's very refreshing.'

'I told you!' Pulchra laughed and as she pulled him back across the sand to the dining couches, he noticed that even the Patron wore wet clothing.

Felix and his wife occupied the central couch at the base of the blue pine's trunk. On their left Voluptua and Vopiscus shared a couch, then came the couch Pulchra had chosen. Lupus shared the end-couch opposite Jonathan and Pulchra with the two little blonde girls. He was in a cheerful mood and did not seem to mind their giggling attention.

'Where's Flavia?' said Jonathan, looking around. 'And Flaccus and Annia Serena?'

Felix extended his tanned arm towards the low promontory to the north. 'Here they come,' he said, and resumed stroking Voluptua's panther. The creature was chained to Voluptua's couch but had come to lie on the sand in front of him.

The garlanded yacht came gliding into sight and a

few moments later Jonathan saw Flaccus help Flavia and Annia Serena down the gangplank.

Pulchra leapt off their couch and ran down to the water's edge. Jonathan could hear her giggling and he felt his chest tighten as she took Flaccus's hand and pulled him into the water. The little girls and Lupus had run down to the water, too. Lupus plunged straight in, then turned to float on his back. Pollinilla took Flavia's hand and Pollina took Serena's, and the little girls tugged them towards the sea. Annia Serena resisted but Flavia kicked off her platform shoes and allowed herself to be pulled in. At that point Annia Serena gave in, too, squealing as Lupus splashed her.

When the dripping guests finally emerged from the water to join the other diners, everyone applauded. Annia Serena joined sleepy-eyed Vopiscus and Voluptua at the end of the couch nearest Felix. Jonathan saw her give the Patron an undisguised honey-look.

'Valerius Flaccus is going to recline on our couch,' announced Pulchra to Jonathan. She was laughing and dripping wet. Her bright blue eyes were lined with kohl, like the older women.

'Salve, Jonathan,' grinned Flaccus, and stretched out his muscular wet body on the other side of Pulchra.

Now there was more applause as three of the Villa Limona's prettiest slave-girls and the two long-haired slave-boys came along the sand carrying light wicker tables. On each table was a silver platter containing what appeared to be a flat round turbot surrounded by a garnishing of radishes, onions, olives, and celery. These were set before the diners and duly tasted by the girls.

Then one of the slave-boys handed out silver goblets

and the other followed him round with two silver jugs, one filled with chilled water, one with wine. Before they reached Jonathan, he heard Nubia cry out in alarm and her cup fell on the sand. She was reclining on a bench with Tranquillus and Flavia.

'My cup has skull person on it,' she said, and made the sign against evil.

'They all do,' said Felix, snapping his fingers and directing one of the slave-boys to retrieve her cup. 'The skeletons remind us to live while we are alive.'

Jonathan examined his own cup and saw a relief figure of a skeleton on it.

'*Dum vivimus, vivamus,*' quoted Vopiscus, his eyes fixed on Voluptua.

'Indeed,' said Felix, and Jonathan saw him wink at Annia Serena.

When the slave-boy had filled all their cups, Felix tipped some wine onto the sand. 'To you, O Neptune, and to you, Bacchus, we offer libations of thanks,' he prayed. 'Now let us eat, drink, and rejoice for, as our great poet Virgil says, *Death is near and he would say, "I'm coming soon, so live today."*'

After everyone poured a libation onto the sand, they began to eat.

The fish smelt strange, so Jonathan tasted it cautiously. Then he smiled in surprise. It was not turbot at all, but a delicious paste of chicken liver and onions. He used sticks of celery to spoon it into his mouth. Parthenope, Leucosia and Ligea attended the diners, while the two long-haired slave-boys stood to one side and played soft music. One strummed a lyre and the other played the softly buzzing aulos.

After the gustatio of chicken-liver turbot, the diners took a second dip in the sea. Most went up to the chest or neck, but Felix, Flaccus and Lupus went right under. They returned to find their skeleton wine cups refilled and succulent slices of wild boar on the tables. It was crispy and salty on the outside but tender and sweet inside and had been dressed with fig and myrtle sauce.

'Delicious boar, Jonathan,' said Felix, licking his fingers, and the others raised their cups to him.

Jonathan flushed with pleasure.

After the boar, everyone took their third bath in the sea.

As the blood-red sun melted into the horizon, the slave-girls brought the secunda mensa, the dessert. Parthenope carried a tray laden with pastry dormice which had been glazed with honey and stuffed with nuts. Leucosia passed round a silver bowl full of plump red cherries, and Ligea set down two platters of shiny green apples.

Remembering what Locusta had said about apples coated with poisoned wax, Jonathan took one and examined it. It was surprisingly cold and it had been dipped in wax. Jonathan scraped off some of the wax with his fingernail, then sniffed, then tasted. No sharpness or bitterness. Just wax. He breathed a sigh of relief and replaced the apple. There was little danger of anyone attempting to poison Polla this evening; so far all the food and wine had been shared.

Jonathan bit the head off a pastry dormouse and relaxed. The two boys were playing soft music again and the temperature of the air was perfect.

'Oh, isn't it a lovely evening?' said Pulchra with a sigh of happiness. 'All pearly pink and blue!' She dimpled prettily at Flaccus.

'That's a lovely sight, too,' murmured Vopiscus, and Jonathan saw him leering at Voluptua, whose wet tunic clung to her body.

Jonathan put down his half-eaten dormouse to study the other diners. He observed that Annia Serena was using the forefinger of her right hand to trace letters in wine on the back of her left. She held up her hand for Felix to see, then erased the message by sensuously licking it off. Felix raised one eyebrow and gave her a lazy smile. Voluptua didn't seem to mind, or even to notice; she was too busy whispering in Vopiscus's ear. But Polla was gazing at Felix with a pained expression on her face. Jonathan saw that Nubia and Flavia were watching him, too, and that Flavia's pastry dormouse lay untouched on the table before her.

Suddenly Voluptua squealed with laughter and playfully slapped Vopiscus, who had taken a bite of apple and let it drop onto her lap.

Jonathan knew it was a coded proposition and he wondered what his father would make of a banquet where men and women shared couches wearing wet, clinging garments and flirted openly. He remembered Seneca's warning: *stop up your ears with something stronger than wax*, and the thought occurred to him that he should probably close his eyes as well.

Captain Geminus had warned Flavia about the licentiousness of Baiae, but as Jonathan looked around, he realised this place was just as bad.

*

'Lemon snow! Lemon snow!' chanted Pollina and Pollinilla together. 'We want lemon snow!'

Flavia smiled sadly at their childish innocence.

'Don't be greedy, my dears,' murmured Polla. 'You haven't finished your honeyed dormice.'

'Oh pater, please?' they cried, ignoring their mother.

Felix smiled at his little girls. 'Very well. You may have lemon snow,' he said.

'Euge!' They cheered.

'What is lemon snow?' asked Nubia.

Jonathan frowned. 'It sounds a bit suspicious.'

Pulchra smiled at Jonathan. 'Underneath the villa,' she said, 'we have a huge block of ice. Sometimes pater chips a little off and puts it in a linen bag and pounds it with a wooden mallet. Then he mixes it with lemon juice and honey and it becomes lemon snow! It's the most divine thing you've ever tasted, and it's fabulously expensive to make.'

'Why?' asked Flavia. 'Why is it fabulously expensive?'

'Because of the cost of transporting the ice down from the mountains. You have to do it in winter and then keep it cool all year round.'

'How do you keep the ice block from melting?' asked Tranquillus.

'It's big enough to cool itself,' said Felix, 'as long as I keep it locked up in the coolest room of the store-house.'

'You keep it locked up?' said Flavia. 'Why?'

'It's worth half a million sesterces,' said Felix.

Annia Serena gasped and glanced over the top of her fan at him. Flavia saw Felix wink back at her.

Polla sighed. 'It's not really such an extravagance as it sounds,' she said. 'It will last us several years.'

'Can we see it?' asked Tranquillus. 'I'd love to see a block of ice worth that much money.'

'No,' said Pulchra with a mock pout. 'Pater's very jealous of it. He's the only one with the key and he never lets any of us down there.'

'So you're the only one who goes down there?' said Flavia to Felix. She felt a sick twist in her stomach.

'Yes,' said Felix, standing up and smiling down at her. 'Only me.' He slipped on his sandals and looked around at the others. 'I may be a little while. It takes some time to prepare. Please continue the feast without me.' He started down the beach towards the waiting yacht and then turned casually to one of the slave-girls standing discreetly nearby. 'Oh, Leucosia,' he said, 'will you come with me? I need you to pluck a dozen lemons from the tree and bring them to the storeroom.'

The girl nodded and smiled at him, and just before she turned to follow him down to the boat, Flavia saw her toss her hair and flash Parthenope a look of triumph.

'What's the matter, Flavia?' said Jonathan. 'Are you all right?'

Flavia had left her couch to run into the olive groves. Jonathan, Nubia and Lupus finally found her in the shrine of Hercules. She was sitting on the cushions staring at the carpet.

'You look nauseous,' said Nubia.

'I feel nauseous,' whispered Flavia.

'Do you think you've been poisoned?' cried Jonathan.

'What have you eaten tonight? Was it the cherries?' He slammed his right fist into the palm of his left hand. 'Pollux! I *knew* it was in the cherries. They were probably injected with aconite.'

'It's not anything I ate,' said Flavia. 'It's Felix. I think he's in love with Annia Serena.'

Jonathan exchanged a quick glance with Nubia and Lupus. They sat on the carpet beside her.

'Why do you think that?' Jonathan asked. The shrine was dim and hot and smelt of roses.

'This afternoon,' said Flavia, 'there was a woman down in the storeroom where the block of ice is, the storeroom where Felix says only he ever goes. She was with someone. I didn't see them, but I heard them. I'm sure it was Annia Serena. I could smell her. She was . . . he was . . . they were . . .'

'Very kissing?' said Jonathan.

Flavia laughed, but it turned into a sob. 'Yes!' She hung her head.

Jonathan took a deep breath. 'Flavia, when we were in Baiae we found out some things about Felix. We were afraid to tell you, because we know you admire him . . .' He glanced at Lupus and Nubia, and they both nodded.

'I'm sorry, Flavia,' he said, 'you're not going to like this.'

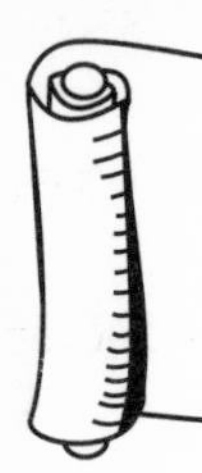

SCROLL XXII

'Where have you been?' cried Pulchra as Jonathan, Nubia and Lupus emerged from the olive grove and resumed their places beneath the shaggy blue pine. 'Pater's just come back with the lemon snow and Leucosia has brought garlands.'

'Where's Flavia?' asked Tranquillus.

'Flavia felt sick,' said Jonathan, accepting a garland of ivy, mint and jasmine from the slave-girl. 'She's having a rest in the . . . olive grove.'

'Is she all right?' Flaccus half rose from his couch. He was already wearing his garland.

'Yes,' Jonathan lied. 'She just had too many pastry dormice.'

'Sit down, Gaius,' said Pulchra, tugging Flaccus's tunic. 'I'm sure she's fine. Now try this lemon snow. Finish your wine and hold out your empty cups and Leucosia will give you all some.'

Jonathan held out his silver skeleton-cup to the slave-girl as she extended a jug. Although the light was fading fast, he noticed her cheeks were flushed and her copper hair tousled. He glanced sharply at Felix, but the Patron looked as elegant and composed as ever. Wearing his ivy garland and stroking Voluptua's panther, he looked like Dionysus reclining on a couch.

Jonathan took a sip of the ice-cold slush in his cup. 'Edepol!' he breathed. 'That's delicious!'

'Isn't it marvellous?' laughed Pulchra. 'I call it nectar of the gods.'

Polla rose shivering, even though the evening was still warm.

'Are you all right, my dear?' asked Felix.

'You don't feel sick again, do you, mater?' cried Pulchra, jumping off her couch in alarm.

'No, dear,' said Polla, putting up a hand to adjust her garland. 'Just a little tired. I'm going back to the villa to rest before the ceremony if you don't mind.'

'Of course you must,' said Felix. 'Parthenope, will you accompany your mistress back to her rooms?'

'Yes, master!' Parthenope spoke with such bitterness that all the diners turned to stare at her in astonishment.

It was quite dark now, but Jonathan was sure that Polla's slave-girl had been crying.

'Flavia? Are you in here?'

Flavia looked up from her wax tablet.

'Who's that?' she said, wiping her wet cheeks with her left hand. She could only see a garlanded silhouette framed between the twin columns of the shrine's portico.

'It's me. Tranquillus. I came to tell you they're lighting the bonfire.'

'I don't care.' She shook some teardrops off her wax tablet and continued to write.

'You should light a lamp. It's not good to write in the dark.'

'Go away. I'm trying to solve a mystery.'

Without replying, Tranquillus went past her to the altar. Flavia heard the distinctive scratch of a sulphur-stick and a moment later he sat down beside her with a freshly-lit bronze oil-lamp in his hand.

'Have you been crying?' he said, holding the lamp up to her face.

'No,' she lied, pushing away the lamp.

'What are you doing?'

'Making a list of the suspects,' said Flavia. 'Somebody's got to solve this mystery.' She pressed so hard with her stylus that the wood beneath the layer of beeswax crunched.

'Why don't you do that later and come back down to the beach.' Tranquillus set the oil-lamp on the carpet. 'The men are going to soak themselves in seawater and then run through fire.'

'I don't care.'

'They say Felix is going to ride through on horseback. Apparently it's more dangerous the higher up you are.'

'What makes you think I give the tiniest bit of wool fluff about Felix?' said Flavia fiercely.

Tranquillus opened his mouth, then closed it. 'May I see your list of suspects?' he asked politely.

Flavia sighed and looked up at the dark ceiling of the shrine. Then she handed him the wax tablet and sniffed.

'This is very good,' he said after a long moment.

'You think so?' She sniffed again and wiped her nose

on her arm. Without looking up from the tablet he pulled out his handkerchief and extended it to her.

It was still damp from his last soaking but Flavia took it and blew her nose and looked over his shoulder at the tablet. She was quite pleased with it.

FLAVIA'S WAX TABLET – PRIVATE

Who is trying to poison Polla Argentaria? The five remaining suspects are:

Publius Pollius Felix *aged 35, poet and patron*
Motive? *Wants Polla out of the way so he can marry one of the dozens of women he is involved with? Also to inherit her substantial wealth?*
Argument against: *He could simply divorce her as he is very rich in his own right.*

Annia Serena *aged 23, a widow (husband died of a fever):*
Motive? *Loves F, and wants Polla out of the way so she can marry him?*
Argument against: *She had plenty of opportunities over the past three days to poison Polla.*

Voluptua *aged 22, a widow (husband died of old age):*
Motive? *She loves F, etc? Or is a legacy-hunter who wants his wealth?*
Argument against: *she seems to prefer Vopiscus as a prospective husband.*

Parthenope *aged 15, slave-girl:*
Motive? *She loves F and wants him to set her free and then marry her?*

Argument against: *She likes Polla, and punishment for murdering her mistress would be torture and death. Also, Felix would probably not marry a slave-girl; he can have them whenever he wants.*

Leucosia *aged 15, slave-girl:*
Motive? *She loves F and wants him to herself.*
Argument against: *(see above)*

Ligea *aged 17, slave-girl:*
Motive? *She loves F and wants him to herself.*
Argument against: *(see above)*

'You're missing another likely suspect,' remarked Tranquillus.

'Who?'

'You.'

'WHAT?'

'You haven't put yourself on the list of suspects,' he said, handing back the tablet.

'What do you mean?'

'You love Felix, too, don't you?'

'That's the most ridiculous thing I've ever heard. Who told you that?'

'It's obvious,' he said.

'Is it?'

'Yes.' There was a pause and then he said. 'Don't worry. I can wait.'

'Wait for what?'

'For you to get over him.'

'I *am* over him!' said Flavia fiercely. 'I mean I was never under him. I mean . . . you know what I mean!'

'Then kiss me.'

'WHAT?!'

'Just give me a quick kiss. I'm a very good kisser.'

Flavia couldn't help laughing.

'Seriously,' he said, in an injured tone. 'I'm a good kisser.'

'No, thanks.'

'If you're really over Felix then you'll give me a kiss. After all, we're going to be married one day. Also . . .' He cleared his throat: 'You look very pretty this evening.'

'I do?'

'Yes.'

'If I give you a kiss will you promise to go away and leave me alone?'

'I promise.' Tranquillus took off his garland and spun it up towards the cult statue standing behind the altar. By some fluke it fell neatly over Hercules's head and came to rest around his wooden neck. In the flickering lamplight the hero-god's archaic smile seemed to broaden.

Flavia laughed. 'All right, then. I'll give you a kiss.'

SCROLL XXIII

Flavia put down the wax tablet and twisted to face Tranquillus. 'You may kiss me,' she said, and closed her eyes.

Tranquillus put a hand on each of her shoulders and she allowed him to pull her gently towards him. Then she felt his mouth on hers.

For a few moments it was not unpleasant. Suddenly she recoiled.

'Ewww! You put your tongue in my mouth!'

'That's how they do it.'

'But it's disgusting. It's like being choked with a hot mackerel!'

'Well, I'm sorry, but all the other girls like it.'

'All what other girls? What other girls have you ever kissed?'

'Well . . . my cousin for one . . . Was it really disgusting?'

'It wasn't too bad.' She giggled. 'Until the hot mackerel.'

'So now will you come and watch the bonfire? If you come I'll run through the fire for you.'

'You'd do that for me?'

'Yes,' he said. 'I really like you, Flavia.'

'I like you, too, Gaius,' she said, blushing as she used his praenomen for the first time.

'Come on, then.' He took her hand and pulled her off the cushions. And in the portico of the shrine he stopped and stood on tiptoe and kissed her again.

Flavia and Tranquillus were still holding hands when they emerged from the olive grove and walked down onto the beach. It was almost dark now and the flames of a crackling bonfire threw a golden light on the people standing around.

Flavia saw everyone turn and stare as she and Tranquillus came into the circle of firelight hand in hand. Felix raised an eyebrow and while he was still watching she deliberately turned and gave Tranquillus a kiss on the cheek. Then she saw Flaccus watching, too. Wearing his ivy garland he looked like a handsome young bridegroom and she felt a sudden twinge of something unpleasant. She quickly let go of Tranquillus's hand and smoothed her hair. To her horror she realised it was falling loose around her shoulders. She had unpinned her painfully tight bun when she had run to the shrine. What must people think? What must Flaccus think?

She looked up at him, but he was walking down to the water with the other men, his garland discarded on the sand.

'Do you really want me to run through that bonfire?' said Tranquillus beside her.

'Of course not,' she said absently, her eyes still on Flaccus. 'Anyone who runs through fire must be crazy.'

'Then I'll do it. For you.' He kissed her quickly on the cheek, then turned and ran down to the water.

*

'Lupus,' said Jonathan, 'I beg of you. Don't run through the fire. It's insane.'

With his too-large ivy garland and eyes flickering green in the yellow firelight, Lupus looked like a young Pan. For a moment he hesitated, then he shrugged off Jonathan's restraining hand and ran towards the sea with a whoop.

'No,' said Jonathan, slowly shaking his head. 'No. I can't watch this.' He turned and stumbled across the beach to the ancient blue pine tree and slumped down on the far side of its trunk. His heart was pounding and he could hear himself wheezing. As he rested his head in his hands, he felt the ivy from his garland tickling his forearms. With a grunt he took it from his head and threw it down.

A cool hand on his arm made him jump.

'Oh, Pulchra! You startled me.'

'Jonathan, what's wrong?'

'Nothing.' He dropped his head again.

'Jonathan. Why are you so sad? A year ago you were so funny and happy. Now you seem so . . . tortured.'

For a long time he was quiet.

'What is it, Jonathan? You can tell me.'

Finally, without lifting his head he said, 'I killed twenty thousand people.'

'What?' she breathed, in a tone more of awe than horror.

He glanced up at her. 'You heard about the fire in Rome? The one a few months ago?'

Pulchra nodded, her blue eyes almost black in the

moonlight. She was kneeling on the sand and still wearing her garland. He could smell the jasmine.

'It was my fault. I started the fire.'

'Oh, Jonathan. How terrible!'

'And . . .' He wanted to tell someone – anyone – but it was so difficult.

'What?' she said softly, stroking his back. 'Tell me.'

'I saw a man on fire,' he managed at last. 'It was terrible. The most terrible thing I've ever seen. I dream about it. I dream about it almost every night.' He hung his head again.

'So that's why you can't stand to watch pater and Lupus and the others running through the flames. Oh, Jonathan!' Pulchra leaned forward and took his face between her cool hands and kissed him on the mouth.

Once Jonathan had accidentally touched a dead jellyfish and it had given him a mild tingling shock. Pulchra's kiss was like that, only pleasant. And tasting faintly of lemon and honey. As he began to kiss her back, all the terrible images slipped out of his mind like water in desert sands, and for a time it was just him and her in the warm, jasmine-scented night, and nothing else existed.

Flavia glanced up as Nubia came to stand beside her. Her friend's eyes glowed golden in the firelight.

'Are you feel better?' Nubia said.

'Yes, thank you, Nubia. I feel a little better. I'm just confused.'

'I too am confused,' said Nubia. 'You like Felix. Flaccus likes you. Then you come hands in hands with Tranquillus. Now everybody is confused.'

'I'm allowed to hold hands with Tranquillus. We're going to be betrothed soon and— What do you mean: "Flaccus likes me"?'

'Flaccus likes you. Very much. I can tell.'

'Don't be silly,' said Flavia. But her heart was suddenly pounding and she felt sick again. 'Does he? Oh, great Juno's peacock. This is bad,' she said, as one of Felix's soldiers ran out of the sea and curved back around towards the fire. 'This is very, very bad.'

As the dark-haired man leapt through the flames and ran back into the sea, everyone cheered. Three more of Felix's soldiers ran through the bonfire and now Vopiscus emerged dripping from the sea and circled round to follow their example. He ran through the flames, but instead of running back into the water like the others, he went straight into the arms of Voluptua. For a moment they clung together in a passionate embrace, then they ran off into the darkness of the olive groves.

Flavia barely had time to register this scandalous behaviour when she saw Flaccus run through the fire. As he emerged from the other side, the hem of his tunic suddenly flickered with flames and Flavia gasped. But a moment later he was safe in the sea and the flames were out and the other men were cheering and slapping his back. Flavia was almost certain he was looking in her direction so she waved at him and clapped her hands, but he had already turned away to talk to the other men and wait for the next runner. Flavia kept her eyes on him, willing him to look her way again. But he didn't.

'Flavia!' hissed Nubia. 'You miss Tranquillus! He just now runs through flames.'

'Oh!' cried Flavia, and then shouted, 'Euge! Tranquillus!' in case he thought she hadn't noticed.

'Behold! Now it is the Lupus!' said Nubia. And then she screamed.

SCROLL XXIV

'Nubia, what is it?' Flavia's voice was faint, as if it came from a great distance. 'What's wrong? Lupus is fine. He made it through the fire. Nubia, speak to me!'

But Nubia couldn't speak. She felt a weight on her back and knees gripping her sides and someone whipping her and urging her to jump through the terrible flames. But she couldn't. She knew if she went forward, her tail and mane would catch fire and she would die. She had never felt such great thudding waves of fear before. She had always obeyed her rider but now her whole being screamed with the desire to rear up and throw off the master.

And so she did.

'What's that noise?' said Jonathan, pulling away from Pulchra's embrace. He could hear shouts of alarm rather than cheers. 'Something's happening.'

They both stood up and moved out from behind the pine-tree.

'Pater!' cried Pulchra, clutching Jonathan's arm. 'I think that's pater in the water with Pegasus.'

'Who's Pegasus?'

'His best stallion.'

They paused for a second. They could hear Felix's men shouting and see them crowding around a horse thrashing in the water. Jonathan had never seen such a striking horse: dark with a pale mane and tail.

'Oh, no!' cried Pulchra. 'Pegasus just kicked pater. I think he's hurt!'

They ran down the beach together, but smoke and excitement tightened Jonathan's chest so that he had to stop and breathe from his herb pouch. When he reached Pulchra at the water's edge she was helping some men lead her father out of the sea. Felix's garland was askew. He tore it off and threw it angrily onto the dark water.

'What happened?' wheezed Jonathan.

Pulchra glanced at him. 'Pegasus threw pater and kicked him in the ribs. That horse is dog meat!' she said fiercely, glaring at the beautiful stallion being led out of the water. 'Don't worry, pater,' she said, 'I'll take care of you.'

'No,' cried Felix, his eyes dark with pain. 'I've got to do this. I can't let my soldiers down. Safinius! Chrysanthus!' he called to the two grooms. 'Get that cowardly beast out of here and bring Puerina!'

'Yes, master,' they replied.

'No, pater!' cried Pulchra. 'You can't ride! Your ribs might be broken!'

'Leave me alone, Pulchra!' said Felix, shaking off her hand almost roughly. 'You can't be here right now. Jonathan, take her away.'

'Yes, sir,' said Jonathan, and took Pulchra's hand. 'Come on,' he said. 'He needs to do this for his men.'

'His stupid men!' muttered Pulchra, but she allowed

Jonathan to lead her back up the beach towards the fire. 'What does he care what they think?'

'He cares the world what they think,' said Jonathan, 'because they worship him.'

Flavia helped Nubia sit up on the soft warm sand.

'What's wrong?' said Tranquillus, coming up out of the darkness. His face was still glowing from his recent triumph.

'I think she fainted,' said Flavia. 'Please can you bring her a beaker of posca or well-watered wine?'

'Right away!' He grinned and ran off towards the row of low tables on the beach. They had been carried down to the shore and laden with fresh wine and refreshments.

'Nubia,' whispered Flavia. 'What happened?'

'I do not know.' Nubia had a dazed look in her eyes. 'It was as if someone wants to make me go through flames.'

'Don't worry!' said Flavia, and gave her friend a reassuring squeeze round the shoulders. 'Only the men do that. Nobody will make you run through the fire.'

'He will,' said Nubia fiercely.

Flavia followed the direction of her friend's gaze and her eyes widened as she saw Felix riding a pretty little grey mare out of the dark sea towards the bonfire. The beach was suddenly quiet as the cheers and laughter died and all eyes turned towards the Patron as he urged his mount in a curve back around towards the flames. He wore nothing but a wet tunic and he rode bareback. His knees and heels gripped the mare's heaving flank and his fingers twisted in the flowing locks of her mane.

In the firelight she saw his handsome face suffused with wild joy, his dark eyes unfocused, his chest heaving. Then rider and horse were leaping through the bonfire and it seemed to Flavia that time stopped. For a moment Felix and his mount were suspended in the flames. Then they were out and into the sea and the surface of the warm black seawater was churned into a milky froth by her thrashing legs.

Felix's men were running towards him now, cheering him, helping him off the mare, clapping him on the back, touching him and kissing the ring on his hand. He was laughing with pure pleasure at their adoration.

'Oh, dear Venus!' prayed Flavia. 'Don't let me love that dangerous man.'

'What?' said Nubia. Her eyes were fixed on the little grey mare being led out of the water.

Flavia smiled at her friend. 'Nothing,' she whispered, as Tranquillus came hurrying up with a skeleton-cup. 'Nothing.'

Although the beach banquet was finished and it was long after midnight, Flavia could not sleep. She was thinking about Felix. She remembered something a wise young woman had said to her the previous winter: *half the women in Campania are in love with him.* How true that statement had proved. Flavia felt sick.

She rolled over onto her side and Polla's words came back to her: *Don't love the dangerous man, love the safe man.*

Why couldn't she love someone like Tranquillus? He

was safe. He was also clever and funny and he thought she was pretty. But she didn't love him. There was no passion. Kissing Felix's statue had been more exciting than kissing Tranquillus. Was there something in between? A safe man she could feel passionate about?

Immediately she thought of Gaius Valerius Flaccus. At the beginning of their trip to Rhodes he had been arrogant and rude. And she had passionately hated him. But by the end of the voyage she had come to admire him. She closed her eyes and imagined kissing him and was surprised to find her heart thumping.

Could she ever love Flaccus? Rich, handsome, noble Flaccus?

No. Not as long as she felt this way about another. For, despite the awful revelations of the day, she knew she still loved Felix.

'Felix!' cried Flavia, starting suddenly out of sleep. 'Don't!' She sat up on her bed, her heart pounding and her body damp with sweat.

She had been dreaming of him again.

In her dream, Felix was Aeneas and she was the beautiful young princess Lavinia. It was their wedding night. He wore a garland and his toga and he laughed as he caught her up in his arms and carried her over the threshold. She was dressed in flame-coloured silk and wore jasmine and lemon blossom in her hair. In their bridal chamber, flickering torches lit a low wide bed sprinkled with yellow saffron and pink rose-petals. He laid her gently on the perfumed covers and he was just bending his head to kiss her when there was a soft scratching at the door.

He turned his head.

'Don't answer it,' whispered Flavia, slipping her arms around his neck and pulling him back down.

'I must,' he said. 'It's her.'

'No!' cried Flavia in her dream. 'Don't!'

But he was already off the bed and moving toward the door.

It was at that point that Flavia had woken.

'No!' she whispered, 'No!' Even though her dream was over, she knew what lurked at the door of her mind. And she could not let it in.

She threw off the damp sheet and rose and stumbled out of the bedroom. She ran along the deep-blue colonnade past the boys' bedroom. She took the stairs two at a time and ran through the torchlit atrium, then along the moon-striped peristyle of the lemon-tree courtyard. When she reached the southern entrance of the villa, a sleepy door-slave let her out and she ran up the path towards the olive groves.

She ran blindly, as if pursued by the Furies. Finally she stumbled and fell and she could no longer keep out the image.

The door from her dream opened and Flavia saw the ghost of Dido standing there, an accusing look on her face. Her tunic was stained with blood and there was a terrible gash where she had fallen on the sword. And Dido's ghost looked exactly like Polla Argentaria.

Nubia found Flavia on the moonlit path. She was lying face down, sobbing into the dirt.

Scuto and Nipur ran to her and sniffed the back of her neck and wagged their tails and whined.

Flavia raised her tear-streaked face from the dusty olive-littered path.

'Nubia? What are you doing here?'

'I hear you cry out. So I am taking the dogs to find you. What is wrong?'

'Oh Nubia! I'm a terrible person.'

'No,' said Nubia. 'You are a good person. You are good to help people and to solve mysteries.'

'No,' Flavia laid her head in the dust again. 'I'm bad.'

Nubia sat on the ground beside her friend. 'Tell me,' she said. 'Why are you bad?'

'I had a dream and it made me realise . . .'

'Yes?'

'I love Felix.'

'Yes.'

'And . . . and . . . part of me wishes Polla was dead.'

'Yes.'

'No! Don't you understand?' Flavia raised her head again. 'Part of me wishes she was dead so I could marry him. I'm no better than the person trying to poison her. I have the heart of a murderer. I'm a horrible person.'

'Every person has bad secret thoughts,' said Nubia, putting her arm around Flavia. 'You cannot help your heart. But not every person is brave to say behold, I think such things.'

'Oh, Nubia!' Flavia sobbed in Nubia's lap for a long time.

'Come,' said Nubia at last. 'Let us go back.' She helped Flavia to her feet and they began to follow the dogs back down the path.

It was nearly dawn and the world around them was a vibrant milky blue.

'Land of Blue,' murmured Nubia. 'It almost sings with blue. Except for the shrine of Venus, which is like a pearl in the moonlight.'

'I think I must have upset Venus,' muttered Flavia, 'for her to torture me like this. Maybe I should bring her a special offering.'

'Hark!' said Nubia. 'Do you hear that? Someone is weeping in shrine.'

'Don't go there,' said Flavia bitterly. 'It's probably Felix and Annia Serena again, and trust me: they're not weeping.'

'No. I am sure it is weeping. Come.'

The dogs must have heard it, too, for they hurried down towards the circular shrine.

'Nipur! Come back!' called Nubia. 'Scuto!' She ran after the dogs and as she caught Nipur's collar she saw Scuto sniffing a girl kneeling at the foot of the altar before the cult statue. The girl's curly head was down and her arms outstretched before her.

'Parthenope!' said Nubia. 'What is matter?' She shooed the dogs away and sat beside the slave-girl. The marble floor of the shrine was hard and cold.

'It's not Polla, is it?' cried Flavia, stopping between two of the columns. 'Has she been poisoned?'

'No.' Parthenope shook her head. 'My mistress is well. She is sleeping.'

'What is wrong?' said Nubia softly.

'Yes,' said Flavia. 'What's wrong?'

'What do you care?' Parthenope raised her head to look at Flavia. 'Don't pretend to care about me. You made me try food you thought was poisoned.'

'But that's what slaves are supposed to do . . .' Flavia's eyes filled with tears again.

'Flavia,' said Nubia firmly. 'Take dogs back to our room. I will come soon.'

Flavia brushed away fresh tears, then nodded. 'Come on, Scuto,' she said miserably. 'Come on, Nipur.'

When Flavia and the dogs were out of sight, Nubia turned back to Parthenope.

'What is wrong?' she said softly. 'Can you tell me why do you grieve?'

'I'm pregnant,' said Parthenope after a long pause. 'I'm going to have my master's child.'

Nubia nodded. She was not surprised. Walking the dogs past the slave-quarters, she had seen several toddlers with Felix's dark eyes. Home-grown slaves, they called them.

'What will your mistress say when you become big with child?' said Nubia.

'She knows about it,' said Parthenope, wiping her face on the hem of her tunic. 'My mistress is very kind. I tell her everything.'

'She is not vexed?'

'No,' said Parthenope. Her lovely face looked as pale as ivory in the growing light of dawn. 'She has often told me she doesn't love him any more and that I must tell her everything that happens between us. She told me I can keep the baby and nurse him myself, until he is weaned.' Parthenope lifted her chin proudly. 'My son will grow up as a slave in this household but one day I know he will be my master's best soldier.'

'Then why do you weep?' asked Nubia. 'And why do you pray to Venus?'

'Because my master doesn't love me any more.' Parthenope began to cry again. 'He used to say that of all the girls in the household I was the most beautiful, and he loved only me. But now he's gone with her.'

'With Leucosia?' said Nubia.

'Yes. With Leucosia!' Sobs wracked the slave-girl's body and all Nubia could do was to sit beside her and stroke her arm.

'Are you sure that's what she said?' asked Flavia, when Nubia finished telling her what she had learned. 'That Polla doesn't love Felix anymore?'

Nubia nodded. 'That is what she said.'

'No,' said Flavia. 'That's not right. Something here is wrong.' She stood up and went to the door of their bedroom and gazed out through dark columns at the lemon-yellow sky of dawn. Then she turned and looked back at Nubia. 'I've got to solve this mystery,' she said fiercely. Her eyes were still swollen from crying, but in the pearly light Nubia could see determination in them. 'But how, Nubia? How can I find out who is trying to poison Polla?'

'I do not know,' said Nubia. 'I have never known a place so full of Venus as this one. And Venus is very dangerous.'

'Eureka!' said Flavia, clutching Nubia's arm. 'That's it! Venus is the answer. We'll make the poisoner come to us. We'll set a trap, like we did for the dog-killer last year. But this time we can't use gold as bait. We'll use something else!'

'Venus?' said Nubia. She didn't understand.

'Not Venus,' said Flavia, 'but something that comes

from her name! Thank you, Nubia. Not only did you give me the idea for the perfect bait, but you just told me the best place to leave it.'

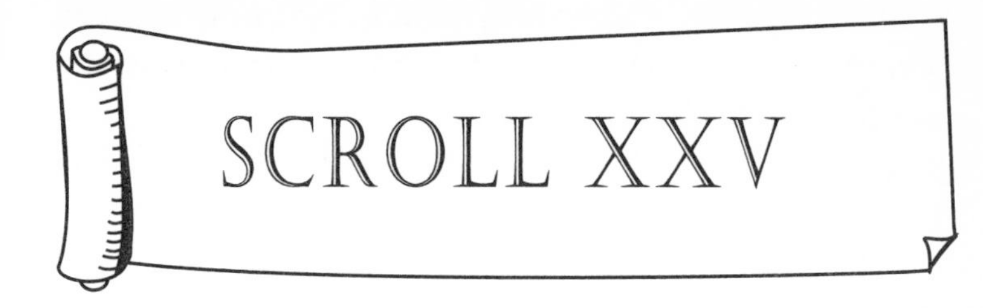

'You may wonder why I've called you all here,' said Flavia Gemina later that day. It was mid-morning in the shrine of Hercules. Flavia, Jonathan, Nubia, Lupus and Tranquillus were sitting on the faded carpet, eating a breakfast of brown rolls, white cheese and apricots. The cult statue of Hercules had a roll and an apricot, too, but they lay untouched on his altar.

Scuto, Tigris, Nipur and little Ajax lay panting happily in the shady portico of the shrine. Over the ridge, the adults of the Villa Limona slept late after the previous night's festivities.

'Is it because you have a plan?' said Tranquillus, taking a bite of his brown roll. 'Is that why you've called us here?'

'Yes,' said Flavia. 'I have a plan to catch the poisoner.'

'Why isn't Pulchra here?' said Jonathan suddenly. 'You said you'd tell us why we haven't included Pulchra.'

'Because Felix is not only a possible motive, but he is also our main suspect.' Flavia took a deep breath, then told them about Locusta's fatal accident on the broken stairs.

'Edepol!' breathed Tranquillus after a pause, 'that's extremely suspicious.'

'Even if her death was ordered by Felix,' said Jonathan, 'that still doesn't prove he's the one trying to kill Polla. He might have just wanted revenge on Locusta because she almost poisoned his daughter. And I can't say I blame him. That woman was insane.'

Lupus raised his hand and wrote on his wax tablet: SHE SAID SYMPTOMS DIDN'T MATCH ANY KNOWN POISON?

'Yes,' said Flavia, 'but only according to Felix's soldier. We'll never know if that's what she really said. And there's more.' Flavia told them about Parthenope's pregnancy.

Jonathan gave a low whistle. 'Pulchra would be devastated if she knew what her father's been doing,' he said.

'She'd be devastated if she knew what he used this shrine for,' remarked Tranquillus, biting into an apricot.

Flavia looked up sharply. 'Felix knows about this place?'

Tranquillus nodded. 'I was talking to the two grooms last night. They'd had too much to drink and . . . well, you know the saying: *in vino veritas*. Apparently every time Felix and Polla have house-guests, and it looks like rain, Felix suggests a hunting expedition where the women are included. He always makes sure he stays near the most beautiful house-guest and if it starts to rain he brings her in here to seek shelter.'

'And then?' said Flavia.

'Then they play Dido and Aeneas!'

'Dido and Aeneas,' said Flavia. 'Again.' She stared up at the ceiling. *'From the highest peaks the nymphs cried out in ecstasy. That was the first day of death and the cause of future evils.'*

'What?' said Jonathan, and Lupus gave Flavia his bug-eyed look.

'She's quoting from the *Aeneid*,' said Tranquillus, spitting an apricot stone out through the columns of the portico. 'Dido and Aeneas went hunting and when a sudden rainstorm came, they sheltered in a cave. That was when they first um . . . consummated their relationship.'

'So that's what the cushions and wine and food and blankets are doing here,' said Jonathan.

Tranquillus nodded. 'It's the grooms' job to make sure everything is ready.'

'Great Juno's peacock!' cried Flavia, her grey eyes wide. She rose to her feet and stared out through the bright doorway of the shrine. 'Great Juno's peacock,' she repeated. 'There's one person I've never even suspected!'

'Who?' they asked.

Flavia looked round at them for a moment and then shook her head. 'No. It's a crazy idea. And yet . . . The more I think about it: Aeneas and Dido . . . Yes! That's got to be the answer!'

'Tell us!' they cried.

Flavia shook her head and sat down again, hugging her knees to her chest. 'If I'm wrong then I'd feel like a fool. We'll find out soon enough, if my trap works.'

'What is your trap?' they asked.

'Jonathan,' said Flavia, 'do you remember how we caught the dog-killer last June? We smeared a vegetable dye on the gold, and as soon as the thief stole it we were able to catch him red-handed?'

Jonathan nodded. 'Of course,' he said. 'My father provided the dye.'

'Do you remember what the dye was? And more importantly, do you remember if it was poisonous?'

'No, I don't know what it was. I'm sorry.'

'Oh,' said Flavia, and her face fell.

'What?' said Tranquillus. 'Tell us what you were thinking.'

Flavia looked around at them. 'Nubia gave me the idea for the perfect bait last night. Poison. *Venenum.* Venom. Named after Venus because most poisons were originally love potions. We need poison as our bait. One that's harmless but will stain the fingers. Or mouth,' she added.

'I know what might work,' said Jonathan after a moment. 'Saffron stamens. They stain your hands bright yellow and of course saffron is edible.'

'Perfect!' cried Flavia. 'The only problem is that saffron is very expensive. Where can we get some?'

'You are having some in your birthday make-up box,' offered Nubia.

'Not enough. We need more.'

'Coqua,' said Nubia. 'The cook. She has a pot of saffron in kitchen on highest shelf. She might let us have some.'

'They'll beat her if they find any missing,' said Tranquillus. 'But I can give her some gold coins to replace what we use. I'm rich as well as clever and good-looking.' He grinned and wiggled his eyebrows at Flavia.

'Brilliant,' said Flavia, and gave Tranquillus a weak smile.

'If we mix it with a little charcoal powder,' said Jonathan, 'then it won't look and taste so much like saffron, but it will still leave a mark.'

'Excellent,' said Flavia. 'I can mix it myself with the little mortar and pestle in my new make-up kit.' She paused and looked round at them all. 'We have to put this plan into effect tonight at dinner. We don't have a moment to lose. Now listen very carefully, everybody, here's what we'll do . . .'

'Where have you all been?' said Pulchra as they emerged from the olive groves and descended towards the slave's entrance of the Villa Limona. She stood with her arms folded and a scowl on her pretty face.

'We've just been taking the dogs for a walk,' said Flavia. 'Look, we took Ajax with us. And we hardly had to carry him at all.'

'Why didn't you wake me?' Pulchra snatched Ajax from Nubia's arms.

'You were fast asleep,' said Flavia.

'You should have woken me. Now you've missed Gaius. He's gone.'

'Who?'

'Your precious Flaccus left a few moments ago. He barely said goodbye to me. He was too busy looking for you.'

'Oh no!' cried Flavia. 'Did he have a message for me, I mean, for any of us?'

'No,' said Pulchra. She turned her back on them and started back down towards the villa.

'Pulchra!' said Flavia, running to catch up. 'Wait!'

'What?'

'We have a plan to find out who's trying to poison your mother. But if we tell you it might spoil it.'

'Why?' Pulchra stopped and turned on Flavia. 'Why do you always leave me out?' Her blue eyes were full of tears.

'Pulchra.' Jonathan came up, wheezing a little. 'Trust us. We know what we're doing. We don't want to exclude you. We just want to help your mother. Please trust us?'

Pulchra glared at Jonathan with red-rimmed eyes. 'All right!' she said at last. 'But I'm not happy about all this. I don't see why I can't be part of it.' She put Ajax on the ground and wrapped his gilded lead around her wrist.

'Pulchra,' said Flavia. 'Is there any way we can dine with the adults again, like we did last night?'

'No. They're having a symposium tonight.'

'A what?'

'A dinner-party where all the house-guests recite their latest compositions.'

'There aren't that many guests left,' said Flavia. 'There's only Vopiscus, Voluptua and Annia Serena.'

'Pater is going to sing his latest composition,' said Pulchra, 'and apparently Annia Serena has written a love poem. Even mater said she might recite something.'

'Will they all be together?' said Flavia suddenly.

'Of course.'

'With the three pretty slave-girls attending?'

'What are you talking about?'

'Parthenope, Leucosia and Ligea. Will they be serving?'

'I suppose so.'

'Good,' said Flavia, with a glance at Tranquillus. 'Then I think we can still put our plan into effect.'

SCROLL XXVI

Later that evening in the red triclinium of the Villa Limona, before the lamps had been lit, five adult diners and two slave-girls looked up as a fair-haired girl caught the wrist of a brown-haired boy in the inner garden. The girl and boy were framed in the bright doorway of the triclinium and apparently unaware of the adults watching them from the shaded room.

'You shouldn't have bought that poison, Gaius!' cried the girl angrily, wresting a small dark sack from the boy's hand. 'Locusta said it was the most powerful poison she had! A tiny pinch of this can kill a bull.'

'I'm sorry,' said the boy, hanging his head in shame. 'I wanted it for research purposes. I don't know what I was thinking.'

'It's ill-omened. You should get rid of it now!' said the girl. 'Take it somewhere nobody can accidentally find it or use it.'

'I know!' cried the boy. 'Let's take it to the shrine of Venus and dedicate it to her. She'll protect us from bad luck and nobody would take an offering from the altar of such a powerful goddess.'

'Good idea,' said the girl, and the two of them hurried out of the bright garden.

*

'OK,' said Flavia a short time later. She was standing with Nubia, Lupus and Tranquillus beside the circular shrine to Venus, and she was still breathing hard. 'They all heard us and they all know where the "poison" will be. Lupus, your job is to hide here and see who takes the bait. Only somebody very desperate would dream of taking an offering from an altar. You might have to wait all night to catch that person. Is that all right?'

Lupus shrugged and nodded, as if to say he didn't mind.

'Jonathan's keeping Pulchra occupied until she goes to bed, then he'll join us in our vigil. He'll go up to the library where he can keep watch over the whole villa. Nubia, your post is in the kitchen, near the domestic slave-quarters. Tranquillus, you patrol the terrace. But keep hidden. I'm going to take the most dangerous hiding place: Polla's dressing room. I'll have to go soon, before their symposium is over. Any questions?'

They all shook their heads. The blood-red sky of sunset cast an eerie pink light on the white marble columns of the shrine and on their faces.

'Can we all give the secret signal Jonathan taught us?'

They nodded.

'Show me,' said Flavia.

In turn, each of them cupped their hands together and pressed the thumbs bent side by side until there was only a tiny crack. Then they blew into this to make the deep fluting cry of an owl.

'Yours is the best, Lupus,' said Flavia, after she herself had tried it. 'Just as well,' she added, looking at the others. 'Lupus's signal is the one we all have to listen for.'

She looked up at the marble statue of Venus. Unusually, the goddess of love was shown fully clothed. The sculptor had shown her dressed in a long palla which covered her head and shoulders, and then fell in heavy folds right to the ground. Flavia knew that this version of the goddess was known as Aphrodite Sosandra, Venus who saves men.

'Forgive us, dear goddess,' said Flavia, placing the black silk pouch on the altar. 'Accept this offering and grant that it may help us to find the culprit.' Flavia gazed up at the goddess's stern and beautiful face and under her breath she added. 'Forgive me, Aphrodite Sosandra, for all the wrong desires in my heart. Please help me find the truth. If you do,' she added, 'I promise to dedicate my bulla to you on the day I get married.'

In the pink light of the setting sun, the goddess's expression seemed to soften.

Flavia turned to her friends and gestured towards the black silk pouch, lying on the altar beside a freshly-lit oil-lamp. 'There's our bait,' she said to the others. 'A pouch filled with the most deadly "poison" known to man: saffron!'

Polla's dressing room had a mosaic floor with a honeycomb pattern and panels of deep Egyptian blue on the walls. It also had a clothes niche like Felix's, with hanging tunics and cloaks.

'Domina?' said Flavia softly, as she stepped into the room. But the room was deserted and dim, with only one small bronze oil-lamp burning on the dressing table. Flavia breathed a sigh of relief, even though her heart was beating so hard she thought she might be sick. She moved quickly to the clothes niche and pushed some of Polla's cloaks towards one corner. Then she used the same trick she had used in Felix's room a few days before. She slipped her feet into a pair of Polla's boots – they fit perfectly – and stood in the darkest corner behind the cloaks. Carefully she parted them to make a narrow vertical slit, then nodded with satisfaction. From here she could see most of the dressing room and even a corner of the low mattress in Polla's inner bedroom.

When she was comfortable, she took a few deep breaths and leaned back against the wall. Then she tried to convince her heartbeat to return to normal.

The cry of an owl started Lupus awake. Pollux! He had fallen asleep.

He gripped the smooth sides of the marble column and pulled himself cautiously up. Then he peeped round it.

Praise the Lord, the little sack still lay on the altar, clearly lit by the oil-lamp.

The soft hoot came again: a real warning cry from a real owl.

The cicadas were creaking steadily, for it was a warm night, but above their steady pulse his sharp ears caught the crunch of sandalled feet on the dirt path. He quickly looked around for the moon and found it almost at its zenith. It was nearly midnight, the darkest part of this short summer night. Whoever was coming had taken pains not to be seen. It must be the poisoner! Flavia's trap had worked.

Then he saw the flicker of an oil-lamp and a shape separated itself from the olive trees behind.

As the figure passed between the marble columns and went straight for the altar and grasped the small black pouch, it was all Lupus could do to stop himself gasping in surprise. It was the last person he had expected to see.

Flavia was wondering whether she dare make a quick visit to the latrine when she heard the call of an owl. Was it the culprit at last? It must be nearly midnight and so far nobody had come to Polla's room.

Then she heard the scuff of a sandal on the marble floor of the colonnade. She stiffened and held her breath as a figure moved into the dim room.

The flame in the oil-lamp on the table was low, but she could see it wasn't Polla. It was a man holding a wine-jug in one hand and two stemless glass goblets in the other. He moved to the dressing table and put down the jug and cups. As he picked up the lamp and turned, she saw his face.

It was Felix.

Lit from below, his face looked strange and dangerous, almost sinister.

'Polla?' he said softly, taking the oil-lamp towards the bedroom. 'Are you here?'

He disappeared into the bedroom but re-emerged a moment later and used the oil-lamp to light two torches in their angled wall-brackets.

Now the room was lit with a soft golden light, and he looked like himself again.

'Domina, where are you?' came a low female voice.

Felix turned in surprise as the slave-girl Parthenope came into the room.

'Is my mistress here?' whispered the girl.

Felix shook his head and bent to put down the oil-lamp. As he stood up again she threw her arms around him.

'Oh, master, I love you!' she cried.

'Careful, my little dove,' he said. 'I've got two cracked ribs.' Then he bent his head to kiss her.

Flavia watched them, her mouth open and her heart thudding.

'Mmmm,' said Felix presently. 'You smell like nutmeg.' Suddenly he thrust her away. 'Someone's coming!'

He reached for the Odysseus wine-jug and busied himself filling the two glass wine cups; one was amber and the other cobalt blue.

'Ah, so you're here,' said Polla, coming into the room.

'Hello, my dear,' he said, straightening up. 'I've brought you some wine to help you sleep.' He turned to face her, a scyphus in each hand, then glanced at Parthenope. 'Your mistress won't need you any more tonight. You may go.'

The slave-girl's chest was still rising and falling and her cheeks were flushed. She looked from Felix to Polla, then pulled up the shoulder of her tunic and ran out of the room.

'Were you enjoying yourself?' said Polla.

'I don't know what you're talking about,' he said, putting the goblets down and going to her. He started to take her in his arms.

'No,' she said coldly, twisting free and going past him to the table. 'You're not coming to my bed tonight.'

'Very well. But at least have a drink with me. It's from an amphora of ten-year-old Falernian that Flaccus gave us before he left. I know you don't usually like sweet wine. You prefer your Surrentinum, your noble vinegar.'

'On the contrary, this looks perfect,' said Polla, and bent over the glass wine cups. She had her back to Felix, but Flavia could clearly see her take a small black silk pouch from beneath a fold of her ice-blue stola. Her hands were shaking as she opened it.

Polla bent over the wine cups and carefully emptied the contents of the pouch into the blue scyphus. Flavia's heart was pounding like a drum. Had her theory been right? She was about to find out.

'What are you doing?' said Felix, coming up behind Polla and stroking her bare right arm. His hand looked very brown against her creamy skin.

'I'm just stirring the wine,' said Polla without looking round, 'there are some dregs in it.' She dropped the silver spoon on the table and stood straight, then closed her eyes as he kissed the back of her neck.

'A fine . . . vintage . . . wine,' he said, removing a hairpin with each word, 'often . . . needs . . . stirring . . . up.' As her honey-coloured hair tumbled free, he turned her and kissed her full on the mouth. This time she did not resist, but responded hungrily.

Flavia shook her head in amazement. How did he do it?

Presently they pulled apart, both breathing heavily.

'You do still love me, don't you?' he said. 'You wouldn't kiss me like that if you didn't.'

'I love you more than you'll ever know, my darling Aeneas,' she whispered, stroking his cheek with a trembling hand.

'What?'

'Here, my love.' She handed him the amber goblet. 'Drink.'

'To Venus,' he said, tipping a small libation on the floor, 'and to us.'

'To Venus,' said Polla. 'May her name be cursed!' Then Polla raised the blue goblet to her lips and drained it dry.

SCROLL XXVII

'Polla!' cried Felix, as the blue scyphus fell to the floor and she slumped forward into his arms. 'Polla!' he repeated, lifting her up. 'What's wrong?'

'Nothing's wrong with her,' said Flavia, pushing aside the cloaks and stepping out into the dressing room. 'She's probably just fainted. She thought there was deadly poison in her wine. But it was only saffron mixed with charcoal.'

'By Jupiter!' he exclaimed. 'What are you doing here? How long have you been spying on us?'

'Long enough!' said Flavia. Although her heart was pounding like a drum, she tried to make her voice confident. 'Long enough to solve the mystery of who's been poisoning Polla!'

'Who?' he said, and winced as he lifted Polla into his arms. 'Who's been poisoning my wife?' In the golden torchlight his hair seemed blond. He looked young and vulnerable and impossibly handsome.

'Take her into the bedroom,' said Flavia, 'and I'll tell you.'

Felix obediently carried his wife's unconscious body into the next room and laid her out on the low bed.

'Sit down,' commanded Flavia, 'and listen to me.'

Felix sat on the bed beside his unconscious wife.

With only the flickering torchlight from the other room it was dark in here. She knew that if she stood with her back to the doorway he would not see the emotion on her face. That was good.

'Who's been trying to poison my wife?'

'She's been poisoning herself,' said Flavia.

'What?!'

'She's been trying to commit suicide, like Arria or Seneca's wife, but she botched it. She's been using hemlock and she's built up a resistance to it. I don't think her heart was really in it. Until tonight.'

'But why on earth would my wife want to kill herself?'

'Because of you.'

'What are you talking about?'

Flavia tried to find the words to tell him, then a sudden inspiration took her. '*Treacherous one!*' she whispered. '*Did you really believe you could hide such terrible wickedness and depart quietly from my land?*' Flavia took a step towards him. '*Will love not keep you with me? Or the right hand once given as a promise of marriage? Not even the terrible death I am about to suffer?*'

'The *Aeneid*,' whispered Felix. 'You're quoting the *Aeneid*.'

Flavia nodded. 'Book four,' she said. 'Dido's plea to Aeneas before she killed herself. She knew he was about to leave her and she couldn't face life without him. She loved him that much.'

On the bed Polla moaned and stirred, her fair hair pale against the dark bedspread.

Felix looked down at his wife and gently stroked a

strand of hair from her cheek. 'But why should Polla want to die? I'm not going to leave her.'

'Treacherous one!' said Flavia, and she was glad he couldn't see the tears filling her eyes. 'Every time you go with a slave-girl or a beautiful house-guest or some girl in Baiae, every time you do that, you leave her. Every time you do that, you wound her.'

'Dear gods,' he said. 'You know about all that?'

'Everybody in Campania knows about it!' cried Flavia. 'Each time you're unfaithful to Polla it's like a sword in her breast. And it does hurt, Paetus!' she cried, before turning to run out of the room. 'It does hurt!'

'Great Juno's beard!' breathed Jonathan the next day as Flavia and the others sat cross-legged in the shrine of Hercules. It was late in the afternoon because Pulchra had stayed close to them all day. At first she had not believed Flavia's explanation that it had all been a mistake and that nobody was trying to kill her mother and that Polla would be fine now.

But when a meek Felix and a radiant Polla appeared arm in arm in the mid-afternoon, Pulchra was finally convinced, saying her mother looked better than she had in years. And when the three sisters received an invitation to have dinner with just their parents, Pulchra had seized it. As soon as Pulchra left, Jonathan and his friends had taken the opportunity to meet in their secret den.

'Great Juno's beard,' he repeated. 'I can't believe Polla Argentaria was trying to kill *herself* all this time.'

'But you guessed that, didn't you?' said Tranquillus, looking at Flavia. 'How did you know?'

'The moment I first suspected,' said Flavia, 'was when Nubia told me Parthenope said that Polla had told her she didn't love Felix. I knew that wasn't true because when you were all at Baiae, Polla said her love for Felix was the greatest tragedy of her life.'

'But Parthenope could have been lying,' said Jonathan. 'Maybe Polla never said she didn't love Felix anymore.'

'I think Polla probably did say something like that,' said Flavia. 'It's just the sort of thing a wife would say to get more details about her husband's infidelity.'

'Even if the details caused her pain?' said Tranquillus.

Flavia and Nubia nodded.

'Like picking a scab, I suppose,' said Jonathan thoughtfully. 'You can't help doing it even though you know it will hurt and be messy as Hades.'

'You must have had more clues than that,' said Tranquillus to Flavia.

'I did,' said Flavia. 'Polla was always praising women who were willing to commit suicide, like Seneca's wife, and Arria. And she also identified herself with Dido, and Felix with Aeneas. It was right in front of me,' Flavia sighed. 'I should have realised ages ago.'

'Just as I choose a ship when I am about to go on a voyage,' said Jonathan, *'so I shall choose my death when I am about to depart from this life.'*

They all stared at him.

'Seneca,' Jonathan explained. 'They made us memorise a lot of his sayings at gladiator school. It gives the men courage when they face death.'

'If Polla wanted to commit suicide,' said Tranquillus, 'why didn't she just fall on a big sharp sword like Dido?'

'I don't think she really wanted to die,' said Flavia. 'It was more like a cry for help. Also, whenever she was ill Felix paid her lots of attention. But on the night of the beach banquet he was flirting openly with Annia Serena, and then he went off so blatantly with Leucosia. After that humiliation, I think Polla really did want to end her misery.'

Lupus raised his hand. He was frowning.

'Is there something you still don't understand, Lupus?' said Flavia bitterly.

He nodded. Then he mimed stomach-ache and fainting.

'That's right,' said Jonathan. 'What about the night of your birthday, when Polla collapsed? Was she trying out a new poison on herself?'

'I don't think so,' said Flavia. 'Claudia was about to accuse Felix of something bad. I think Polla just pretended to faint to distract everyone and avoid humiliation. That's why the doctor couldn't find anything wrong with her,' she added. 'And maybe why her symptoms made no sense to Locusta.'

'What about Locusta dead?' said Nubia quietly.

Flavia frowned. 'Maybe it was just an accident.'

Jonathan raised an eyebrow. 'Or maybe she shouldn't have given poison to the Patron's daughter.'

'You're brilliant.' Tranquillus gazed at Flavia. 'You should be proud you found the truth.'

'Sometimes the truth hurts,' said Flavia picking dejectedly at a loose thread in the carpet. 'I almost wish I hadn't found out that Felix is no better than a satyr and his wife a would-be suicide . . .'

'So this is where you've all been hiding,' said Pulchra

from the door of the shrine. Ajax panted and wagged his tail as the other dogs rose to greet him.

'Pulchra!' Jonathan jumped up and went to her. 'What happened? I thought you were having dinner with your parents . . .'

'An old man with a wispy beard just brought this urgent message for Tranquillus.' She tossed a folded sheet of papyrus onto the carpet, then looked at Jonathan with wounded eyes. 'None of the slaves knew where you were so I said I would try to find you. Ajax led me straight here. I'm sorry I interrupted your secret meeting!' she added bitterly, and turned away.

'Pulchra!' he cried reaching for her arm, 'Wait! Don't go!'

But she had twisted away and was running back up the hill through the olive grove. Ajax waddled after her on his stubby legs, his gilded lead trailing in the dust behind him.

'Pollux!' cursed Jonathan. He sat down and began to strap on his sandals. 'Do you think she heard what we were saying about her parents? I'd better go after her.'

Suddenly Tranquillus leapt to his feet and pounded the wooden wall of the shrine with his fist, letting out a torrent of Greek swear words that made them all freeze in astonishment.

Jonathan stopped lacing his sandals and stared as Tranquillus pounded the wall of the shrine.

'Gaius!' cried Flavia. 'What's wrong?'

'My stupid father!' cried Tranquillus, his back still turned to them. He cursed in Greek again, and thumped the wall of the shrine until ribbons of dust drifted down from the ancient wooden beams overhead.

Flavia stood up and put her hand on his shoulder.

'Gaius, what is it?'

Without turning around, he pressed the folded piece of papyrus into her hand.

Flavia took it and as she began to read it, Jonathan saw her face go pale.

'Read what my blockhead of a father says,' cried Tranquillus. 'Read it out loud!'

'I can't!' whispered Flavia. She let the papyrus fall from her fingers and sat down heavily on the carpet.

Jonathan picked up the papyrus and began to read it out loud:

M. Suetonius Laetus to his son C. Suetonius Tranquillus.

I have just received disturbing news. One of the promising young lawyers I sometimes meet in the forum stopped me today to remark that he had recently seen you and that you were well. Apparently this young man had been at the villa of Pollius Felix with you only the day before and he said you seemed to be having a fine time. He mentioned in passing that you were seen hand-in-hand with a young girl of the equestrian class and that she had kissed you in public. When I grew angry, he tried to defend you and the girl, saying you were soon to be betrothed. But I must tell you Gaius: I was deeply humiliated. Upon strongly pressing him for further details I discovered that you and this girl had been alone in an olive grove for some time and that when you reappeared hand-in-hand this young woman's hair was unpinned. *I cannot tell you the shame I felt at this revelation from a young man of undisputed character and reputation. I could tell he was distressed by my reaction, and this made his report all the more believable. Furthermore, that such scandalous behaviour should take place in the household of a man as deeply respectable as Pollius Felix is like adding vinegar to soda. I have since made other inquiries about the young woman in question. I have discovered that in the past year she has been allowed to run wild in the most disgraceful fashion. No doubt you are not the first young man for whom she has 'unpinned her hair'—*

Jonathan paused, then put down the letter. 'There's more,' he said, 'but I won't read it.' He looked at Flavia, who was staring blankly out the shrine door. 'I'm sorry,' he said. 'I'm really sorry, Flavia.'

'So am I!' said Tranquillus and turned his face to look at her. Jonathan was surprised by the passion in his eyes. 'It's so unfair to you, Flavia. You've done nothing but good. You kept your vow, you solved the mystery, you saved a woman's life – maybe a whole family . . . And you always seek the *summum bonum*.' He stared at the ground. 'My tutor Archileus is probably the old man with the wispy beard who brought the message. He'll certainly thrash me, but that doesn't bother me. What does bother me is that I'll have to go home with him right now. I'm a good, obedient son,' he said through gritted teeth.

After a few deep breaths he said, 'Goodbye Lupus, goodbye, Nubia. I'll never forget you. And Jonathan,' here he turned and held out his hand and shook Jonathan's firmly. 'Thank you again for saving my life.'

Then he went to Flavia and pulled her to her feet and hugged her.

'Goodbye, Flavia,' he said. 'I wish . . . I'll try to explain it to pater, but he's as stubborn as—' Emotion suddenly overcame Tranquillus and he turned and ran out of the shrine.

Half an hour later, the four friends returned to find the Villa Limona in turmoil. Tranquillus had departed with his tutor, but Pulchra had not yet returned.

As they entered the lemon-tree courtyard, Polla Argentaria came up to them, her face paler than usual and her hair slightly dishevelled. She was holding Ajax in her arms; he looked dusty and exhausted.

'Flavia!' she breathed. 'At last! Tranquillus told us that Pulchra found all of you at some disused shrine and that she delivered his message. He said she started back to the villa before he did. But Pulchra never appeared and a short time ago a door-slave found Ajax scrabbling at the slave's entrance. The poor little creature seems very distressed. Something must have happened to Pulchra. My husband and his soldiers are searching the hills and we have every slave scouring the villa and outbuildings. Even the house-guests are searching for her. Oh, Flavia! Do you have any idea where she might have gone?'

'No,' said Flavia, with a glance at her friends. 'But Jonathan's dog Tigris is excellent at tracking a scent. If we give him one of her tunics to sniff he'll find her.'

'Oh, thank you, Flavia!' said Polla, 'Please hurry! It will be dark soon.'

Flavia looked at Polla and then handed Scuto's lead to Lupus. 'Nubia, will you get a piece of Pulchra's clothing? Something she's worn recently? Jonathan, you and Lupus take Scuto and Nipur to your room and get Tigris to smell the tunic. Then meet me back here. I want to talk to Polla privately.'

As their footsteps receded, Flavia kept her eyes on Pulchra's mother.

'I know what you're going to say, Flavia,' said Polla, looking down at Ajax and stroking him distractedly. 'Please don't think too badly of me. I just wanted to end the anguish.' She glanced up at Flavia, then quickly looked down again. 'You don't know the pain Felix caused me.'

'You told me once about Seneca's wife,' said Flavia, 'and Arria. You admired them because they were brave.'

'Yes!' said Polla, looking up eagerly. 'I wanted to be brave like them.'

'Let me tell you about bravery,' said Flavia, trying to keep her voice steady. 'Nubia's parents were killed by slave-dealers. But she has never once complained about her fate, though she often cries in her sleep. That is bravery. Lupus saw his father murdered and was torn from his mother's arms and had his tongue cut out to stop him talking when he was only six. Last month he finally found his mother and he saw her for just one night. Then he left her to help us solve a mystery. That is bravery. For ten years Jonathan believed his mother was dead. When he found out that she was alive and a slave in Rome he risked his life to save her and bring her home. That is bravery.' Flavia blinked away the tears filling her eyes. 'My own mother died in child-birth when I was only three years old. I'd give anything to have her back for just one day. Anything. But you! You have an opulent villa and slaves and more money than you know what to do with and three beautiful daughters who adore you. How could you!' Flavia angrily wiped her wet cheeks with her fingers. 'Shame on you, Polla Argentaria! You aren't brave. You are a coward!'

Tigris led them down a rocky path beside the stream to a little inlet on the south side of the Villa Limona. Felix's yacht was berthed here, in a man-made grotto carved in the limestone cliff. Not far from this boat-cave, where the rocks met the water, they found a neatly folded pink tunic and gilded sandals. Tigris looked up from sniffing them and whined.

'Oh, no!' cried Flavia, clenching her fists. 'She's decided to end it all!'

MAYBE SHE GOT ON A BOAT wrote Lupus on his wax tablet.

'No,' said Flavia. 'You don't strip off to get on a boat, but you take your clothes off if you're going to drown yourself.'

'Pollux!' swore Jonathan. 'What a stupid thing for her to do!' He turned away, his eyes brimming.

'Behold!' said Nubia suddenly, pointing towards the Sirens' rocks silhouetted against the magenta sky of dusk. 'I think I see the Pulchra!'

'Nubia! You're right! Oh, praise Juno!' cried Flavia. 'She didn't kill herself. She just went swimming!'

Lupus nodded vigorously and Jonathan started to strip off his tunic.

'No, Jonathan,' said Flavia putting a restraining hand on his shoulder. 'I think it would be better if I go.' She pointed down at the pink tunic lying on the rocks. 'She's completely naked.'

'Pulchra!' gasped Flavia, pulling herself out of the sea onto the lowest of the Sirens' rocks. 'What in Juno's name are you thinking: going for a swim at this hour? It will be dark soon.'

Pulchra looked at Flavia with swollen eyes.

'Pulchra? What's wrong?'

Pulchra did not reply.

'You heard us talking, didn't you?' said Flavia. 'About your parents.'

Pulchra nodded. Then her face crumpled and she began to sob. 'I was so miserable I wanted to drown myself. I swam way out beyond the rocks but the current is so strong and cold out there. I got frightened and swam back here. Flavia, I almost *did* drown.'

'Oh, Pulchra!' Flavia put her wet arm around Pulchra's bare shoulders and let her friend weep. In the west, the lemon-shaped sun was dissolving into a purple and pink horizon.

Flavia tried to think of something she could say to console Pulchra but for once she had no words.

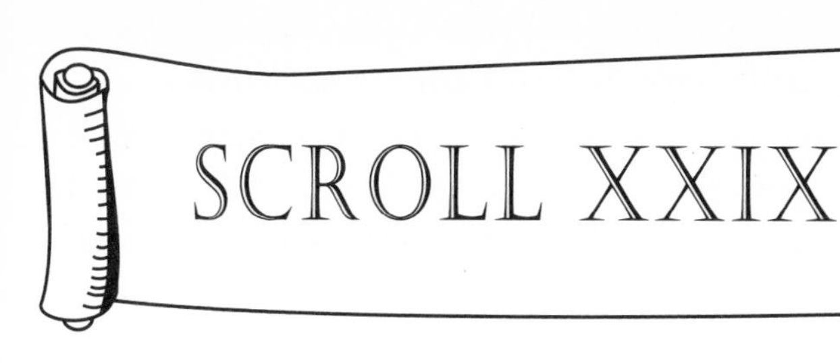

'Look, Pulchra!' said Flavia presently. 'Here come the boys in a rowing boat. They're trying to get another look at you naked!'

Pulchra gasped and turned to look.

'Just joking,' said Flavia. 'The boys are rowing so they have their backs to us. Nubia's navigating. That's why they haven't run aground. And look! She's holding up your tunic.'

Pulchra hid her face in her hands. 'How can I go back, Flavia?' she whispered. 'My father is a satyr and my mother a would-be suicide. How can I face them?'

'It won't be easy,' said Flavia gently, 'but you have to.'

'You don't understand. I worshipped pater. To find out he's been with every slave-girl and female guest in the house . . . And everybody knew about it except me! It's so humiliating . . .' Pulchra raised her swollen face. 'And mater! She was going to kill herself and leave me and my little sisters alone and motherless!'

'I know. Your parents have behaved very badly. But Pulchra, you have to set an example to them.'

'An example? Of what?'

'Of the *summum bonum,*' said Flavia. 'You have to be wise, just, self-controlled and brave. Especially brave.'

Pulchra shook her head. 'I'm not brave. I'm a coward. I couldn't even kill myself.'

'I think sometimes it takes more courage to live than to die,' said Flavia. 'Come back to the Villa Limona, Pulchra. Come back and live a brave life.'

A sea breeze ruffled the water and although it was still warm, Pulchra shivered. 'I don't think I can.'

They were both quiet for a moment.

Then Pulchra looked up at Flavia. 'If you were to stay here with me, then I might be able to do it. But without you I have nobody to pull me up to the higher good.'

'Yes, you do. I think that deep down, your mother is noble and good. If she can only make her peace with Venus, she would be a wise mentor. And I believe your father really loves her. After what's happened, he'll think twice about looking at another girl.'

'Do you really think so? Do you think he's reformed?'

'I'm sure of it,' said Flavia. 'He won't risk losing your mother again.'

'Oh, Flavia! That would be so wonderful!' Pulchra smiled through her tears at Flavia. 'How did you get to be so wise?'

'I'm not wise,' said Flavia. 'And if I am a little wise, it's always about other people. I need somebody to be wise for me.'

'Flavia!' cried Pulchra suddenly, 'Let's write letters encouraging each other. Like Seneca and his friend Lucilius!'

'Oh, Pulchra! What a wonderful idea! And it will be

easier than keeping a diary because I'll be writing to somebody else, not just to myself. We can include a wise saying or an encouraging motto in each letter. Just like Seneca.'

'And beauty and grooming tips,' said Pulchra. 'Not like Seneca.'

Flavia laughed. 'Good. It's agreed: we'll encourage each other to strive for both inner and outer beauty.'

'And the *summum bonum,*' said Pulchra. 'Like good Stoics.'

'But no drowning ourselves,' said Flavia.

'Or dashing our heads against the triclinium wall,' said Pulchra with a giggle.

'Or drinking cups of hemlock.'

'And definitely no opening of our veins!'

'Especially no opening our veins,' agreed Flavia. 'Not unless absolutely necessary.'

And when Nubia climbed onto the rock with Pulchra's pink tunic and an ecstatic Ajax, both girls were still giggling.

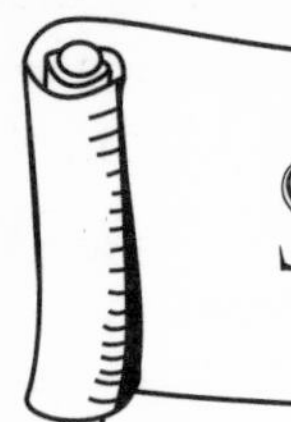

SCROLL XXX

'I am so grateful for what you did,' said Felix to Flavia the next morning. 'You saved my wife and my daughter. You really are a most extraordinary girl.'

The Patron had invited Flavia up to his tower library to thank her in private. He stood with his back to her, looking out of an arched window. Flavia sat on a cushioned bench of yellow Numidian marble. She was wearing her short blue summer tunic, the same colour as his.

Felix turned to look at her and a breeze ruffled his grey hair. His gaze was less focused than it usually was, and his presence less intense. Perhaps it was because of the pain of his cracked ribs, or maybe he was still shaken by the events of the past few days.

He came over and sat on the cushion beside her.

'You really are a most extraordinary girl,' he repeated, and patted her knee. 'A bright, brave and beautiful girl.'

Flavia looked down at his hand and for the first time she saw the design on his gold and sapphire signet-ring. It was a strutting cockerel. She looked back up at him. Up close, in the harsh light of day, his face wasn't smooth and bronze. She could see slight pouches underneath his eyes and a cut on his cheek where the barber-slave had nicked him. For the first time she noticed that his chin was weak. And beneath his trademark scent of citron she caught the faint stale whiff of his underarms.

Had he changed? Or had she? She didn't know. But something was different and she suddenly felt afraid. She wished he would take his hand away. But it remained there, resting on her knee. Could she move it? No. It would be impolite. He was still smiling at her, his eyebrows slightly raised, as if everything was normal.

But everything wasn't normal.

'Do you still have that kylix I gave you last summer?' he murmured, slowly bending his head towards her.

'NO!' she cried, jumping up and taking a step away from him. 'I'm sorry, but . . . but I have to use the latrine! I'm sorry.'

She turned and ran out of the library, and she was halfway down the pink marble stairs before his reply sunk in.

'I'm sorry, too,' he had said.

But the look in his eyes had been cold.

When Flavia reached the latrine she bent over it and was sick.

Later, Nubia found Flavia on her bed, sobbing into Scuto's woolly neck.

'What is wrong?' asked Nubia, perching on the side of Flavia's bed.

'It's him,' said Flavia. 'I think he was going to kiss me.'

'Felix?' said Nubia.

Flavia nodded into Scuto's fur. She could not bring herself to meet Nubia's gaze. 'I've always dreamed of him kissing me but when he almost did . . . It was horrible.'

'He is horrible,' said Nubia, 'to do such a thing after you are helping him.'

'But, Nubia,' Flavia raised her head and turned swollen red eyes on her friend. 'Don't you see? Maybe he knew I loved him. Maybe someone told him. Or maybe he saw it in my eyes.' Flavia's voice was barely a whisper. 'Maybe it was *my* fault.'

'Never!' said Nubia fiercely. 'Even if he knows you love him, it is wrong of him to do such a thing because you are young and he is old. And he should be wise and . . . not do such a thing. It is never your fault. He is overweening. He is . . . he is . . .' Nubia thought for a moment and then she said, 'He is ithyphallic!'

Flavia's jaw dropped. 'Nubia! Where did you learn that word?'

'Tranquillus tells me in Baiae. Tranquillus says Felix is ithyphallic and that he should be tied to the mast of his own ship.'

Flavia burst out laughing. 'Oh, Nubia! What would I do without you?'

Nubia's eyes were still blazing with outrage on behalf of her friend. 'I do not know. But I recommend that we will go away from this place soon.'

'You know, Nubia,' said Flavia, giving her friend a quick hug. 'You may not be a philosopher, but you are very, very wise.'

Flavia Gemina to her dearest pater M. Flavius Geminus.

This will be my final letter from Surrentum, pater. Although we solved the Mystery, some bad things happened. I'm afraid my betrothal to Gaius Suetonius Tranquillus is off. His father completely misunderstood something reported to him by Gaius Valerius Flaccus. Dear pater, if Rumour whispers bad things about me in your ear please do not believe her!!! I came here innocent and happy and I am leaving sad and wise. But rest assured: my Virtue is still intact.

Remember you said if anything went wrong, we could send for Aristo to come and fetch us? Well, I have sent him a message asking him to meet us at Three Taverns tomorrow afternoon. We will all spend the night at one of the taverns there and then return to Ostia the following day. I promise we will stay indoors and be very good and study diligently until you return from Sicily.

One day when I am older I will tell you all that happened. But it is still too tender and painful.

Farewell, dearest pater, from your sadder but wiser daughter. Cura ut valeas.

'I'm sorry,' said Polla Argentaria the next day, as Flavia and her three friends stood beside a white carruca trimmed with gold leaf. 'My husband was called away suddenly on business. He deeply regrets not being able to bid you goodbye in person. But he sends his warmest thanks for all your help and wishes you the blessings of Mercury and the Twins on your journey home.'

Flavia suddenly realised that Polla was not murmuring, but speaking in a normal voice. She seemed to have a new strength about her.

'Mater and I made an offering for you at our lararium this morning,' said Pulchra. 'And guess what? Mater has agreed to give me and my sisters lessons every morning in poetry, music, maths and philosophy. We're starting today. Isn't that wonderful?'

Polla smiled at her eldest daughter and then turned back to Flavia. 'I was very impressed by your knowledge of the poets. So was my husband. It was his idea that I take the girls' education in hand, and that I become a patroness to poets again. Oh, that reminds me.' She extended a parcel wrapped in lemon-yellow silk and tied with a blue ribbon. 'He wanted you to have this.'

Flavia took it. She knew Felix was trying to bind her in a debt of obligation. The package was heavy and round and she knew without opening it what it would be. Another fabulously expensive vase. Probably the *oenochoe* which showed Odysseus tied to the mast so that he would not succumb to the Sirens' song. She almost laughed out loud as she remembered what Nubia had said the previous day. Instead, she smiled politely and handed the parcel back to Polla.

'Please tell him that our stay at your lovely home was thanks enough,' she said as brightly as she could. Then she added, 'I'm not very good at taking care of precious things. I'd only lose it or break it.'

Polla looked surprised for a moment, and studied Flavia's face. Flavia's smile must have been convincing because Polla's forehead relaxed and she took back the parcel.

'Very well, Flavia Gemina,' she said. 'I'm sure he'll be disappointed that you refused his gift, but I'll pass on your message.'

'Thank you,' said Flavia. 'And tell him I hope you have a long and happy life together,' here she looked at Pulchra and smiled, 'with lots and lots of highborn grandchildren.'

Pulchra gave Flavia a pretend smack on the arm and then hugged her awkwardly, for she was still holding Ajax. 'Don't forget to write to me, Flavia,' she said, pulling back. 'You too, Jonathan. You promised.' Her blue eyes were suddenly brimming, and she gave him a quick kiss on the cheek.

Lupus gave Jonathan a bug-eyed look, then grinned and wiggled his eyebrows at Flavia and Nubia.

Smiling, the four friends climbed up into the carruca, where three panting dogs sat patiently beside the luggage.

'Wait!' cried Polla Argentaria, as the driver raised his whip. She went to the side of the carruca. 'I want to thank you all,' she said, looking up at each of them in turn, 'for teaching me what true bravery is.' She looked at Flavia last and gave her an almost imperceptible nod. Then she went back to Pulchra and put her arm around her daughter's shoulders.

The driver flicked the mules into motion and as the carruca moved off up the hill they waved and called out their farewells until Pulchra and her mother disappeared from view.

The grinding rumble of the iron wheels filled the covered, colonnaded roadway, but above it Flavia thought she could hear a cock crowing exultantly.

'Behold the graffiti,' said Nubia in Flavia's ear, pointing to big red letters which someone had scrawled on the inner wall of the covered road.

Lupus guffawed and Jonathan read it in a loud voice: 'EVERYBODY LOVES FELIX.'

'Not everybody,' said Flavia to herself.

Presently, the carruca left the resounding colonnade and turned onto the relative silence of the Surrentum road.

It was a beautiful bright summer morning. The sea was blue, the sunshine was warm and the sky above seemed infinite and pure. Flavia put her arm around Scuto's woolly neck and as she looked ahead her spirits began to rise with the sun. The road ahead promised adventures and mysteries, myths and stories. Later in her life there would be time for love and romance.

But for now those things could wait.

FINIS

Acerronia (ak-air-*oh*-nee-uh)
female friend of Nero's mother Agrippina, she died during Nero's first botched attempt to assassinate his mother

Acte (*ak*-tay)
beautiful freedwoman (ex-slave) who was loved by Nero and hated by Nero's mother Agrippina

Aeneas (uh-*nee*-ass)
Trojan hero who fled his burning city and eventually settled in Italia, becoming the father of the Roman race

Aeneid (uh-*nee*-id)
Virgil's epic poem about Aeneas, the hero whose descendants founded Rome

Agrippina (ag-rip-*pee*-nuh)
Julia Agrippina was the sister of Caligula, the niece and wife of Claudius, and the mother of Nero; in AD 59 she was murdered at Baiae on Nero's instructions

Amazon (*am*-uh-zon)
mythical female warrior; they reputedly cut off their right breasts to more easily fire bow and arrows, giving them their Greek name: *a*=not, *mazon*=breast

amphitheatre (*am*-fee-theatre)
an oval-shaped stadium for watching gladiator shows, beast fights and the execution of criminals

amphora (*am*-for-uh)
large clay storage jar for holding wine, oil, grain, etc.

Aphrodite (af-ro-*die*-tee)
Greek goddess of love; her Roman equivalent is Venus; Aphrodite Sosandra ('who saves men') was unusually presented as clothed and solemn

apodyterium (ap-oh-di-*tare*-ee-um)
changing-rooms of the baths, usually with wall-niches for clothing

arete (ah-ret-*tay*)
Greek word meaning 'excellence', 'courage', 'moral strength'; equals the Latin word 'virtus'

Argonautica (arr-go-*not*-ik-uh)
story of Jason's quest for the golden fleece on his ship the *Argo*; a Latin version was begun by the poet Gaius Valerius Flaccus around AD 80

Arria (*ar*-ee-uh)
Stoic wife of Paetus who encouraged him to commit suicide by doing it first

Atalanta (at-uh-*lan*-tuh)
mythological girl who could run faster than any man until distracted by love

ataraxia (at-are-ax-*ee*-uh)
Greek word meaning 'freedom from passion'; Epicureans indulged not to excess, but only until the absence of physical and/or mental discomfort was achieved

Athena (ath-*ee*-nuh)
Greek goddess of wisdom and war; her Roman equivalent is Minerva

atrium (*eh*-tree-um)
the reception room in larger Roman homes, often with skylight and pool

Augustus (awe-*guss*-tuss)
Julius Caesar's adopted nephew and first emperor of Rome

aulos (*owl*-oss)
wind instrument with double pipes and reeds that made a buzzy sound

Bacchus (*bak*-uss)
Roman equivalent of Dionysus, the Greek god of wine and revelry

Baiae (*bye*-eye)
pretty spa town on the Bay of Naples west of Vesuvius, notorious for its decadence (modern Baia)

bird-lime
a sticky yellow substance made of mistletoe berries: if small birds alight on rods smeared with it, they cannot fly away.

bulla (*bull*-uh)
small ball-shaped amulet of leather or metal worn by many freeborn Roman children as a good-luck charm to protect them until they come of age

caldarium (kald-*are*-ee-um)
hot room of the baths, usually with heating under the floor and a hot plunge

Campania (kam-*pane*-ya)
fertile region around the Bay of Naples

carruca (kuh-*roo*-kuh)
a four-wheeled travelling carriage, usually mule-drawn and often covered

Castor (*kas*-tor)
one of the famous twins of Greek mythology (Pollux being the other)

Catullus (ka-*tul*-uss)
Gaius Valerius Catullus (c.84–54 BC) was one of Rome's most famous poets

Cerberus (sir-burr-uss)
mythical three-headed hound of Hades who guarded the underworld

Claudius (*klaw*-dee-uss)
fourth emperor of Rome (AD 41–54), husband of Agrippina, stepfather of Nero

clyster (*kliss*-tur)
an enema (where water is squirted up the bottom to help elimination); from the Greek word meaning 'syringe'

colonnade (kal-uh-*nayd*)
a covered walkway lined with columns at regular intervals

Cupid (*kyoo*-pid)
god of love and son of Venus, he is often shown as a baby or boy with bow and arrows

depilatory (dip-*ill*-ah-tor-ee)
something which removes unwanted body hair

Dido (*die*-doe)
Phoenician queen of Carthage who fell passionately in love with the Trojan Aeneas, then killed herself when he left her to pursue his destiny

Dionysus (die-oh-*nye*-suss)
Greek god of vineyards and wine; he is often shown riding a panther

domina (*dom*-in-ah)
a Latin word which means 'mistress'; a polite form of address for a woman

dum vivimus, vivamus (*doom* viv-*ee*-mus viv-*ah*-mus)
Latin: 'While we live, let us live'; a quote from Epicurean philosophy

edepol! (*ed*-uh-pol)
exclamation based on the name Pollux, probably rather old-fashioned by the late first century AD

ephedron (*eff*-ed-ron)
herb mentioned by Pliny the Elder and still used today in the treatment of asthma

Epicurean (ep-ik-yoor-*ee*-an)
follower of the philosophy of Epicurus, by Roman times this usually meant a retreat from public life in order to achieve a pleasant and tranquil existence

Epicurus (ep-ik-*yoor*-uss)
Athenian philosopher (341–270 BC) who taught that as there is no afterlife we should strive to avoid pain and gratify our physical desires during our lifetime

euge! (*oh*-gay)
Latin exclamation: 'hurray!'

Falernian (fa-*lair*-nee-un)
highly-esteemed sweet Roman wine of amber colour, from a wine-growing region northwest of Naples

Felix (*fee*-licks)
Pollius Felix was a rich patron and poet who lived in a maritime villa south of Surrentum; he is mentioned by the poet Publius Papinius Statius in several poems

Flaccus (*flak*-uss)
Gaius Valerius Flaccus, poet who began a Latin version of the *Argonautica* around AD 80

Flavia (*flay*-vee-a)
a name, meaning 'fair-haired'; Flavius is another form of this name

Fors Fortuna (forz for-*toon*-uh)
goddess of luck and good fortune; her festival is celebrated in Rome on July 24, three days after the mid-summer solstice

forum (*for*-um)
ancient marketplace and civic centre in Roman towns

freedman (*freed*-man)
a slave who has been granted freedom, his ex-master becomes his patron

frigidarium (frig-id-*dar*-ee-um)
the cold plunge in Roman baths, often under a domed roof

fulcrum (*full*-krum)
curved part at the head of a couch, (usually a dining couch)

Furies (*fyoo*-reez)
also known as the 'Kindly Ones', these mythical creatures looked like women with snaky hair; they tormented people guilty of particularly terrible crimes

Galba (*gal*-bah)
one of the three Emperors who ruled for a short time after Nero's death in AD 68

garum (*gar*-um)
very popular pungent sauce made of fermented fish parts, not unlike modern Worcestershire sauce

Germania (jur-*man*-ya)
Roman province west of the Rhine

gladiator
man trained to fight other men in the arena, sometimes to the death

glirarium (glir-*are*-ee-um)
Latin 'home for dormice'; container for holding and fattening dormice in preparation for eating

gustatio (goo-*stat*-yo)
first course or 'starter' of a Roman banquet; the main course was called *prima mensa*, 'the first table', and dessert was called *secunda mensa*, 'the second table'

Halicarnassus (hal-ee-car-*nass*-uss)
(modern Bodrum) ancient city in the region of Caria (now part of Turkey)

Helios (*hee*-lee-oss)
god who drove the sun across the sky in a chariot; *helios* is Greek for 'sun'

Herculaneum (herk-yoo-*lane*-ee-um)
town at the foot of Vesuvius, buried by hot mud in the eruption of AD 79

Hercules (*her*-kyoo-leez)
very popular Roman demi-god, the equivalent of Greek Herakles

Hypnos (*hip*-noss)
Greek god of sleep who touches the forehead with a branch to bring sleep

Ides (eyedz)
thirteenth day of most months in the Roman calendar (including June); in March, May, July and October the Ides occur on the fifteenth day of the month

impluvium (im-*ploo*-vee-um)
a rectangular rainwater pool under a skylight (com-pluvium) in the atrium

in vino veritas (in *vee*-no ver-i-*tass*)
Latin for 'in wine there is truth', a well-known saying in the first century AD

Italia (it-*al*-ya)
the Latin word for Italy
ithyphallic (ith-ee-*fal*-ik)
showing evidence of the male state of arousal
Juno (*joo*-no)
queen of the Roman gods and wife of the god Jupiter
Jupiter (*joo*-pit-er)
king of the Roman gods, husband of Juno and brother of Pluto and Neptune
Kalends (*kal*-ends)
the first day of any month in the Roman calendar
kohl (*coal*)
dark powder used to darken eyelids or outline eyes
kylix (*kie*-licks)
elegant, Greek, flat-bowled drinking cup, especially for dinner-parties
lararium (lar-*ar*-ee-um)
household shrine, often a chest with a miniature temple on top, sometimes a niche
Lavinia (la-*vin*-ya)
Italian princess whom Aeneas had to marry so that he and his followers could settle in Italy
lectus (*lek*-tuss)
bed or couch; looking into a dining room, the lectus imus (lowest couch) was to the left of the middle couch and the lectus summus (highest couch) was on the right; the place of honour was usually the lectus medius.
Leucosia (loo-ko-*see*-uh)
name of one of the mythological sirens, also the name of an island near Paestum
Ligea (li-*gay*-a)
name of one of the mythological sirens

Limon (li-*mone*)
second property belonging to Pollius Felix; 'limon' can mean 'meadow' or 'lemon', or both; nobody knows exactly where it was, but it might have been between the Lucrine Lake and Puteoli, near modern Arco Felice

Livia (*liv*-ee-uh)
wife of Rome's first emperor, Augustus, whom she may have poisoned.

Locusta (lo-*koos*-ta)
notorious female poisoner from Gaul who helped kill several emperors and would-be emperors, she was given an estate by Nero as thanks for helping him

Lucan (*loo*-kan)
Marcus Annaeus Lucanus (AD 39–65) talented poet, nephew of Seneca, and husband of Polla Argentaria, he was forced to commit suicide after being implicated in the Pisonian conspiracy against Nero in AD 65

Lucilius (loo-*kill*-yuss)
young ex-Epicurean turned Stoic to whom Seneca addressed many of his letters

Lucrine Lake (*loo*-kreen)
small lake near Baiae, it was famous for its fisheries and oyster beds; Nero's mother Agrippina had a villa nearby

metopium (met-*ope*-ee-um)
exotic perfume made of cardamom, myrrh, balsam, honey and bitter almond oil

Minerva (min-*erv*-uh)
Roman equivalent of Athena, the Greek goddess of wisdom and war

Misenum (my-*see*-num)
Rome's chief naval port on the bay of Naples

Mithridates (myth-ri-*date*-eez)
King of Pontus who fought the Romans in the first century BC and lost; he committed suicide by stabbing himself, because poisons had no effect on him

mithridatium (myth-ri-*date*-ee-um)
universal antidote invented by King Mithridates (see above) who lived in fear of being poisoned

mortarium (more-*tar*-ee-um)
stone or clay bowl used to hold things while they are being ground with a pestle

names of citizens of Rome
praenomen = first name – there were only about a dozen of these in Roman times; girls did not have one; they took the feminine form of their father's nomen and cognomen. For this reason they often used diminutives like Pollina and Pollinilla
nomen = family name denoting clan (*gens*) e.g. anyone named Flavius or Flavia belonged to the Flavian clan
cognomen = nickname to distinguish clan members, it often described a trait (Geminus means 'twin') or characteristic (Felix means 'prosperous' or 'lucky')

names of freedmen
freedmen took their master's first two names and added their own slave name as cognomen: e.g. Publius Pollius Justus

names of slaves
slaves usually had only one name, e.g. Nanus or Parthenope

Neapolis (nee-*ap*-o-liss)
the major city of Campania; it was still very Greek in the first century (modern Naples)

nefas (*nef*-ass)
Latin word meaning 'wickedness', 'sin' or 'shame'

negotium (neg-*oh*-tee-um)
Latin for 'business' or 'work'

Nero (*near*-oh)
Emperor who ruled Rome from AD 54–68

oenochoe (ee-*nok*-oh-ee)
Greek word for a wine jug

Orestes (or-*ess*-teez)
son of Agamemnon and Clytemnestra, he was commanded by Apollo to avenge his father's murder by killing his mother; he was then pursued by the Furies

Ostia (*oss*-tee-uh)
port about 16 miles southwest of Rome; Ostia is Flavia's home town

otium (*oh*-tee-um)
Latin word for 'leisure', 'relaxation', 'quiet'

Ovid (*ov*-id)
Publius Ovidius Naso (43 BC–c.AD 18); Roman poet whose works include love poetry as well as the famous *Metamorphoses*

Paestum (*pie*-stum)
Greek colony south of Sorrento, famous for its roses and Greek temples

Paetus (*pie*-tuss)
Caecina Paetus was implicated in a conspiracy against the emperor Claudius and had to commit suicide; his wife Arria encouraged him by doing it first

palaestra (puh-*lie*-stra)
exercise area of public baths, usually a sandy courtyard open to the sky

palla (*pal*-uh)
a woman's cloak, could also be wrapped round the waist or worn over the head

papyrus (puh-*pie*-russ)
papery material made of pounded Egyptian reeds, used as writing paper and also for parasols and fans

Parthenope (parth-*en*-oh-pee)
name of one of the mythological sirens, also a poetic name for Naples

pastille (*pass*-til)
from Latin *pastillus* 'little loaf'; a lozenge or pill made of moulded substances

patrician (pa-*trish*-un)
a person from the highest Roman social class

Pausilypon (pow-*sil*-lip-on)
modern Posillipo, a coastal town near Naples across the Bay from Sorrento; the name means 'rest from troubles' in Greek

pax (packs)
Latin for 'peace'

pergola (purr-gole-uh)
covered area formed by plants climbing over columns and/or trellis-work

peristyle (*perry*-style)
a columned walkway around an inner garden or courtyard

Philodemus (fill-oh-*dee*-muss)
Lucius Calpurnius Philodemus could have been a descendent of Lucius Calpurnius Philodemus, the

Epicurean philosopher who may have lived in the so-called Villa of the Papyri near Herculaneum which was destroyed by Vesuvius in AD 79

Piso (*pee*-zo)
Gaius Calpurnius Piso led an attempt to depose Nero but was discovered and forced to commit suicide along with nearly twenty of his alleged fellow-conspirators; the plot against Nero is called the Pisonian conspiracy after him

Plato (*play*-toe)
famous Greek philosopher who wrote about Socrates and described his death

Pliny (*plin*-ee)
(the Elder) famous admiral and author who died in the eruption of Vesuvius; his only surviving work is a *Natural History* in 37 chapters or scrolls

Polla Argentaria (*pol*-luh ar-gen-*tar*-ee-uh)
widow of the poet Lucan and patroness to several first century poets, she may or may not have been the same Polla who was married to Pollius Felix

Pollux (*pol*-luks)
one of the famous twins of Greek mythology (Castor being the other)

portico (*por*-tik-oh)
roof supported by columns, often attached as a porch to a building

posca (*poss*-kuh)
well-watered vinegar; a non-alcoholic drink particularly favoured by soldiers on duty

praenomen (*pry*-no-men)
see: names of citizens of Rome

prima mensa (*pree*-ma *men*-sa)
Latin for 'the first table' or main course of a meal, the

starter was called *gustatio*; and dessert was called *secunda mensa*, 'the second table'

Propertius (pro-*purr*-shuss)
Roman poet and contemporary of Virgil and Ovid; he wrote many poems about love

pugnate! (pug-*nah*-tay)
Latin second person plural imperative: Fight!

Puteoli (poo-tee-oh-lee)
Rome's main port on the Bay of Naples; also the birthplace of Pollius Felix (modern Pozzuoli)

Ravenna (ruh-*ven*-uh)
seaport in northeast Italy where part of the Roman fleet was based

Scamander (ska-*man*-der)
according to Homer's *Iliad*, this river ran close to Troy

scroll (skrole)
a papyrus or parchment 'book', unrolled from side to side as it was read

scyphus (*skif*-uss)
drinking cup, usually with no stem and two horizontal handles

secunda mensa (sek-*oon*-da *men*-sa)
Latin for 'the second table' or dessert course of a meal, the starter was called *gustatio*; and the main course was called *prima mensa*, 'the first table'

Seneca (*sen*-eh-kuh)
Lucius Annaeus Seneca (c.4 BC–AD 65) was Nero's tutor and Lucan's uncle; a Stoic philosopher and author of tragedies, he often wrote about how to die a good death

sesterces (sess-*tur*-seez)
more than one *sestertius*, a brass coin; about a day's wage for a labourer

Sicily (*siss*-ill-ee)
large island off the 'toe' of Italy; known as Sicilia in Roman times

Socrates (*sock*-rat-eez)
Greek philosopher who lived in Athens in the fifth century BC, he was made famous by Plato, who wrote accounts of the dialogues Socrates had with his pupils and disciples

Sosandra (so-*sand*-ruh)
see 'Aphrodite'

Stabia (*stah*-bya)
modern Castellammare di Stabia, a town to the south of Pompeii (also known as Stabiae)

Stoic (*stow*-ik)
a Greek philosophy popular in ancient Rome; its followers admired moral virtue, self-discipline and indifference to pleasure or pain

stola (*stole*-uh)
a long sleeveless tunic worn mostly by Roman matrons (married women)

stylus (*stile*-us)
a metal, wood or ivory tool for writing on wax tablets

summum bonum (*soo*-mum *bone*-um)
Latin for 'the highest good'

Surrentinum (sir-wren-*tee*-num)
wine from the region around Surrentum, dry and thin and almost vinegary

Surrentum (sir-*wren*-tum)
modern Sorrento, a pretty harbour town on the Bay of Naples south of Vesuvius

susinum (*soo*-sin-um)
expensive perfume made of lilies, saffron, roses, myrrh and cinnamon

symposium (sim-*po*-zee-um)
Greek-style dinner-party with drinking, discussion and recitals at the end

synthesis (*sinth*-ess-iss)
garment worn by men at dinner parties, probably a long unbelted tunic with a short mantle of matching colour

tablinum (tab-*leen*-um)
room in wealthier Roman houses used as the master's study or office, often looking out onto the atrium or inner garden, or both

Tartarus (*tar*-tar-uss)
the underworld, especially the part reserved for those deserving punishment

tepidarium (tep-i-*dar*-ee-um)
the warm room of the baths, where bathers were often massaged and anointed

tesserae (*tess*-ur-eye)
tiny chips of stone, pottery or glass that make up the picture in a mosaic

Titus (*tie*-tuss)
Titus Flavius Vespasianus, 40 year old son of Vespasian, has been Emperor of Rome for almost a year when this story takes place

toga (*toe*-ga)
a blanket-like outer garment, worn by freeborn men and boys

Tranquillus (tran-*kwill*-uss)
Gaius Suetonius Tranquillus, the famous Roman

biographer, was probably born the same year as Flavia Gemina: AD 69

triclinium (trik-*lin*-ee-um)
ancient Roman dining room, usually with three couches to recline on

tunic (*tew*-nic)
a piece of clothing like a big T-shirt; children often wore a long-sleeved one

venefica (ven-eh-*fik*-uh)
a sorceress who uses drugs, potions and poisons

venenum (ven-*nay*-num)
Latin for 'poison'; some scholars think it came from the name Venus (goddess of love) because it was originally a love-potion

verna (*vur*-nuh)
Latin for 'home-grown' slave; i.e. person born into slavery because their mother was a slave; it was not unknown for the master to be the father

Vesuvius (vuh-*soo*-vee-yus)
volcano near Naples which erupted on 24 August AD 79 and was still smouldering a year later

Virgil (*vur*-jill)
author of the *Aeneid*, considered by many to be the greatest of all Latin poets

Vopiscus (vo-*piss*-kuss)
Publius Manilius Vopiscus, a rich Epicurean who became consul in AD 114

wax tablet
a wax-covered rectanglar piece of wood used for making notes

LAST SCROLL

Pollius Felix was a real person. We know about him from the poems of Publius Papinius Statius, another native of the area around Naples. On at least one occasion, Statius was a house-guest at his patron's villa and he describes it in great and loving detail. From Statius we learn that Felix was a rich Epicurean, a patron, born in Puteoli and that he was a grandfather by the year AD 90 (ten years after this book takes place). We also know that Pollius Felix was married to a woman named Polla who may or may not have been Polla Argentaria, the widow of Lucan. The rest of the things about Pollius Felix in this book (including his first name), are made up.

The accounts of the conspiracy to assassinate Nero after he murdered his mother Agrippina, and of the suicide of the Stoic philosopher Seneca and his nephew Lucan, are true. You can read more about these events in the *Lives of the Caesars* by Gaius Suetonius Tranquillus, better known as Suetonius.

If you go to the Capo di Sorrento in Italy, and follow signs pointing to the 'Ruderi Villa Romana di Pollio Felice' (ruins of the Roman villa of Pollius Felix) – you will come to the ruins of a Roman villa on the very tip of the promontory. Terraces of olives and vineyards rise up behind these ruins and the sea lies on three sides around. From here you can see Ischia, Prochida, Misenum, Vesuvius and the Milky Mountains. You will find a secret cove behind the site and four rocks in the sea in front of it. Not far away is a crescent beach called Baia di Puolo, possibly named after Pollius.

Despite the signs, we do not know for certain that this was the site of the villa of Pollius Felix. But I like to think it was.